BREAKEVEN

MICHELLE DIENER

ECLIPSE

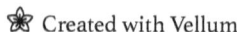

THE STORY SO FAR . . .

Readers don't have to have read Breakaway to enjoy Breakeven, but they will understand the references to what happened to Dee on Garmen better, and understand exactly what's happening at the start of the book, which opens in the middle of a Caruso attack.

Throughout Breakaway, Dee and her boss, Leo, discover that the Core Companies of Garmen have made a devil's bargain with the Caruso, a warlike alien race. Dee is on the Deck of Felcitos, Garmen's tethered way station, to warn Leo's business associate, Ruanne, of an impending Caruso attack on Ruanne's planet, Lassa, but before that happens, the Caruso attack Garmen, trying to take the Deck to gain control of the whole planet.

Breakeven opens just as Dee takes cover after the Caruso open fire . . .

ONE

THERE WAS VERY little sound to the massacre.

Dee thought it should be louder, but the laz fire, shooting out in uninterrupted streams from the massive weapons wielded by the Caruson soldiers, simply created a buzz.

There weren't many screams, either.

There had been at the start, when the Caruso had suddenly appeared in their midst on the Felicitos Deck, but people soon worked out screaming just drew attention.

Those who could hunker down and get out of sight, did. And they kept quiet, too.

Just like her.

She angled herself so she could see out of the door of the pleasure cruiser she'd taken cover in. A Caruson soldier walked past, his body and his gaze facing away from her.

Initially, the Caruso had attacked the workers and traders dealing with ship maintenance and the loading of goods, but as soon as the Cores had gotten over their shock at the assault, they'd sent a unit of guards up to the Deck to engage the attackers.

The move forced the Caruso to deal with armed, trained fighters, a little more challenging than the civilians and deck crew they'd ambushed minutes before.

Dee waited until the Caruson soldier was out of her line of sight, and then glanced behind her, down the long, narrow passageway of the cruiser. She'd heard nothing from within, and had the sense she was alone on the ship, but she didn't want to be taken by surprise from behind.

All she knew about the crew and owners was this was a Lassian Cores-owned pleasure cruiser, and one person who worked on the ship was a member of the Lassian resistance.

She knew this because the leader of the Garmen resistance, Zyr, had arranged to meet him today. To warn them of a potential Caruson attack on Lassa.

Dee's mouth gave a wry twist at the irony.

She was on the Deck for the same reason, to pass what she knew about a Caruson attack on Lassa to the head of the largest independent contractor on Lassa, Ruanne.

She and Zyr had come up together, although she'd passed him without acknowledgment as she'd walked over to meet her contact, while Zyr was busy talking to his own.

Little had they known Garmen was first on the Caruson attack list, not second.

Alternatively, the Caruso could be attacking Lassa at this very moment, as well. A double action that would take out both Breakaway planets at the same time.

While the Garmen Core Companies, who'd invited the Caruso onto Garmen in the first place, must have been taken by surprise at this attack, they'd been very quick to mobilize their troops in response.

Her boss, Leo Gaudier, had long thought trying to overthrow the Cores with a military conflict would be too costly in terms of loss of life, and it looked as if he'd been right.

The Cores were more ready to fight and kill at a moment's notice than even she'd imagined, though.

The laz fire, which had died down for a few minutes, started up again, blinding and smelling of ozone.

Her comm set buzzed, and she slid back a little into the cover of the cruiser's entryway, and accepted the contact.

"Dee?"

It was Leo.

She looked behind her, checking again there was no one sneaking up on her from behind. "Yes."

"Are you somewhere safe if the enviro and grav fail on the Deck?" Leo's voice was a little faster than usual--an edge of panic to it which she'd seldom heard before from her boss. "If not, find a place, because Sofie's about to flick the kill switch."

"That's . . . good."

That was very, very good. Dee'd heard about the fabled kill switch that could shut Garmen's tethered way station down. She hadn't realized Leo's lover, Sofie, had access to it. "I'm in the Lassian pleasure cruiser. Look for me afterward."

She cut off the connection.

If Sofie was about to flip the switch, that meant the enviro and gravity generator would shut down. The Deck sat like a hat at the top of the tethered way station, just poking out of Garmen's lower atmosphere.

When the power went off, there would be no air, no gravity.

The only way to survive would be to get the pleasure cruiser's door closed, and time was wasting.

She checked outside one last time, and saw a woman running toward the ship.

Long dark hair streaming behind her, arms waving, the woman foolishly screamed as she ran. Her eyes were wild, but with a glassy sheen, as if she was drugged as well as terrified, and she was wearing an outfit that Dee could only describe as fantastical.

It was dark blue and sheer, a body suit that was tight in places, ruffled in others.

She was wearing one high heeled shoe; the other foot was bare, and she ran in a strange, off-kilter stride, not just because of the missing shoe, Dee thought, but possibly because she'd never had to run before.

She didn't know how.

Dee thought for a moment they looked a little alike, although, if this pleasure cruiser belonged to her, the woman and Dee had nothing else in common.

Dee hesitated a moment, wondering if she should stay by the door, help the woman in, when she noticed a man running beside the woman, laz out, his stance protective.

Bodyguard.

She would know, she was one herself.

And then the guard went down, taken out by the heavy firepower of the Caruso.

He pitched forward, body caught in mid-stride, and as he knocked into the woman, she was thrown off balance. She stumbled, fell, her legs caught beneath his body.

She rose up on her elbows and tried to get out from under him, her screams even more panicked and high pitched.

Dee took a single step forward onto the ramp, about to run and get her, when the woman suddenly fell backward, body dancing a little under the onslaught of hits.

Too late.

Dee shrank back, out of sight, and edged deeper into the cruiser. Then she turned and ran for the bridge.

If the grav and enviro cutting off didn't kill her, the Caruso might.

It was time to lock this cruiser up tight.

THE VERDEN, the Lassian pleasure cruiser he'd been tracking for days, had landed early.

Sebastian led his small team around crates of goods and dodged the utility carts piled with ore, weaving his way through the obstacles toward his goal, keeping low to avoid laz fire.

The Verden's early arrival had initially messed up his plans, but he should have been bracing for it.

Nothing Rina Fattal did should surprise him by now. Her mercurial and changing whims had made kidnapping her difficult. This stopover on Felicitos had been something he'd had to scramble to take advantage of, and he was determined to make it work.

Early arrival or not. Caruson attack or not.

Although, he conceded, the Caruson attack had come out of nowhere, and was one thing he couldn't blame on Rina Fattal.

No doubt she was hunkered down, nice and safe in her executive suite onboard the cruiser, paid for with the blood and tears of the Lassian people, throwing back drinks or sniffing up drugs.

He would have to find out from his intelligence how they could not have heard even a whisper about Caruson interest in Garmen, but that was for later--he pushed it aside and focused on what was a months-long goal.

To grab Rina Fattal and use her to manipulate her scumbag of a father.

The Caruson attack might even work to their advantage. It might just make it easier to get onboard the Verden and slip away in the chaos.

"Seb." Lucia touched his shoulder, and the dread in her voice caught him by surprise.

She was pointing in the direction of the pleasure cruiser, and as he followed her gaze, he saw what had caught her eye.

Harvey lay sprawled on the ground near the pleasure cruiser's back engines.

Sebastian crouched lower, and did a visual sweep of the area.

Toward the front of the pleasure cruiser he saw the flash of laz fire, and he motioned the team to follow him to the rear of the ship.

Harvey had been going to open the maintenance hatch for them to sneak aboard from the back, and as he reached the fallen informant, Sebastian saw the hatch was still closed.

He crouched beside him, and then looked up at Lucia and shook his head.

The man who'd been their inside informant was dead.

Karr moved over to the hatch and started fiddling with the keypad, but after a minute he stepped away, frustrated.

From his position beside Harvey's body, Sebastian could see through the Verden's struts to the front of the ship. The laz fire had stopped, the Caruson soldiers had obviously moved on to engage with the Cores guards who were still spilling out of successive hovers coming up the hoverway.

"We go in the front?" Lucia asked.

He took in the team; Lucia, Karr and Vavi all dressed in the dark gray standard ship crew overalls that made them indistinguishable from any other crew on the Deck, and gave a nod.

If the maintenance hatch was closed, there was no other choice but the front ramp.

He rose up and moved around the side of the ship facing away from the hoverway. It gave them cover from the laz fire that was still lighting up the indigo sky of Garmen's lower atmosphere.

As he edged around the ship, he glanced outward and saw the Deck's viewing platform and the planet of Garmen below.

This was his first time on the tethered way station, and he had to admit that Felicitos was a wonder of the galaxy. An achievement he would have to begrudgingly give to the Garmen Cores.

He stopped at the final corner of the ship and peered around, then drew back in surprise as three crew ran up the ramp.

He'd thought most of the crew would stay onboard, given Harvey had told them Rina was here to do a false trade--stopping on the pretext of picking up something small from the Garmen Cores, but really here to buy something illicit from another ship, also here on the pretext of genuine trade.

The fact that there were other Lassian ships on the Deck meant the less anyone saw, the better.

But the mystery of what the crew were doing outside was something he'd have to deal with later, because the ramp started retracting.

"Go, go, go." He sprinted along the front of the ship, and leapt onto the ramp, relieved to hear the thump and reverberation of the others landing behind him.

He flung himself into the ship and everything darkened as the ramp closed behind him.

They were in.

TWO

DEE HEARD shouts and the thunder of footsteps past the closed door, and pressed herself against the wall, waiting for someone to burst into the haven of luxury and excess she'd found herself in.

The room was beyond anything she'd ever seen, and she'd worked for one of the richest people on Garmen, Leo Gaudier.

But then, Leo was from her home town, Phansi, Garmen's mining center, and had grown up just like her.

He'd never wasted his money on ridiculous fripperies, but whoever lived in this room certainly did.

She'd found herself here because she couldn't get onto the bridge to close the ship up.

It had been locked tight, and there was no way she was getting into it. She'd been overly optimistic to think it would be open and would have no bio or code locks.

The only door that had slid open at her touch had been this one, which didn't make sense at all, as it looked like the master suite, but she wasn't going to complain.

If the grav and enviro went on the Deck, she'd at least have enough air to survive for a few hours.

It was better than nothing.

A lot better.

She heard the hum of the ramp retracting and relaxed a little, because that meant the onboard enviro would kick in, providing air no matter what happened on the Deck.

Whoever was onboard had obviously gone straight to the bridge.

As she straightened, though, she was sure she heard more footsteps.

Some last minute arrivals. They must have just made it in before the ramp closed.

She kept very still, but they moved past the door as well, although far more quietly than their colleagues, and she waited until it sounded as if they'd moved on before she moved herself.

Her first stop was the door lock.

The laslock hadn't been set, and she gave it a try, swiping her finger through the narrow band of pink light.

The system flashed once in acceptance, and she stared down at it in surprise.

She hadn't expected it to work, but now, she was able to stay locked in here, and no one could get in until she allowed them access.

Safe for the moment, she turned to face the rest of the room.

The bed took up most of the far wall. It was an impractical oval, but large enough for at least three adults to sleep comfortably.

The rest of the space was furnished with plush couches in various shades of teal, and strewn over everything were clothes and accessories, none of which Dee would ever consider wearing.

She began picking the clothes up, clearing the space to see what might lie beneath them.

She suddenly remembered that Carver was up on the Deck, keeping watch from the hidden passageways Leo's lover, Sofie, had given them access to, and worry gripped her at the thought of him or anyone else on her team stepping out to help those in trouble from the Caruso attack.

She looked over at the blank wall to one side of the room, and then walked over to it. She ran her finger down the pale pink line of light that was set into the wall about halfway down, and the solid cream of the upper part of the wall faded away, to reveal a window out onto the Deck.

The fight still raged.

She stood for a long moment, carefully looking at all the fallen bodies that littered the ground, but there was no sign of Carver, Sam, Finkle or any of her other colleagues.

The ground beneath her feet suddenly vibrated, and Dee widened her stance to brace for take-off, but it wasn't the ship starting up, she realized. Suddenly everything not tied down was flying, sucked into space, including the ship she was on.

She was flung across the room as the cruiser cartwheeled upward. She slammed into the top of the wall, and then slid down to lie dazed as the world spun.

She reached out her hands and grasped the leg of a table that seemed to be bolted to the floor, drew herself into a ball, and rode it out.

TAKING the Verden had been easy.

Sebastian had been braced for more than just three panicked crew all focused on getting the cruiser ready to fly.

By the time he and his team reached the bridge, systems had been engaged.

He stepped in, laz raised, and all three crew froze.

Their gazes skipped over Sebastian to the three other team members behind him, and he could see the moment they gave up.

"Let us get clear of the Deck, then we'll take the lifepod, and you can have this thing." There was defiance, but also desperation in the eyes of the woman who spoke up first.

Sebastian hesitated. He'd planned to force them out, but he couldn't square that with his conscience. They'd be killed by the Caruso out there.

He inclined his head.

She relaxed a little against the console. "We're ready to go."

There was an urgency to her voice he sympathized with.

There was nothing to be gained by hanging around right now.

"Then let's go." As he said it, there was a strange vibration through the ship, and everyone's gaze went to the wide front screen of the cruiser.

Suddenly they were thrown upward.

Everyone was flung up and then down again.

Sebastian caught a glimpse of a small hover and a body flying past the front screen, and then they were out in the black of space.

"Power up." Sebastian pulled himself to a crouch and gripped the handhold on the back of a chair. "We need the grav generator. Power up."

One of the Verden's crew lunged forward, forehead bleeding, and slapped a hand on a scanner.

The soft hum of power purred through the cruiser, and everything tumbled back down.

"What happened?" Vavi was lying awkwardly against a console, and Sebastian saw the side of her face was bruised.

She manipulated her jaw and winced.

"Someone turned off the enviro and grav generator on the Deck." One of the Verden's crew flopped down into a chair. "Someone sent out a warning to all registered ships' crew. That's why we risked running back to the Verden, even though we had to get past some Caruso to do it."

"The Garmen Cores did this on purpose?" Lucia looked out of the front screen, eyes wide. "More than half the dead are their own guards."

"And there goes their profit," Karr pointed as a cargo box floated past them.

Of course, what was a little lost profit, when they had also surely killed every Caruson solider attacking the Deck? Sebastian wasn't so sure the Cores wouldn't make a decision like that, no matter how many of their guards were killed.

"I don't think it was the Cores." The Verden crew member tapped the screen in front of her. "Sounds like Arkhor has taken control of Garmen."

Sebastian was there instantly, looking over the woman's shoulder to read the announcement.

"They say to remain calm, and they'll come fetch us all and tow us back to the Deck when they've reset the generators." The woman seemed to find comfort in that.

"That's what's going to happen to you," Sebastian told her. "Not to us. Unless . . ." He leaned past her and tapped to access the ship personnel locator. Grunted in satisfaction when he saw the master suite was occupied.

"Unless what?" One of the other crew watched Sebastian from his own console.

"Never mind." Sebastian smiled at him. "You're free to go. Karr and Vavi will see you to the lifepod. Have a good life."

The three crew got slowly to their feet.

"What about Rina Fattal?" The woman who stood beside him glanced sidelong at the ship locator.

Sebastian smiled again. "Don't worry. We'll take good care of her."

THREE

THE SHIP'S power humming to life had been one of the sweetest sounds she'd ever heard.

Dee noticed they weren't going anywhere, though, just drifting with the engines idling, which suited her fine.

She got up tentatively, and rubbed her upper back as she walked toward the window.

She winced as her fingers encountered a raised welt across her shoulders that must have been caused by hitting the edge of the table.

Her forehead and left side of her face was bruised, and when she feathered her fingertips over the skin, she found it was swollen and extremely tender.

Ouch.

But at least she was alive and breathing.

Leo would come for her. She knew that.

She just had to sit tight, and wait for him or Fink.

She reached the window and braced herself for a view of carnage and destruction, but there was nothing to see but space.

Either she was on the wrong side of the ship, or they were much further from Garmen than she thought.

It could be either, she conceded.

Footsteps sounded in the corridor behind her, and she tensed, looking toward the door, although she knew no one could get in.

No one stopped though, and suddenly she realized that was strange.

Wouldn't they at the very least check to see if anyone was in here, and if they were all right?

She recalled the screaming, glazed-eyed princess who'd been killed running toward the Verden, and guessed this was her room, and most likely, her cruiser.

Even more reason for the crew to check on her.

She took a step toward the door, and then paused.

No doubt the crew would be surprised to find it wasn't their employer in here, but rather a stowaway.

Her mouth twisted into a grin. Probably surprise would be the very least of their reactions.

And she needed to give Leo and Finkle time to find her--although given the chaos below on Garmen, with Felicitos out of action-- perhaps she'd better come up with her own plan than rest her hopes on a speedy rescue.

Her friends and colleagues would come for her, but how long would it take them?

She checked her comm set, but she wasn't able to reach Leo or anyone else.

Either the Caruso had taken out the comm systems, or flipping the kill switch had rendered them useless.

Another possibility was that she was too far from Garmen.

She didn't want to think about that. At all.

She had piled the clothes and shoes she'd found littered about the room on the teal couch, but out of the corner of her eye she noticed the pile was moving.

She turned, heart suddenly beating fast, as the whole thing toppled, and something wriggled amongst the clothes.

She approached carefully, lifted up a thin shirt, and then frowned in surprise when she couldn't see anything.

She bent closer, and something hissed at her, almost right in her face.

She jerked back, and looked more carefully.

Two angry eyes stared up at her, the whole iris a dark blue, and then she saw pink gums as it bared its tiny white teeth.

She wasn't someone prone to sentimentality, but she crouched down, entranced.

"Aren't you a cutie?"

The hissing stopped.

"Did Princess Messy keep you as a pet?" She put out a hand, moving slowly and smoothly.

She felt the cautious touch of a tiny clawed paw, and then the creature scrambled up onto her palm.

It was almost completely invisible. Up close, Dee could see it was about the size of her palm, with incredibly fluffy fur that seemed to have no color of its own, but rather to reflect the color around it.

When it had snarled at her, its teeth had been tiny but sharp-looking, although Dee guessed they wouldn't do much damage, even if it bit her.

She carefully lifted a finger and ran it down the little creature's body, from head to tail, and it arched under the stroke and made a tiny little purring sound.

Dee hadn't seen any bowls or food that would indicate the princess had a pet at all, so she walked to the food and drink station. There was nothing she could find that was small or shallow enough to be useful, so she poured a little water into her other palm and held it out.

The creature leaned forward delicately, bracing its front paws on her hand and lapped at the water, and Dee laughed as the roughness of its tongue tickled her skin.

When it had drunk its full, she looked for something to give it to eat, and eventually settled on cutting up a piece of exotic fruit she'd never seen before.

When she offered it to the little animal, it snatched it in its enthusiasm, and turned away from Dee on her palm, as if to protect the food from being taken back.

"Either that is a natural reaction of your species, or the princess wasn't a very nice pet owner." Dee walked back to the window to see if she could catch a glimpse of Felicitos now that the ship had drifted a bit more, but she couldn't see anything. Not even Valdos, the big water planet that lay close to Garmen in the solar system.

It worried her.

While she tried to work out where they might be from the position of the stars she could see, a lifepod spun out from below the ship and powered away.

She stared at it, openmouthed.

Was something wrong with the ship, and because she'd hidden here, they'd evacuated without her?

She strode to the door, disengaged the lock, and stepped out.

Almost straight into a man standing with his hand raised, as if to open the door himself.

"Oh." She put her hand to her chest. "I thought there might be something wrong with the ship when I saw the lifepod. What's going on?"

The man looked at her with cool eyes. "For you? Nothing good."

SEBASTIAN SAW Rina Fattal's eyes widen in surprise as he spoke, and then she jumped backward, leaning to the right to hit the button to close the door.

The speed with which she'd moved took him completely by surprise and he lunged forward to follow her into the room, but he was too late.

The door closed in his face.

"What happened?" Vavi asked as she and Karr walked toward him.

Sebastian glanced at them. He had a deep sense of unease about his brief encounter. "Rina Fattal stepped out of the room, but when she saw me, she jumped back in."

"Faster than you could grab her?" Karr asked, and Sebastian heard the skepticism in his tone, and gave a nod.

"Yes. Which doesn't jibe with anything Harvey told us about her. She moved fast." And she had the sleek, muscled body of a woman to whom physicality came naturally. A grace and a balance that said guard or special forces to him. Not spoiled princess.

"She was injured. There was a bruise on her face, and a welt across her cheek, probably from when we were sucked up off the Deck. She might also have injured her arm. She was holding it against her body when she jumped back, and even though the button to close the door is on the right, she used her left hand."

"But it *was* Rina Fattal, right?" Vavi asked.

Sebastian looked thoughtfully at the closed door. "From what Harvey told us, her coloring was right. Dark hair, dark eyes. It seems very unlikely there'd be someone so similar who just happens to be in Rina Fattal's bedroom who isn't Rina Fattal."

But there was something queasy in his gut, telling him maybe they had screwed up. Seriously screwed up.

There was a long moment of silence.

"You're kidding, right?" Karr put a hand on his hip. "You can't honestly be thinking this *isn't* her?"

"She looked me directly in the eye, and she was absolutely shocked to see me, but not rattled. She moved like she knew how to handle herself. She's had some training. There's no doubt about that."

No one wanted to tell him he was wrong, he could see it in the way they shifted uncomfortably, but they also didn't want him to be right.

They'd lost Harvey, put everything on the line for this.

If this wasn't Rina Fattal, he didn't know how they could recover.

And the stakes couldn't be higher.

Vavi pushed past him and hit the open button he'd already tried twice. Nothing happened.

"Harvey said this door was never locked because she was so often high, they had to have access in case she passed out."

"Well, she's obviously decided to lock it." Sebastian shrugged. "Given the Caruso were on a rampage, she probably was more concerned about them getting in than someone not being able to revive her from a substance fugue."

Vavi acknowledged the logic of that with a nod and a wry twist of her lips.

"We can speak to her, though. Talk her out." Karr pointed down the passage to the bridge. "There'll be an internal comm system."

That was true. And if that didn't work, there was no way there wasn't a workaround for the door lock. An override switch, or he could just crawl through the venting and drop into the room.

Talking wouldn't hurt to start, though.

Sebastian made his way to the bridge.

He'd left Lucia in control, although there wasn't much to do right now. They were just drifting along at this point. He wanted to get a comm to Rina's father before he decided on a destination. And he knew the top exec of the most powerful Core Company on Lassa would not simply accept anyone's word that they had his daughter.

He'd want proof.

A live comm with her speaking to him at the very least.

Which meant Sebastian needed to get Rina Fattal out of that room.

Lucia swore softly, then turned to look at him over her shoulder. "We've just been pinged by what looks like an Arkhoran warship."

"Ignore it," Sebastian said.

She shook her head. "I mean, personally pinged. They want contact with this ship in particular."

Sebastian stepped up beside her and looked at the message.

Felt a chill in his gut again. "Fire up the engines, and head as fast as possible in the opposite direction to the warship."

"What are the Arkhorans doing in all this?" Vavi asked.

"You think Arkhor would let Garmen fall into Caruso hands?" Sebastian shook his head. "They somehow knew what the Caruso were planning. I wouldn't be surprised if it wasn't them who switched the enviro and grav generator on the Deck off."

"Why are they interested in us, particularly, though?" Karr asked.

Sebastian looked out the door, down the passage to where Rina Fattal's room lay.

And thought he knew the answer.

FOUR

DEE STEPPED out of the shower in the lavish private bathroom off the executive suite, and heard the internal comm chirp again.

She dried off with towels made of something almost as soft and fluffy as her new little friend, and ignored it.

They'd be coming for her soon enough.

She knew she couldn't stay here forever. They'd either break in or override the door. It was inevitable.

She suppressed a shiver of fear.

She was as vulnerable as it got.

But imagining what might be in store for her wasn't doing her any good. Leo and Finkle would come for her, and she just had to hold on until then.

She'd decided she might as well have a hot shower first.

The warm water had soothed her aches and pains from when the ship had been thrown into Garmen's nearspace, and she had rummaged through the pile of clothes and found some that were not too ridiculous.

As she pulled them on, she looked around for Fluffy, and spotted her sitting next to the basin.

"Do you want a little wash?" she asked. She turned on the taps until the water was warm, and filled the sink.

It seemed Fluffy did want a wash.

She dived in, and Dee noticed with interest that with her fur wet, she could see pale gray skin beneath.

When Fluffy hopped back on the counter, she gave herself a shake and Dee gently rubbed her dry, then extended her hand so the little creature could climb up her arm and onto her shoulder.

She felt a lot better as she made herself a cup of jah, gave Fluffy some more fruit and water, and then finally turned to the internal comm again.

She pressed the button, waited for someone to pick up. "You wanted to talk?"

There was surprised silence on the other end. "Yes. We've been waiting." The man who spoke was definitely the same one she'd encountered outside her door. His tone was wry.

"Should I not have taken seriously your threat to me?" She kept her own tone even.

He hesitated. "You should have taken it seriously."

"That's what I thought."

"We're going to get you out of there. It's just a matter of time."

She took a sip of jah. "I know. What's this all about?"

"We have a problem with the way your father is running Lassa. If he wants you back, he's going to have to change course." His voice was deep, and she could hear the passion in it.

"My father was killed in a mine explosion in Phansi, the mining center of Garmen, twelve years ago. If you can contact him, Lassa has made some scientific leaps ahead I didn't know about."

There was silence. "Are you saying you're not Rina Fattal?"

"I don't even know who Rina Fattal is. My name is Dee Vanuka, and I'm the inventory manager for Gaudier Transport." Well, that was her official title. She was actually one of Leo Gaudier's lieutenants, running interference on the core companies of Garmen; undermining them whenever she could. But she wasn't going to go into detail.

The silence was even longer this time.

Talking amongst themselves, she guessed.

"What are you doing on this ship, if you work on Garmen?"

"I was checking a transport ship on the Deck when the Caruso attacked. I ran to the nearest open door, which happened to be this ship, and hid. I got a warning on my comm that the enviro and grav were about to go, so I tried to close the ship up, but I couldn't. For some reason, the room I'm in now was open and uncoded, so I locked myself in here."

"What happened to Rina Fattal?" The man's voice was deeper now. As if he was fighting some emotion.

"I saw a woman and what looked like her bodyguard being shot down as they ran for the ship. She was certainly dressed like she belonged in the room I'm in now. She could have been Rina Fattal."

"How convenient for you."

Dee sighed. "No, it's not convenient for me at all. But I'm betting not nearly as inconvenient as it is for you if I'm telling the truth. You've taken the wrong woman, and your plan is dead."

The comm cut off, and Dee ran her finger down Fluffy's spine. "I don't think he wanted to hear that."

For some reason, that struck her as funny, and she laughed.

Then she set down her cup, straightened the dark blue jacket she'd found in Rina Fattal's wardrobe, and headed for the door.

She wasn't going to wait for them to find a way in. She'd meet them on her own terms.

———

"DO YOU BELIEVE HER?" Lucia was staring at the comm panel, her lips a tight line.

Sebastian didn't want to, but yes, he did believe her.

He nodded slowly.

"Shit!" Karr kicked the nearest chair.

"She could be lying," Vavi said, but even she didn't sound like she believed it.

"Do you think Rina Fattal would have talked like that? Would even be capable of talking like that, from what we've been told about her?" Sebastian hadn't thought so since he'd first seen that quick, intelligent face, looked into those quick, intelligent eyes.

"I'm glad you've come to that conclusion." Dee Vanuka was standing in the doorway, leaning against the doorjamb.

Karr took a step toward her, but Sebastian shook his head. He wasn't going to restrain her. What would be the point?

"You're pretty sure of yourself," he said. "Aren't you worried about us?"

She lifted a shoulder. "You'd have gotten into the room if you wanted to. I could hardly hide in there forever. And as it happens I want you to turn this cruiser around and take me home to Garmen."

There was silence.

"Take you home?" Lucia asked.

"You took me away from it." Dee shrugged.

"That doesn't really suit us," Sebastian said.

She gave a dry laugh. "Then at least let me contact my boss so someone can pick me up."

Sebastian gritted his teeth. That was all they needed. Coordinating with another group would slow them down, and he didn't trust anyone enough, anyway. They didn't have time for it.

Of course, if Rina Fattal really was dead, everything they'd planned for was shot to hell.

"We could put her in a lifepod, like we did the other crew," Vavi suggested.

Before he could respond, the comm panel lit up.

"Something's coming up on us, fast." Lucia sat down. "Something big." She turned to look at him, eyes wide. "Caruson warship."

"Running from the Arkhorans, most likely." Sebastian turned to look at the screen himself.

"Maybe they'll just scream past us," Vavi said, her voice hopeful.

"Maybe." Sebastian thought they'd be lucky if that was the outcome.

"Arkhorans?" Dee took her first step onto the bridge.

"They were hailing us earlier. I thought they might be looking for you." Sebastian looked across at her.

"Oh." She tapped her lip. Then gave a sudden smile. "Garmen is in the hands of the Arkhorans? And they have the Caruson on the run?"

"The question is, why are they running toward us?" Sebastian looked down at the panel. "I think it's time we pinched to the black."

"Too late." Lucia's fingers danced over the screen. "They're too close. We don't have the space we need."

"But the system only just warned us they were coming." Vavi leaned over Lucia's shoulder. "How could they be on us so fast we don't have room to pinch out?"

"They've got tech we don't know about." Dee stood a little apart from them all. "I saw some comms feed of an incident at Cepi, where a warship fired on the ruins there and then raced off at speeds faster than anyone had seen before. I saw Caruso techs working on an identical warship in a Garmen Cores warehouse just the other day. My guess is the extra speed was a technical upgrade thanks to the Caruso, and I'm sure they wouldn't give the Garmen Cores an advantage they don't already have in their own ships."

"How they did it isn't as important right now as whether they'll just pass us by or not." Sebastian's gaze was fixed on the screen.

The warship was bearing down on them so fast he could scarcely track it, and then suddenly it was above them, and completely still.

There was a long moment of silence.

Dee looked up at the ceiling. "Looks like they aren't going to pass us by."

FIVE

THE MAN the others called Sebastian was tall and lean, his face almost hawkish, and looking at him without the lens of fear and panic, Dee realized he was a little *too* lean.

They all were. Like food was rationed.

Her fear of them had faded, superseded by the cold terror of the Caruso warship hovering above them.

She'd seen what the Caruso had done on the Felicitos Deck and she still couldn't understand the hubris of the Garmen Cores to have thought they could go into a deal with the Caruso and not somehow end up under fiery attack.

Though it seemed, thanks to her boss Leo and his lover, Sofie, Garmen was now out of both Cores and Caruson hands, and in the much firmer and fairer hands of the Verdant String Coalition.

They had won.

She would do a little victory dance, except that wouldn't go down well right now. Everyone in the room was tense as they watched the screen to see what the Caruso would do next.

There was surely no good reason for them to stop, especially if they were being pursued.

"If you know anything about this, tell us now."

Sebastian had turned, and was staring at her with dark, hostile eyes.

Fluffy had been curled up under her hair at her nape, but at the tone of his voice, she stiffened, and rose into a crouch on her hind legs.

No one had said anything about Fluffy, and Dee wondered if they might genuinely not have noticed her.

"I could ask you the same." She winced a little as Fluffy grabbed a lock of her hair to balance. "They don't even know who I am or that I'm onboard. It must be you they're interested in."

There was silence, and then they all heard the clang of a clamp engaging.

"They're going to tow us?" Vavi clutched the back of a chair.

"Be grateful this ship doesn't have inter-ship connectivity, or they'd be in here right now." Sebastian looked directly up at the ceiling, where the thumping was coming from.

Dee cocked her head. "That sounded like boots."

Lucia threw herself into a chair and her fingers danced over screens. She swore quietly. "Two individuals. Coming through the maintenance hatch."

"The hatch I couldn't get into?" Karr sounded disbelieving.

"Either they know something you don't, or they've got better tech." Vavi was checking the charge on her laz.

No one said anything to that, and Dee guessed that whoever these people were, they didn't have better tech.

Their clothing was dark gray--standard Deck crew gear--but Dee bet they'd stolen it, and the laz in Vavi's hands looked old and battered.

If there was a confrontation, no matter what happened, they were still clamped to the warship. Right now, there was no way to win this.

Sebastian and Karr had their weapons out, too. And Dee found herself adopting a defensive pose.

Lucia glanced over at her. "No laz?"

She shook her head.

Lucia pulled her own out from the neat little holster at the small of her back.

They spread out evenly through the room, all putting themselves in front of Dee.

She would have smiled if the situation wasn't so serious.

Usually, she was the one doing the protecting. As part of Leo Gaudier's security management team, she put herself on the front line every day.

It was . . . strange to be the one standing at the back.

She realized she didn't like it.

Fluffy tugged a little on her hair again, and she lifted her hand and ran a soothing finger down her back, then arranged her hair to cover the little creature more completely.

She heard the thump of boots hitting the floor in the corridor just beyond the door.

Fluffy hissed in her ear, and she could only guess she had picked up on the tension everyone was feeling.

Sebastian glanced back at her at the sound, a frown on his face, but he turned back as a second pair of boots joined the first.

The Caruson soldiers moved straight to them, so Dee guessed they had scanned the ship and knew everyone was on the bridge.

They entered weapons first, and there was no question they had the upper hand. They were armed with the massive laz guns she'd seen the Caruson wield on the Deck to deadly effect.

They stepped into the room and seemed to relax a little.

"Good, you kept the daughter of Hanran Fattal safe." The Caruson who spoke stumbled a little over the words, but he was completely understandable.

His gaze had gone straight to her, but when he spoke he addressed Sebastian, who'd stepped into lead position.

Dee knew her mouth dropped open a little. Had they really stopped while fleeing the Arkhoran Special Forces to see if Rina Fattal was in the cruiser and doing all right?

Surely not?

Sebastian had said Rina's father was running Lassa, which meant he was a top Cores exec. And while she knew there was an insidious alliance between the Caruso and the Cores, surely not on this level?

She was wearing Rina's clothes, and from what little she'd seen of the woman, they did have similar coloring. The way Sebastian and his team stood, ranged in front of her, the Caruso might be forgiven for assuming they were her crew, protecting her.

It occurred to her that right now, the Caruso thought of them all not as prisoners, but as allies.

If they learned the truth, that could change in a heartbeat.

She wet her lip and sucked in a deep breath.

They had a better chance of surviving as long as the Caruso believed she *was* Rina Fattal.

So she would have to be Rina Fattal.

SEBASTIAN HAD JUST PROCESSED the Caruson soldier's words about keeping Rina Fattal safe when the Garmen woman seemed to explode behind him.

"No thanks to you!"

He turned, trying to keep the shock off his face, and found her with hands on hips, head angled in defiance.

"I was on the Felicitos Deck, looking at the view, and I nearly *died*." She drew in a deep, outraged breath. "And let me tell you," she pointed her finger straight at the Caruson soldiers, "the people who were shooting at me looked a lot like *you*."

The soldiers lowered their weapons.

"We didn't know you were there." The second soldier spoke up. "There is a reason we asked your father for your flight plan."

"Last I heard, I didn't have to check in with you on everything I do."

Sebastian watched entranced as Dee Vanuka, if that was her real name, gave a contemptuous head toss.

"And what do you think you're doing coming aboard without permission? And clamping us?"

Sebastian saw Vavi was watching the display with wide-eyed admiration, but Karr was scowling.

Lucia kept her features schooled, and he hoped he was doing as good a job.

Then he heard it again, the strange hissing he'd heard earlier. Dee wasn't making it, though, something that made him unaccountably pleased. He shouldn't care if the woman was crazy strange or not, but somehow, he did.

Her arm was also fine, she was waving it around without a hint of pain, yet he was sure earlier she'd held it close to her body.

He couldn't figure her out.

She looked magnificent. Sleek and powerful. Far more fit and energetic than the description he'd had of Rina Fattal.

He couldn't decide if they'd all been played, and this really was his target, or whether Dee Vanuka was giving the performance of her life, and saving them all while she did it.

The hiss sounded again, and she tilted her head to the left, and made a shushing sound, her finger running down what looked like thin air.

Except, it wasn't. Now he was focusing, he noticed two dark eyes, almost lost against her dark hair, and the white of fangs and pink of gums as the tiny creature perched on her shoulder snarled and hissed again at the Caruso.

"You have a pet?" The Caruson soldier frowned, leaning forward a little to try and see it.

"Yes. And she's a very pretty girl, aren't you, sweetie?" Dee lifted the creature off her shoulder and rubbed her cheek against the top of its head.

It made a sound Sebastian guessed was a purr.

"What is it?" The Caruson asked.

For the first time he saw Dee look nonplussed. She covered it well, though, ducking her head to kiss the little creature on the head, although now it was no longer hissing, it had disappeared completely and it looked as though she was kissing thin air.

"What does it matter?" She raised her head, her eyes narrowed. "Answer the question. Why have you clamped us?"

"Your father was worried you'd come to some harm on Felicitos."

"Well, I'll let him know I'm fine. Be on your way." She shooed them with a limp hand.

Vavi nearly choked, and covered it with a coughing fit.

"We've been instructed to tow you to Lassa. Our ship is faster than yours." There was no give in the voice of the soldier who spoke.

Sebastian heard the steel in it. Knew the Caruso were probably under orders. There would be no changing their mind.

At least they were considered allies, not enemies.

For now.

Sebastian had no doubt they would be dead without the performance Dee was putting on.

"Instructed by who?" Dee cocked a hip.

"By your father. We'll let him explain to you." The other soldier pulled out a screen and tapped it.

Dee froze, and he heard her draw in a sharp little breath.

She straightened up. "Isn't he too busy to deal with something this minor?" Her voice was softer, now, less strident.

"He requested an update." The soldier flipped the screen over, holding it toward Dee, and she stepped closer to it.

She bent her head over the screen, obscuring most of her face with her thick, dark hair.

Sebastian tightened his hold on his laz.

The moment Hanran Fattal worked out the Caruson had an imposter, not his daughter, things would go to hell.

Dee pushed a hunk of hair back from her face and frowned. "Well, where is he?"

She sounded so aggrieved, he had to fight back a laugh of admiration.

The Caruson flipped the screen back and shrugged. "Must be interference. The signal is better on our ship. We'll let your father know you're safe."

They turned.

"Wait. Where are you taking us?" Sebastian spoke for the first time.

One of the Caruson soldiers gave him a quick glance. "The Cores hover base." He paused, and looked around the bridge. "I suggest you buckle in. We go faster than you'll be used to."

The Caruson disappeared down the passage, and no one moved as they listened to them climbing back out the maintenance hatch.

Silence reigned until they were gone.

"That was . . . pretty magnificent." Vavi grinned over at Dee, who sent her a smile back.

"A little too good. Who the hell are you?" Karr stood with his arms crossed over his chest.

"The person who just saved your life," Dee responded, her voice suddenly weary.

Silence fell over the group, because there was just no arguing with that.

SIX

DEE FELT tiny shivers of shock course through her as she headed for the door.

She needed to get away from the hostile, accusing stares and--she looked down at her trembling hands--probably drink a big cup of jah.

She'd faced down the Carusons' massive laz weapons knowing the slightest slip on her part and they'd all be dead.

She shuddered as she stepped into the passageway and Fluffy made a kind of crooning sound and patted her cheek.

The gesture forced a smile out of her.

"Dee, wait." Sebastian's fingers curled around her upper arm, and she stiffened as she turned.

"I don't think the Caruso were exaggerating about us needing to buckle up. Lucia says we'll feel it if we're dragged behind them at the same speed they approached us at." He dropped his hand, and gestured back toward the bridge.

She'd forgotten about the warning the soldiers had given before they'd left. She'd been too rattled by the performance she'd had to put on, and Karr's hostility afterward.

She gave a nod, turned more fully to face him, and the floor seemed to fall away from her.

She was flung down the passageway, almost weightless at one point in her trajectory.

She saw Sebastian's mouth moving, but she couldn't hear him. He reached out and grabbed her, then pulled her close, his arms hard bands around her. They fell, and he somehow twisted so that when they hit the floor, he was beneath her.

He gave a grunt as his body absorbed the impact, both of the floor, and her on top of him.

Fluffy was hanging on by her hair, pulling on it hard.

They all slid on the smooth surface of the passage floor, then hit the wall and slid along it, slowing a little.

Sebastian's arms tightened around her, and her nose wedged between his shoulder and his neck.

He was warm and solid beneath her.

Her fingers gripped his jacket reflexively as an invisible hand seemed to press her down, the pressure so intense, she didn't know if she could stand it.

She breathed hard, lying draped across Sebastian's body as she tried to adjust. She could feel Fluffy scrambling off her, her sharp little claws digging into her neck, and then she heard the click of her paws as she ran away down the corridor.

Suddenly, the pressure eased a little, although it didn't go completely away.

Dee edged carefully off Sebastian's chest and fell onto her back. She looked up at the ceiling, her breath coming in pants.

"You all right?" She looked over at Sebastian. Found his head was turned her way, his dark eyes meeting hers.

"Getting there." Sebastian wheezed the words out, his body flush against hers as they lay side by side.

They stayed like that for a while.

It felt nice.

Peaceful.

"Are you all right?" Lucia leaned over them.

Dee hadn't even heard her approach.

"Think so." Sebastian didn't move.

"I cranked up the enviro and grav to compensate for the speeds we're going at, but it can't completely cancel out the effect. The system isn't designed for this kind of speed."

"When we pinch to the black, we go faster, don't we?" Dee asked.

Lucia shook her head. "When we pinch, we bend space time, so while theoretically we may go faster than this, it's only for milliseconds. This kind of sustained pressure will take its toll." As she spoke, the cruiser gave a groan, and Dee felt the floor beneath her vibrate a little.

She tensed up, and beside her, Sebastian did the same.

"Come strap in." Lucia held out her hand to Sebastian.

She sensed him hesitate before he grasped it and let Lucia help him to his feet.

He turned to her, extended his hand, and she gripped it.

As he hauled her up, she realized for the first time since she'd been forced to take shelter in the cruiser that she felt as if she had an ally.

Another long, creaking groan sounded, and they all looked up at the ceiling.

"How long until we get to Lassa?" Dee asked.

Lucia kept her gaze upward, her brow wrinkled in worry. "At least five more hours, going at this speed."

Dee hoped they made it.

"SO, what's your problem with Rina Fattal's father?"

Sebastian looked over at Dee as she spoke, and realized for the first time she had no idea who they were.

The way she'd almost run from the room earlier began to make sense.

"He and the other Cores execs are killing us." Vavi turned to her as she answered, her straps forcing her to twist in her seat.

"Who is 'us'?" Dee asked. "And killing you how?" Her questions were genuine, but Sebastian saw Karr's head come up in outrage, and he cut in before his team mate could alienate her further.

"We're part of the Lassian resistance. The Cores have taken back all the wells and refineries run by independents. Taken over every business that they didn't already own. They've taken control of every means of production on the whole planet. They're starving us to death."

She had looked over at him when he jumped in to answer, and she leaned back in her chair, her expression thoughtful. "The Cores were trying to do that on Garmen as well. Leo thwarted them at every turn, and they started playing dirty." She rubbed her forehead, and he thought she'd gone somewhere dark in her head. "They killed some of my colleagues. Killed them in as ugly a way as they could and left their bodies as a warning. It was the first shot across the bow, and we knew we'd have to fight back. We were getting ready for it when the Caruso attacked."

"Getting ready, how?" Lucia asked.

"We made contact with Arkhor Special Forces. We started getting the independent miners ready to attack, and we'd made deep connections to the gen-pop in Tether Town, so they'd follow us if we asked them to. We also made an alliance with the resistance."

"Why should we believe you?" Karr asked.

She looked over at him, and while Sebastian thought she was taken aback at his hostility, she certainly didn't shrink away from him.

She was quite comfortable holding her own.

"Why should I believe you?" she asked him. "For instance, I know there was a member of the resistance working on this cruiser, and that he was in regular contact with the Garmen resistance leader, Zyr. So I have to ask myself why the resistance would need to send a team to take Rina Fattal when they had the means to do it all along."

There was silence.

"How did you know we had someone onboard?" Sebastian knew his voice was thick with shock.

"Because I just told you, we'd formed an alliance with Zyr, the head of the Garmen resistance. He told me he was meeting someone from the Lassian resistance this morning to pass on the word that the Caruso were planning to take Lassa, and I saw him talking to a member of this cruiser's crew myself."

"Harvey." Lucia spoke up. "His name was Harvey. He was killed by the Caruso just before we boarded."

"He was more an informant than a full member of the resistance." Vavi's voice was quiet. "He was afraid they had too much information on him for him to show his hand. He thought they'd go after his family."

"He was right. They would have." Lucia rubbed her palms along the tops of her thighs. "But without him, we wouldn't have known about Rina or how to find her."

Except, Sebastian never knew he was a liaison between the Garmen and Lassian resistance. And he most definitely should have.

Koan should have told him when he passed on Harvey's details and helped set this whole operation up.

"What did he look like, this person Zyr met with?" Sebastian was aware his tone was harsh.

"Medium height, dark hair with silver at the temples." She folded her arms over her chest, and her gaze was cooler when she met his gaze.

He'd lost some of her trust with the harshness of his questioning, and he was sorry for it. But he was even sorrier that she was right, because she had just described Harvey.

And that meant people were keeping secrets.

Lucia looked over at him, a quick, shocked glance, and Karr risked a look too, scowling deeply.

"You didn't know he was a contact for the Garmen resistance?"

Sebastian turned, noted the interest in Dee's eyes. She was sharp, smart, and saw way more than he was comfortable with.

"The Lassian resistance has been through some upheaval recently." He raised his shoulders as if it didn't matter, but it did. He had a sick feeling in his gut it mattered a lot.

He let the silence between them stretch out.

"What's happened to all the people on Lassa, if the Cores have taken everything?" She changed topic without any sign of annoyance.

"Everyone's doing whatever they can to survive, but things are desperate."

"And desperate people do desperate things." Dee's gaze rested on him, and for the first time he didn't meet it, because he could hear the softer tone in her voice. "Like kidnap silly women in pleasure cruisers."

"There's starving kids in the streets," Vavi said. "Small groups stealing what they can, sometimes from people in worse straights than they are. It's turning people into animals."

"And dying." Lucia's voice was almost toneless. "A lot of people are dying--from starvation, but also because the Cores guards are shooting them. They've been driven to risk everything, and more often than not, they lose. It's an extermination."

Dee drew her feet up on her chair, rested her chin on her knees. "Garmen's better off, and that's because Leo had the power to push back, to give us time to organize. But the Garmen Cores would have done exactly what the Lassian Cores have done if they could have."

"What are you saying?" Sebastian had the sense she was deciding something as she spoke.

"I'm saying, if I can help you when we get to Lassa, I will."

SEVEN

HER HEARTBEAT SPIKED as they came through Lassa's atmosphere.

She stood on the bridge and looked out through the big screen, and was sorry she was arriving under such strained circumstances.

She caught glimpses of tall, tall trees and the flash of color as birds dived between branches--all so different to the open plains and snow-capped mountains of Garmen.

The other glaring difference here was there was no Felicitos. The tethered way station was a wonder, and Garmen was rightly proud of it because it was one of a kind. On Lassa, they had to make do with an orbital way station and hover ports at key positions on the surface.

As they came in, she caught sight of a massive transport hover lumbering up, wide and bulky and graceless as it blasted up above the cloud line.

"The buildings are so spread out." She was astonished to see rough dwellings set below the curve of an elevated hover track that rose above the trees, glinting white in the afternoon sun.

On Garmen there were only two towns, the buildings tightly packed together. Tether Town, which lay at Felicitos's feet, and Phansi, the mining town on top of the escarpment.

"Not too spread out." She'd known the moment Sebastian came to stand beside her, a hard, inconvenient little thrill chasing through her as she remembered the scent of him as she lay with her face buried in the crook of his shoulder.

He pointed at the wide, empty swathes of green. "The houses are usually clustered around a rail stop or along the track. Inbetween there's no way to buy or sell goods because the hover only stops at certain points."

"Did they build the rail for the hover because the forest is too dense?" She couldn't see the ground, even though they were flying low.

He nodded. "They started to clear it, then realized it was going to be quicker and cheaper to build a high-level track."

She leaned against the window and let herself delight in the lush beauty below her, glad that the Cores hadn't cleared it for their transport hovers.

Sebastian lapsed into silence and she glanced up at him. He was watching her with an intense look, one that said he didn't know whether he could trust her.

Unfortunately for him, right now he didn't have a choice.

She and everyone else on the bridge knew she was going to have to pull off the impossible in the next hour or so, and continue to convince the Caruso she was Rina Fattal, and they were her crew.

She felt the tension thrum through her body again, and steadied herself. She'd had to stare down the barrel of a laz many times over the years working as security for Leo, and she'd always come out the winner--but this time, she had no laz to fire back, and nowhere to run if she needed to.

Sebastian tapped lightly on the window with his knuckles. "I've always been glad they chose an elevated track, rather than ground level road, because having a thick undergrowth has given the resistance more places to hide."

On Garmen, she'd liked being out of town, on the open plains between Tether Town and Phansi, but she didn't know if she'd be as thrilled being surrounded by thick vegetation, unable to see very far ahead.

"You don't look convinced."

She heard the amusement in his voice as she glanced over at him.

She smiled. "I'm used to the escarpment, and low, scrubby bushes. I'm not sure about jungle conditions."

"Most likely you won't have to experience them." His voice turned grim. "The Cores hover base is where we flew out from, chasing after Rina. It's hard to get in, and it's very hard to get out."

"My thoughts are that Rina Fattal will have no trouble getting out."

He gave a nod of agreement. "If you can convince them you are her, that will most likely be our only chance."

"So, no pressure." She said it to lighten the atmosphere, but the look he gave her was without any humor.

She didn't know if he intended to respond, but before he could, a warning bell chimed.

"Strap in, we're landing in five minutes." Lucia waved a hand at them.

Sebastian turned on his heel and walked away and Dee followed behind and buckled up.

Sebastian was high in the resistance hierarchy, she decided. Very high. It was in the way his team responded to him, and how much their failure seemed to weigh him down.

He took full responsibility for this, and she hadn't heard a word from him about reporting to a boss.

Which meant this trip must truly have been their last ditch chance.

If Sebastian was here, it was because he thought he could negotiate something meaningful with Rina Fattal's father.

The fact that Rina was no longer available as a bargaining chip told her she was likely walking into a situation on the losing side.

It didn't matter.

When it came to the Cores, whichever side was against them was the right side to be on.

Win or lose.

DEE VANUKA WAS A PUZZLE.

Sebastian didn't like that he found it difficult to look away from her, that his gaze seemed to drift toward her even though he needed to think, to work out what to do as every plan he'd made was shot to hell.

Or maybe he couldn't help himself because of that.

There was nothing left in the tank.

They'd spent every last credit they had left for him, Lucia, Karr and Vavi to take the small freighter they'd used to track Rina and her pleasure cruiser. They had no more backup plans, nothing to fall back on.

This had been it, and it had been an abject failure.

"What's the plan?" Karr seemed to be reading his mind.

"Just getting off this cruiser alive would be a good start." He looked over at Dee. "If you can continue to convince them you're Rina Fattal and we're your crew, we may be able to just walk out of there."

"We'll need to make it realistic, then." She jerked in surprise, and then stroked a hand over thin air, and Sebastian guessed her invisible pet had finally rejoined her. "When we land I'll go pack some bags with clothes to bring along with me. Maybe you can carry them out, Karr?" She smiled sweetly, and Lucia choked back a laugh.

"Agreed." Sebastian nodded. "They think I'm the head of your security, so Lucia and I will play bodyguard. Karr, you and Vavi carry bags and generally look useful."

Karr looked over at him in disbelief, but Sebastian was tired of his shit. Dee had done nothing but save their asses so far. He shot Karr a hard stare, and then looked away.

Vavi walked past him and looked out as the hover port loomed closer. "The Caruso are obviously already in some kind of alliance with the Cores--they seemed to know Rina and they certainly seem to know her father, but do you think this is the first time they're flying down to this base?"

"Has to be their first time." Lucia was concentrating on the controls in front of her. "Or, if not, it only started since we left to follow Rina's pleasure cruiser from Lassa to Garmen."

"Otherwise one of your informants would have told you about it, right?" Dee's hand was raised, and her finger seemed to be scratching under her pet's chin.

"Yes." Vavi looked over her shoulder at her. "I hadn't even heard they were involved with the Cores until they started shooting everyone on the Felicitos Deck, and then I thought it was just a Garmen problem. Now we know it isn't, and that means they must have kept things very quiet before."

"Except, now they're flying into the Cores hover base in broad daylight. That's the opposite of quiet," Dee pointed out.

"Yes." Vavi pointed a finger at her. "Why? What's changed?"

"They've had to step things up because their attack on Garmen failed?" Karr asked.

"You'd have thought that would have made them even more secretive, not more blatant." Lucia frowned as she lowered them down onto a landing pad. "Especially as they've just been smacked down by the Verdant String on Garmen. They won't want the VSC looking this way, too."

Sebastian heard the clamps engaging and rose from his seat.

"What do you think, Seb?" Vavi asked. "What's going on?"

He paused. He didn't like what he thought. He didn't want to even consider it, but he hadn't survived this long by ignoring things he didn't like. "I think we have a mole in the resistance, and they've been actively hiding the Caruso's alliance with the Cores."

Lucia looked up, and he saw there wasn't any surprise in her eyes. She'd worked it out, too.

Karr shoved out of his chair. "I won't believe it until I have solid proof."

Sebastian shrugged. Karr was a die-hard loyalist.

Sebastian didn't have that luxury.

"You were going to pack," he reminded Dee, and she nodded and slid out of her seat, disappearing down the passageway.

"Don't trust her," Karr said, not even trying to lower his voice.

"We don't have a choice," Lucia told him, and Sebastian thought he detected the same irritation in her voice he was feeling himself.

"No, we don't. So we'll play her lackeys." He reached out a hand and clamped it over Karr's shoulder. "And we'll smile while doing it."

EIGHT

DEE TUGGED on the complex filigree ear jewelry that hung almost to her shoulders, and waited for the door to lower into a ramp.

Behind her lay a pile of bags, and she could feel Karr's irritation gathering like a dark cloud at her back.

She smiled at the thought, and at that moment the door slid open.

With a toss of her hair, she strode down the ramp, the fluttering fabric of her shirt a strange feeling against her skin.

She had chosen low heels, in case she had to run, and tight pants that were made of a fabric that shifted color as she walked.

Probably not the best choice if she wanted to be unobtrusive, but there had been nothing in Rina Fattal's wardrobe that seemed understated, so she ended up going with choices that would catch the eye, and take it off her face.

Because the less people looked at her, personally, the safer they would all be.

It would only take one person to claim she was an imposter, and the whole illusion would be ripped away.

Halfway down the ramp, Sebastian and Lucia caught up with her, sliding into place on either side.

She sensed Lucia's amusement at her wardrobe choices, while Sebastian seemed stunned into silence.

He looked at the deep V of cleavage revealed by the frilly shirt and then jerked his gaze away.

She couldn't be sure, but she thought she heard Lucia chuckle at that.

As long as eyes landed on her breasts, they weren't on her face, and that suited her fine.

She hitched her bag strap higher on her shoulder, and made sure it was still open enough that Fluffy could poke her head out if she wanted to.

The docking bay they'd landed on was in the open, on the massive raised disc that was the hover base landing pad.

Above, the sky was a deep blue and warm air brushed her, stirring her hair. Three moons ranged across the sky, one very close, the other two staggered behind each other to the right of it.

She tipped up her face, and let the sun touch her closed eyelids.

It was never this warm on Garmen. It was cold and wet, and when it wasn't, it was cold and dry.

"Looks like we might be free and clear," Lucia murmured beside her, and she opened her eyes again and saw there was no one coming to meet them, no guards or any barrier to them simply walking away.

To the right, the big Caruso warship's engines were still powering down, and all activity seemed to be focused on it.

"Let's go." Sebastian looked hard and dangerous in his dark clothes with dark shades against the bright sun, his mouth a grim line.

He looked like she usually did, she realized. Focused on the task at hand, aware the stakes were life and death.

It was strange to be on the other side of that.

And then Sebastian reached back a hand to stop her, his gaze up ahead, where now she could see four Caruso soldiers walking toward them, their thick-set bodies shimmering out of the heat haze from the warship's engines and the heat of the landing pad.

They were all cradling the massive laz weapons in their arms, and the way they approached, Dee felt an overwhelming sense of menace.

Her heart did a little hop in her chest and then she strode forward, between Sebastian and Lucia.

She heard Sebastian make a sound deep in his throat beside her, and then somehow he was in front of her again, angled slightly to shield her.

She was being a bad client, but she had a feeling Rina Fattal *would* be a bad client.

"You need to come with us." The soldier who spoke addressed Sebastian, not her, and Dee had a feeling Rina would not have taken that well.

"Why are you talking to him? I'm the one in charge." She waved an agitated hand in the air.

The soldier glanced at her, then focused back on Sebastian. "We have transport waiting for you."

Dee crossed her hands under her breasts and pushed them up slightly. She wasn't sure if the Caruso had any interest in Verdant String women, but it was worth a shot. "I'm not going anywhere with you. I've got plans."

"What plans?" At last, the soldier faced her.

"I've got friends to meet up with, shopping to do." She fluttered her fingers. "Although I'm not sure what business it is of yours."

Sebastian's grip on his laz tightened a fraction, and she wondered if he'd sensed a change in attitude amongst the Caruso. Was she pushing them too hard?

From behind her, she heard the bags thump down. Karr and Vavi had obviously caught them up.

"Where we taking them?" Karr asked, and even though he wasn't openly hostile, Dee could hear the resentment in his tone, which probably fit well with how someone at Rina Fattal's beck and call for a few days would sound.

She assumed he was speaking to Lucia, because she was the one who answered with a shrug.

"Your father wants you at a reception tonight in Dar Raca." The

Caruso soldier delivered the line reluctantly, as if he'd prefer to keep her in the dark.

"My father wants me at a function?" Dee gave a derisive laugh. "Then he can ask me himself." She took a step to the side, to go around the soldiers.

The soldiers edged back a little, but one moved subtly into her way, and Sebastian was suddenly very close to him.

Everyone went still.

"We're just passing on the message. Your father has provided a hover to take you to Dar Raca, where you will stay this evening and attend a function with him."

"What hover?" Sebastian asked.

"We'll escort you." The soldier stepped back a little.

"We can find it ourselves." Sebastian's look was flat and dangerous.

"We have orders," the soldier repeated.

Two of them shifted the laz weapons in their arms, going from cradling them to gripping the hilts and pointing them at the floor.

Ready to lift up and shoot at a moment's notice.

The move was lost on no one.

"Well, if we have to." Dee flounced forward, and the Caruso got out of her way.

She could have had another tantrum, but she had no interest in testing how far she could push the soldiers. Even if their orders were to keep her unharmed, she didn't know if they would follow that if they were angry enough.

She sensed nothing but cold hatred from them.

How had the Cores ever thought this would be a useful partnership?

A hover approached, long and narrow, and stopped when it reached her. There were two Cores guards onboard, one on either end.

They stood as the hover came to a stop, their movements stiff and jerky, as if they weren't here willingly. As if they were afraid of the Caruso.

"Good, a ride." She had no idea if she was playing this right, but she cocked a hip and gestured to Sebastian with her fingers, then snapped them. "Help me up."

She could sense his surprise, but he reached out and lifted her up, his hands gripping her hips as he swung her into a seat.

The heat that speared through her as her tight shirt rode up and his fingers pressed into the bare skin of her waist left her almost breathless. She lifted shocked eyes to his as he stepped back.

His own gaze was heated, and then he turned away, grabbing up one of the bags Karr was hauling, and setting it in the baggage area at the front.

One of the Core guards stepped up to the Caruso soldiers and spoke quietly with him, and then took up position on the hover again. She had the sense that they were being guarded rather than escorted.

The dynamics were so strange, she couldn't work them out.

One thing that had her relieved--it seemed the Caruso were not coming along. They were handing her over to the Cores guards.

Sebastian swung up, but he didn't sit, he stood, one arm gripping the back of her seat, his gaze sweeping the area as the hover reversed course, skimming the landing pad as it headed toward a square glass building.

She recognized her own vigilance in the way he made himself aware of their surroundings.

She pretended to fuss with her nails, and kept her own eye on what was happening around them.

Was Hanran Fattal, Rina's father, waiting for them in the building up ahead? And how did he have a warship of Caruson soldiers playing messenger for him?

She knew whatever the answer, she had to avoid meeting him at all costs.

HIS ARM RUBBED against Dee's side, the soft, smooth fabric of her ridiculous shirt making a whispering sound against the coarser fabric of his jacket.

He glanced at her, but she was looking away, and his gaze caught on the curve of her breasts, rising out of the ruffles of her shirt like . . .

He shook his head and faced forward again.

His focus was needed elsewhere.

Nothing about this situation was good.

There would be no quick escape. The Caruso had been waiting for them, and now they were in the hands of Cores guards who didn't look like they would be letting them out of their sight.

He bet what little money he had left that they'd be escorted to Dar Raca as well.

For some reason they wanted Rina Fattal under their control. Whatever deal the Caruso had made with the Cores, Hanran Fattal seemed to be directing it.

Fattal was the head exec of the most powerful Core Company, so that made sense, but their hovering around Rina was something he couldn't understand.

Up 'til now, she'd been a free spirit. Going where she pleased and doing whatever she wanted to do.

A thought had wedged itself into his head that maybe Hanran Fattal been tipped off about the resistance's plans to kidnap his daughter.

It certainly felt like the Cores had always been one step ahead these last six months, as he and the rest of the resistance had stepped up the fight.

There were rumors of moles, but there always had been. And when Vahn had disappeared, and Sebastian had stepped up as leader, he'd tried to follow those rumors down the crazy-making paths they'd led him.

And then they'd found out Rina Fattal would be out of her father's orbit, easy to take, and he'd rushed off, using every port and credit they had left to fund it.

Had he been led here, to this moment, by subtle innuendo and clever prompting?

He would need to think back to the meetings and conversations he'd had before he'd staked everything on this, but he knew he'd be grasping at straws, because there hadn't been a choice.

Since the Cores had started the mass repatriation of the wells and refineries, of every business on Lassa, the resistance had been taking them on the only way it could, in small groups. They'd disrupted transportation, delayed supplies, but every choice to fight was weighed against the cost of that fight to the hungry and the sick.

Their resources were perilously close to zero.

They'd needed a break, and Rina Fattal seemed to be the perfect solution.

As the hover neared the port building, his lips twisted in the parody of a smile.

Instead of their solution, chasing after Rina Fattal might have proved to be their doom.

NINE

DEE WAS TOO afraid of being overheard to ask Sebastian what Dar Raca was.

As the hover they'd been herded into at the hoverport entrance shot along elevated rails leading north, she tried to look bored and spent her time playing with Fluffy.

The little creature seemed to like the bag, hopping in and out of it frequently, and swinging on the straps.

The hover was as plush and luxurious as Rina Fattal's pleasure cruiser, a stark contrast to the shanty town that followed the curve of the elevated rails.

She could see wide pipes twisting through the forest, emerging at random points to curve beneath the rails and turn in the direction of the hover base they'd just come from.

Dee knew the main export of Lassa was a liquid gas that was used in many manufacturing processes. She guessed the pipes were how it was transported from the refineries.

"Dar Raca," Lucia murmured in her ear, and Dee turned in her seat to look.

The city rose in a collection of buildings made up of two or three columns of white, twisted around each other like the trunks of the trees in the forest that surrounded them. One in particular rose up to tower over the others.

She fought to school her features at her astonishment.

She wondered how many Cores execs there were on Lassa to justify buildings on this scale, and then suppressed a cynical smile, because from her experience as a gen-pop on Garmen, the Cores didn't bother justifying anything that meant their own comfort and wellbeing.

And, she supposed, on Lassa they didn't have an equivalent of Felicitos, the tethered way station that was the lifeblood and the hub of Garmen. These buildings, even stacked on top of each other, wouldn't come close to Felicitos' height.

The hover track curved between two of the smaller buildings, and headed straight for the largest one, and they entered through a silver door that opened as they approached.

The hover came to a stop in a massive atrium in which a small interior jungle seemed to thrive. The plants climbed up an artificial slope, and water cascaded down rocks. A living tree rose up at least three stories high, its leafy branches filtering the light pouring in from above into a cool green.

The hover doors opened and the Core guards stepped out. They were joined by two more.

Dee forced her legs to move, putting a little more swagger into her step as she reached the open door.

She waited for Sebastian to go ahead of her, and when he turned back, she put out an imperious hand, and with the tiniest crinkling in the corner of his eyes, he held out his own hand and she took it, as if she needed help stepping over the tiny gap between the hover and the platform.

Her hand still in his, she looked around, trying to appear bored.

The thing that struck her the most was the lack of people.

Felicitos was in a constant state of chaos most of the time, with people pushing and shoving their way onto the hovers to go up or down the hoverway.

There was respite from the scrum up on the Lower and Upper

Reaches, where only the Cores and their top workers were allowed, but everywhere else, including on the streets of Tether Town, there was always what seemed to be a crowd.

Here, she could see well-dressed women and men walking in and out the atrium, but there were none of the workers she was used to seeing bustling around.

A tiny luggage hover arrived, and Karr and Vavi loaded it up as if they did this every day.

One of the guards bent over the control panel, and the tiny hover trundled off in the direction of the lifts.

"Where are you taking my things?" She made her voice sharp.

"To the suite your father arranged for you." The guard's gaze swept over the others. "Your staff is dismissed."

Dee felt the first shot of hope and excitement. Maybe Sebastian and the team could get out of this, at least--but she didn't want to seem too eager to get rid of them. Rina Fattal would want to be served.

She made herself pout, but before she could open her mouth, Sebastian stepped in front of her. "The others can go, but I stay."

"You're not needed, we'll provide security." The soldier didn't change expression.

Dee put a hand on Sebastian's shoulder and hesitated, wondering whether to play along with him or not.

It would be better if he was free to escape as well. She didn't know why he was refusing to leave her, but she didn't want it to be because of a misplaced sense of responsibility to her.

She decided to hedge her bets. "You know I always need you, but maybe run off and have a little break." She made her words into a purr. "I'm sure I can . . . amuse myself."

He glanced back at her, and she almost blinked at the fury and determination in his gaze. "No."

She was so shocked, she let the silence grow too big.

"You need me." He made the words curt.

She looked at him for another beat. What would Rina Fattal do? Would she take what looked a lot like insubordination?

She wondered what he would do if she told him no again, and decided she liked him too much to risk him pushing back even harder, and maybe raising the guards' suspicions.

She forced herself to give a slow, naughty wink.

"Well, then, if you insist." She blew him a kiss, then turned to the guard. "I'm afraid I need this one. He's very . . . useful to me."

She hooked her arm through Sebastian's, and when the guard opened his mouth to argue, she hardened her expression. "No argument."

The guard stared at her, unblinking, and then finally gave a tiny nod, stepping out of the way.

Sebastian stepped away from her, and she saw the other three had formed a small group off to the side. He walked over to them and murmured something.

She could see the resistance on Lucia's face, as if she wanted to fight to stay herself, but eventually they all turned and walked away.

When Sebastian joined her, three of the guards stepped back into the hover and it moved off silently. The fourth one turned and led the way, and she risked a quick look at Sebastian behind his back.

But Sebastian wasn't looking at her, he was being a good body-guard, sweeping the space with his gaze. Never stepping out of character.

She felt Fluffy scramble out of the bag, and picked her up, cradling her close to her chest as they walked toward lifts.

The guard had moved quickly ahead of them, so Dee deliberately slowed her step to be contrary.

Sebastian glanced back at her, realized she was falling behind, and gave a tiny shake of his head.

She didn't think Rina Fattal would rush for anyone, so she gave him a long, slow smile and sent him an air kiss.

She had to suppress a grin when she saw a faint flush of color on his cheeks.

The guard stood stiffly beside the lift door, holding it open, his lips twisted in a snarl as he stared inside it.

There was someone else in there, a man, and he was leaning back against the wall.

From the glimpse she caught of him, arms and legs casually crossed, he seemed unintimidated by the guard.

She turned her back to him as she stepped inside, just in case he was someone Rina Fattal might know.

She put Fluffy up on her shoulder, and the movement caused her earring to jangle.

The man sucked in a sharp breath. "Rina? It's me, Peyt."

She went still, her gaze shooting to Sebastian, and then she angled her head slightly over her shoulder in the man's direction, letting her hair fall across her face. She hesitated, scrambling for what to say to him.

"Rina Fattal is not engaging with others today." Sebastian's voice was cold behind her, and she realized he'd stepped between herself and Peyt, blocking her from view.

"But it's me." The man sounded so surprised, Dee guessed he was a Cores exec or the son of one. Absolutely secure in his own sense of importance. "Is it really you? I thought you were away."

"As far as you're concerned, she still is." Sebastian kept his tone chilly.

"You're welcome to come up to my place tonight. We can catch up." The man's voice was thoughtful. "You can bring your talu."

"Rina Fattal will be attending a reception with her father tonight." The Cores guard spoke for the first time.

The man made a sound of surprise, and then shuffled in place.

Dee barely registered it, because her heart rate had spiked at the reminder she'd be dealing with Hanran Fattal so soon. Fluffy swung down the strap of the bag, and disappeared inside it, and Peyt made another sound of interest.

Then there was silence. It stretched for a long, agonizing eternity, and then the door of the lift pivoted open and the guard gestured them out, leaving Peyt behind them.

Sebastian walked behind her, a warm, solid presence, and she followed the guard down a short passage that opened up into a circular foyer with a massive curved window looking out onto the city. It looked as though a curved bite had been taken out of the floor, and she walked over to it and looked down through a number of similar holes to the atrium and the tree below.

Doors had been set into the curved walls to the right and the left, and the soldier opened one of them and indicated they enter.

Sebastian ignored him and set the laslock to his imprint first.

Dee could see the guard was about to object, and she flounced into the room past him and gave it a derisive glance. "Where's my father?" Her throat was so tight when she said the words, her voice came out husky.

"You'll see him tonight. Someone will fetch you at eight."

The guard turned and walked away, and Sebastian stood by the open door and watched him go.

"Close the door." Dee kept her voice to a low murmur.

Sebastian waited another beat before he stepped back and did as she asked. As soon as it closed, she spun to face him.

"What the hell?" She hadn't realized how angry she was with him, but it exploded out of her. "You should have taken your chance and run with the others." Her words were a low hiss as she stepped toe to toe with him.

His hands came up and gripped her upper arms. "I got you into this, I'll get you out. I'm not going anywhere." His dark eyes held hers.

"You *didn't* get me into this." She narrowed her eyes at him. "The Caruso and the Cores did. I don't hold it against you."

He dropped his hands and took a deep breath as he stepped away and turned. "That makes you a better person than me because I've had to fight hard not to resent you for not being Rina Fattal."

His admission hurt.

Enough to silence her.

She set her bag on the table, heard the click of Fluffy's claws as she scrambled out of it and went off to explore, and forced herself to look at Sebastian.

He was facing away from her, and he stalked to the window and looked out, his broad, muscular back to her.

His hand curled into a fist, and he thumped it softly against the glass.

"So what's your plan, then?" She knew she sounded angry, but she couldn't help it. "Seeing as you insisted on throwing your lot in with me."

"Escape." His tone was short.

She gave a snort at his answer, and turned away from him, taking in the room properly for the first time. She'd been too afraid Hanran Fattal would be in here waiting for her the first time.

It was like everything else--overdone and overwrought. It was as if the Cores execs were intent on spending everything they had on luxury, just to prove they could.

She stepped out of the uncomfortable shoes, and then walked into the bedroom and found her luggage stacked neatly in a walk-in wardrobe.

She had packed all the sensible things in one bag, and she put it on the bed, rifled through it and pulled out dark pants and a dark tunic.

Neither had ever been worn.

She was already in the new pants, and was just lifting the tunic over her head when Sebastian walked in behind her.

She sensed him freeze, but he didn't step back out and she didn't know if he looked away.

She pulled the soft fabric over her head, tugged it down, and turned to face him, eyebrows raised. "Yes?"

He cleared his throat. "Sorry for the temper tantrum. I see all this luxury, and when everyone I know is starving, it makes me a little crazy."

"Are the Cores not hiring, or aren't they paying enough?" She thought back to what she'd seen since she first landed on Lassa. She'd been tense, and focused on threats, but she realized she'd seen hardly anyone here that on Garmen would be called gen-pop--the general population.

Those she had seen had been below the hover rails, looking up at them from the shacks cobbled together on the forest floor.

"They've got automatons doing as much as they can. What jobs aren't suited to that, they've employed more guards, a lot of them from what were the criminal gangs. There are a few jobs where they're employing the gen-pop, but not at living wages."

"Why? What caused the change?" She sat down on the bed and pulled on socks and then boots.

Sebastian leaned back against the doorjamb and watched her with a hooded expression. "They started losing money." He hesitated. "Someone I've got working in one of the Cores' offices told me that since the Faldine War ended, the gas wells on Faldine are finally starting to produce. It's not the same quality as ours, but it can be refined. So that's one thing. Then something happened a while back to make the Verdant String unwilling to do business with us. My contact couldn't find out what."

"Cepi," Dee told him. "Cepi and Var."

"What's Cepi?" She had his interest. He pushed away from the door, dropped his crossed arms.

"Cepi was a moon orbiting the Verdant String planet of Kalastoni. It doesn't exist anymore and the Breakaways, both Garmen and Lassa, seem to be to blame."

Sebastian winced. "And what about Var? That's the capital of Parn, isn't it?"

"Yes. Looks like to cover for their mistake at Cepi, the Cores set loose a fanatic on Parn, gave him a ship and weapons, and he blew up a number of buildings in Var. Killed VS citizens. And unfortunately for the Cores, left enough clues for the VSC to follow the trail right back to them."

"The VSC is boycotting the Breakaways?" Sebastian rubbed his temple.

"And nature abhors a vacuum." Dee thought of the way the Caruso had been so quick to jump in when the VSC withdrew. They must have been watching the Breakaways for a long time to move so quickly.

"Yes, the Caruso didn't take long to worm their way in."

Beside her, Dee felt the brush of fur, and saw Fluffy had curled herself up next to her. Even with the little creature's eyes closed, she thought she was getting used to seeing her better and better. Peyt had called her a talu. She would have to look it up when she was able to find a comm set with interplanetary access.

She stroked the top of Fluffy's head and then stood, putting the small pack she'd found amongst Rina's things on the bed and rolling up clothes to go in it.

"What are you doing?"

She glanced over her shoulder at him. "I thought the plan was to escape?"

He flushed a little. "Yes. But I have a feeling it isn't going to be as easy as walking out."

She shrugged. "I can't meet Hanran Fattal this evening. I'm dead the moment I do. So I'm prepared to take some risks."

He hesitated, then gave a nod. "I won't let you meet him on your own, whatever happens."

She believed he meant it, but it occurred to her that it would be very convenient for Sebastian to have a face-to-face with Hanran Fattal, especially if he was able to get close while armed with a laz.

Because surely that had been his objective all along.

TEN

THEY STEPPED BACK OUT into the light, airy space of the foyer, and Sebastian felt the stir of air coming up from the circle in the floor and the muted sound of the atrium, seven floors below.

He walked over to the massive window and looked out over Dar Raca from the most exclusive address in the city.

He'd never been inside the Tree--the Cores head office--until now. Not once in all the years he'd lived on Lassa.

His reaction to it was visceral.

He couldn't look at anything without thinking of the suffering beyond, in the shacks and shanties that hugged the hover rail, or were tucked away in the forests.

Things had never been good for the gen-pop, but since the Cores had started clawing back every last bit of independent wealth, it had been catastrophic.

"Did you notice the Caruso didn't leave the landing pad?" Dee asked softly as she came to stand beside him. "I don't see them anywhere below, either. They're keeping out of sight."

"Doesn't matter. We have resistance members everywhere, including more than one working at the hover base. I should have known the Caruso were there long before now."

"I'd say that today might have been the first time they came down to land here, but no one so much as blinked an eye at them, so I don't think that's true."

That she'd noticed the reactions of the landing pad crew told him more about her than she probably realized.

This woman was more than just an inventory manager. She held herself with the ready tension of a guard.

One thing was for sure, she didn't live in the same grinding poverty that he'd been forced into these last six months. She had looked at the apartment they'd been allocated and sneered rather than gaped.

Her body, and because he'd walked in on her without knocking, he'd seen more of it than he should have, was exactly as he thought it would be. Muscled. Toned. Sleek.

She hadn't gone hungry in a long time, and she kept herself in peak condition.

"Things are obviously better for the Garmen gen-pop." He was looking down at her as she took in Dar Raca, which glistened white and silver amongst the dark green of the trees.

She glanced up, surprised. "Why do you say that? I've always thought things were pretty bad."

"You don't look like you have things pretty bad, Dee."

She flushed and looked away. "That's true, I don't. I work for the richest independent on Garmen."

He didn't know why, but a flash of jealousy hit him, and he had to look away. "You live with him?"

She nodded. "Most of the--" She paused, looked away. "Yes. Myself and a few colleagues share a wing in his home."

"Most of the what?" He didn't mean his voice to sound so hard, but he couldn't help it.

"None of your business." Her voice was cool. "Let's go, I think I've got a good idea of how things are laid out down there. Where are we escaping to?"

"The forest." He forced himself to step back. "As soon as we make it past the Dar Raca wall, we're safe." Safe, but not comfortable. But he knew the forests better than any Dar Raca Cores guard.

She gave a nod and turned, started walking toward the lift.

He reached out and closed a hand over her shoulder. "Careful. The man in the lift earlier, he worked out you weren't Rina Fattal."

She raised startled eyes to his. "Why didn't he say something?"

"I think he liked knowing something the guard didn't. My guess is he's planning to blackmail you, and it has something to do with Fluffy."

He was getting used to the little creature, because he could see her head peeping out from the top of Dee's pack.

She gave a slow nod. "Well, I'll duck if I see him coming."

Sebastian thought it more likely Peyt was planning to sneak up here and corner her in her apartment.

There was something in the man's demeanor that had his instincts humming. At first, it was the lascivious look in Peyt's eyes as he'd craned to look at Dee.

He'd had a sexual encounter with Rina Fattal at one point, there was no doubt in Sebastian's mind about that. And when he realized Dee wasn't who he thought she was, his focus had turned to Fluffy. It had almost seemed as lascivious as the way he'd looked at Dee.

She was striding ahead of him now, her hair back in a knot at her nape, her dark clothing giving the impression she was a guard.

It was in the way she held herself, in the way she moved. Exactly like him.

Because he'd been a Cores guard himself a lifetime ago, working the pipelines until his conscience rebelled.

Damned if he believed she was an inventory manager.

On that score, he was sure, she was lying.

DEE STOPPED as they neared the lift and turned slightly to Sebastian, waited until he was right beside her.

"I need to access interplanetary comms." She kept her voice low.

"I checked and there wasn't a way to connect in the apartment, but I need to get in touch with my boss on Garmen. I'm assuming once we're in the forests, interplanetary comms aren't easy to come by?"

His lips thinned at the request, but he gave a nod. "We either find a way here, or it doesn't happen."

It was a dangerous side-trip, she knew that. But if there was any hope of getting word to Leo, and having him alert the VSC to what was going on, it would have to be now.

"I think it's worth the risk. With Arkhor taking control of Garmen, Leo can pass what we know about the Caruso on to them, and they can pass it on to Bodivas, and hopefully, they'll send some warships to intervene."

His lips twisted into a wry smile. "Bodivas could have intervened any time in the last six months, and there's been no sign of them."

"Maybe they've been having the same trouble getting the right information that you have." Dee wasn't so enamored of the VSC she'd die on a hill for them, she'd been brought up on a Breakaway, after all, but she couldn't see how it was in their interests for the Caruso to get a hold on the Breakaways. If Bodivas, the closest Verdant String planet to Lassa, had known they had cause to intervene, they would have.

Sebastian blew out a breath and gave a curt nod. "Maybe."

He took the lead, moving beyond the lifts to a narrow door, and shoving it open with his shoulder.

She approved. Using the stairwell in a Cores exec facility was the one sure way to avoid meeting anyone.

She followed him, running lightly down behind him.

He was fitter than she was, faster, and she knew she was in the best shape of her life.

While he could obviously stand to gain some weight, he had honed his body into a weapon.

Perhaps because it was one of the few weapons he had.

Her gaze went to the laz that was tucked into a holster at the small of his back. It was at least a decade old, and she didn't think the others in his team had anything better.

Most likely, Zyr and the men and women of the resistance on Garmen had faced similar issues when it came to lack of resources, but they'd had another option. Their access to the secret tunnels of Felicitos had given them the chance to mess with the Cores in other ways, harming them financially by leaking secrets and knowing what deals were going to be made.

It looked like on Lassa, the resistance had had to take a more confrontational approach.

"The first three floors above the atrium are offices." Sebastian stopped at a door. "This should be the top one of the three. I've never been in this building before today, so I don't know what to expect."

She nodded. "We can play the 'I'm looking for my father' game if someone stops us."

He shot her a skeptical look. "Unless someone actually calls Hanran Fattal. Or if this is the floor his office is on."

She acknowledged that with a nod. "So we play it by ear."

Because he looked so serious and grim, she couldn't help blowing a kiss at him before she pushed the door open. "It'll be fine. You were good at playing the jealous bodyguard earlier."

She caught a glimpse of the shock and surprise on his face, and smiled as she stepped into the Cores offices.

It was early evening, and there was no one around.

Except, down the first passageway to her right, she saw a guard.

Sebastian paused beside her, and as he did, a second guard joined the first, their stance professional and alert.

They were guarding something, or some one.

Before they could notice they were being watched, she started down the main passageway. She could hear the low murmur of voices behind a door to her left, but otherwise things were very quiet.

Sebastian caught up to her, walking by her side.

Up head, a man stepped out of an office, talking on his comm.

He turned away from them, walking toward what looked like a bank of transparent lifts that were set on the outside of the building.

It wasn't necessary for them to speak.

Sebastian turned with her into the man's office without so much as a pause, and he closed the door behind them as she went straight for the comm unit.

"Looks like it has interplanetary comms." She rubbed her hands together in excitement, then slid into the man's abandoned seat.

It took her a few minutes to get out of the internal company system, and then she found Gaudier's Transport's comm platform, and sent a message.

There was no immediate response, and she stood, agitated, and walked to the window, looking out over trees and a smaller building of twisted columns in the distance. Directly below her was what looked like a park and a meandering path.

"Dee?"

The voice that came from the screen was Leo's, and she raced back to the desk, and gestured to Sebastian to join her.

"Leo!" She sank into her chair in relief. "Everyone's all right?"

"Everyone's all right, except for worrying about you."

Dee sensed Sebastian come up behind her, and Leo narrowed his eyes as he looked over her shoulder.

"What's happening, Dee?"

"I'm on Lassa. And things are bad here, Leo. The Caruso are here, hiding with the help of the Corcs, just like on Garmen."

"And your friend?" Leo's gaze was focused beyond her shoulder, on Sebastian.

She turned to him, lifting her brows in a silent question on how many of his secrets she could reveal.

She saw his eyes widened in surprise.

He hadn't expected her to keep his secrets with Leo.

"I'll let him tell you himself," she said, and moved to one side.

"I'm Sebastian Xian. The leader of the Lassian Resistance."

Dee crossed her arms under her breasts and gave a quirk of her lips. She *knew* it. She'd guessed he was high up in the leadership structure.

"And how did one of my most senior employees end up with you?" Leo kept his voice neutral.

"She was hiding from the Caruso on a pleasure cruiser, and we mistook her for Rina Fattal, the owner of the ship." Sebastian lifted his shoulders in a calm shrug.

"That doesn't answer my question."

"I don't have to answer your questions."

Dee stared at Sebastian in astonishment. There was a real edge to his voice. A tone of dislike that surely wasn't warranted.

He didn't even *know* Leo.

She shot him an incredulous look. "Listen, Leo, they're desperate down here. The Cores have taken back all the businesses, cut most of the gen-pop off from access to food and resources. People are starving, they have nothing left, and the Caruso are landing, calm as you please, at the Cores hover base. Because I was hiding in the Lassian pleasure cruiser, the Lassian resistance took me for Rina Fattal, the daughter of a top Cores exec. They were planning to hold her for ransom. While I was explaining I wasn't Rina Fattal, the Caruso arrived, clamped the cruiser to their warship, and towed us to Lassa under orders from Rina Fattal's father. The Caruso think I'm Rina Fattal, too. So before I have to meet face-to-face with Hanran Fattal, her father, I have to get out of here. Sebastian is helping me. I just wanted to get hold of you, and ask you to send the VSC here. The Caruso are going to take over, and there won't be an easy way to blast them into space like you did on Felicitos."

"That wasn't me," Leo said. "It was Sofie." He paused. "I'm going to try and get hold of Ruanne. Get her to help you. She can put you on the next freighter back to Garmen."

"Ruanne Lex?" Sebastian bent closer to the screen.

Leo gave a short nod.

"Far as I know, Ruanne Lex was murdered by the Cores six months ago, because she refused to hand over her assets to them."

Dee drew in a sharp breath. She should have thought of that. If all the businesses had been taken back by the Cores, why would Ruanne's be any different?

The woman was the largest independent on Lassa, and she and Leo had had a longstanding cooperative relationship.

Both cheated the Cores' system as much as possible, and helped each other where they could.

"Did you speak to Ruanne's captain on the Deck before the Caruso attacked?" Leo asked her.

She shook her head. She'd been looking for Vur when the shooting started. "But we've been in touch with some of Ruanne's people in the last six months." She'd spoken to one of them herself.

"I've gotten written messages from Ruanne." Leo leaned back in his seat. "They didn't mention any of this, which seems unlikely. And one of the messages has been within the last two months."

"So that begs the question." Dee glanced over at Sebastian. "Who have we been talking to?"

ELEVEN

HE WAS BEHAVING LIKE AN ASSHOLE, but Sebastian looked at Leo Gaudier's slick, handsome appearance, and wanted to punch the bastard.

He didn't like the proprietary way he addressed Dee, and he didn't like the way the man looked at him with deep suspicion.

"Did they take over Ruanne's business, or close it down?" Dee asked him, and he forced himself to put his animus aside.

"They took it over. They kept everything that was making money running."

"So you were talking to the Lassian Cores, then. We all were." Dee's face was grim as she spoke to Leo.

Leo sucked in a breath and scowled, his eyes cold and angry. "Dee, I want you out of there."

"Send the VSC, Leo. There's a population in crisis here. Even more than on Garmen. People are literally starving to death. And I'm an eye witness to the fact the Caruso are on-planet."

"I'll tell the Arkhorans, but they're not the the Verdant String planet with jurisdiction over Lassa. That's Bodivas." Leo leaned forward on his elbows, his face taking up the whole screen. "According to my connection in the Arkhoran Special Forces, Bodivas is sending a warship to Lassa right now. Is there a way I can get in touch with you later, so I can give them your coordinates?"

"I don't think so." Dee glanced at him for confirmation. "When we get to the forest, we'll be safe, but we'll be out of the loop."

"I'll make a plan to get you to a comm unit." This wasn't Dee's fight, and if there was a chance he could get her out of here, he'd take it. "I'll try to make contact in a couple of days, when the Bodivas warship has had a chance to get here."

Dee shook her head. "That would put us both in serious danger. Where would you even find a comm station in the forest?"

Sebastian met her gaze. "There're a few Cores security facilities scattered along the pipelines." He knew--once upon a time he'd worked in them.

Dee narrowed her eyes. "And I bet they're guarded to the hilt. Give Leo a place where it will be safe for a ship to land, and I can make my way there. Say in three days."

"The closest place is more than three days away. You're looking at at least a week until you reach open ground. The forest is too dense." Sebastian rubbed a frustrated hand over his short hair. "I don't think you'd make it on your own, and I don't have the time to go with you, or the people to spare to send someone in my place. Either the Bodivas land at the Cores hover base, or you take a smaller hover up to meet them. And right now, that's impossible. I don't have access to a hover anymore. The one I had is floating off the Felicitos Deck." He hadn't even thought about how he was going to explain to Seres that the small freighter he had borrowed to chase Rina Fattal was floating around Garmen's nearspace after the Caruso attack.

"Then bribe someone," Leo said.

"I can't." He looked over at Dee, held her gaze as he tried to push away the sick, hopeless feeling that would paralyze him if he let it. "We don't have money left to feed ourselves now, let alone pay a big bribe. We gambled everything on getting to Rina Fattal, and we lost."

"Then you find a way to contact me in three days." Leo had gone back to cold and hard.

Dee opened her mouth to say something, but Sebastian heard a voice just outside the door.

He reached over, switched off the screen, and grabbed her forearm, pulling her with him so they ended up flush against the wall beside the door.

It opened, and the office worker walked in, still talking on his comm set; unaware and blind to the world around him.

Sebastian slid his hand down Dee's arm, closed his fingers around hers, and then when the man had almost reached his desk he tugged her out into the passage.

Sebastian sensed movement as the man turned, but they were already a few steps away from his door, headed for the lifts.

"Good ears," Dee murmured. "Fast moves." There was approval in her voice. She threaded her fingers through his more fully, and squeezed.

He hadn't been happy in a long time, but, he realized with a ripple of shock, he felt close to it right now.

It was ridiculous. They were playing a game here, and none of this was real. And yet, because he'd had so little joy recently, he found he held on to it anyway.

SEBASTIAN LED them through the darkening streets of Dar Raca, keeping to the back ways.

Below the canopy of trees were lower, single and double story buildings that ran in a long, meandering line from west to east and Sebastian was leading them west, where the last, dark orange light of the day lit the sky.

Fluffy had fallen asleep in the bag when they'd left the apartment, but Dee felt her stir and then pop her head out the top as strange birds began calling from the trees as the darkness settled in, and insects started up a whirring sound that seemed to come from all around them.

"Did you see those guards?" she asked him. "Down the passageway?"

He nodded. "They've got someone or something down there. No question."

"I wonder--"

"Trouble." Sebastian's words were low and clipped, and as he said it, she saw for herself Cores guards turning the corner up ahead, coming their way.

"Won't they pass us by?" They weren't doing anything suspicious, after all.

He gave a tiny shake of his head. "I wouldn't count on it."

He was right that the two men heading toward them seemed to be focused on them, and then Dee saw one look down at a screen and then back up at them.

They weren't just doing rounds. They were hunting.

She looked for a way out, saw the narrow gap between two low slung buildings made of the crisp white material everything here seemed to be constructed with.

She took a shallow, quick breath, and then gave a low, husky laugh. "Oh, all right then," she said, tugging Sebastian between the buildings. As soon as they were out of sight, she gave a loud giggle. "Run," she hissed, and took off, ducking around the back of one of the buildings. From inside the bag, she thought she heard Fluffy give a strange chortle of delight.

Sebastian overtook her, turned the next corner, and she almost ran into him as she found him stopped and facing a dead end.

A white wall blocked their way, a blue glow emanating from the top of it, and beyond it, away to the left, she noticed what looked like a massive screen which faced into the forest.

"What's the glow on top?" She measured the height, looked for hand and footholds.

They could maybe get over it with a little luck.

"You don't want to touch it. Chemical compound that burns through skin and bone."

Right. They weren't going over the wall. And she could hear the pounding of boots headed their way.

She set her pack down at her feet.

"Well then, big boy." She crooked her finger. Leaned back against the building behind her. "Let's make it real."

TWELVE

DEE WATCHED him with eyes that dared him, that asked him what they had to lose.

And even though his training, and every sensible, logical part of him, screamed to stand ready for the guards who he could hear running in their direction, he stepped up to her.

She lifted her face to his, slid her arms around him as he backed her flush against the cool, smooth finish of the wall behind her.

He bent his head, his mouth almost brushing hers.

"Real, remember?" She whispered the words, then rose a little, nibbled on his lips.

The sensation slammed through him, almost blanking his brain as he pulled her hard against him, slid his tongue between her lips as her mouth opened beneath his.

She arched against him as he vaguely noted the guards racing around the corner, gasping for breath.

"Told you," one of the guards huffed to the other.

Dee tilted her head back, to break the kiss, and he couldn't help himself, he bent with her, keeping their lips fused, unwilling to break their connection.

She raised her hands, cupped his face, and smiled against his mouth.

Then she turned her head to the guards, so his lips were on the soft skin of her cheek. "Sorry, boys, this is a private party."

She extended an arm in their direction, made a shooing motion with her fingers.

Then she turned back to Sebastian, anchoring those fingers in his short hair as she got impossibly closer.

One of the guards cleared his throat. "I'm afraid your father--"

She made a sound of frustration, turned to them again, while Sebastian got himself back under control.

"We were just out to get something to eat. It's at least two hours until I've got to be at the function my father has ordered me to attend, and I haven't eaten in nearly a full day. This," she twirled her hand between herself and Sebastian, "was just a delicious little side trip before we found a place we liked."

She straightened back from the wall, hooked an arm around Sebastian's waist, and picked up her pack.

Sebastian saw it move a little, but in the gloom of the alleyway, he couldn't see Fluffy poking out the top.

"You said you knew a good place." She was looking up at him. "Somewhere real and gritty."

She was setting it up so he could take her somewhere the gen-pop would go, not the Cores. It would help keep her under the radar a bit longer while they worked a new way out of this, because these guards were not going to leave them now.

He said nothing, just gave a curt nod, and walked straight for the guards.

They eyed him with dislike and what he guessed was disdain, but then, he felt the same about them. He just hid it better.

He'd been taking them toward the gen-pop end of Dar Raca when they'd run, and he did know a restaurant nearby that served food that was traditionally from Bodivas, the closest Verdant String planet to Lassa. Even though it wasn't particularly expensive, it was out of the reach of most gen-pop now, though, so the gritty and real descriptors most likely no longer applied.

Still, that made it more likely to be a place Rina Fattal would frequent, not less.

He stepped a little away from Dee, grabbed her hand rather than be constrained by her arm around his waist if he needed to defend them.

She laced her fingers through his, and while he knew it was for show, he let himself enjoy the feeling.

When you lived as close to the edge as he did these days, you took what you could and held onto it with both hands.

Up ahead, the little place he was taking them to was lit up, but quiet still, because the sun had only just gone down.

He bent his head, put his lips near her ear. "We might have a problem paying for the meal. I spent my last ports buying supplies for the freighter we took to Garmen."

"As it happens, I found some ports in Rina Fattal's bedroom suite on the cruiser." She turned to whisper her answer in his ear, and her lips brushed his skin.

He had to fight the shiver that wanted to run through him.

"Well, then." He held the door to the restaurant open for her, let it swing shut in the guards' faces as he followed her in. "Let's eat."

SEBASTIAN ATE with the single-minded focus of someone who hadn't had a decent meal in far too long.

She enjoyed watching him as she sampled the aromatic traditional dishes of Bodivas, like nothing she'd ever tasted before.

The bowls of colorful food suited the warm, tropical air of Dar Raca and the calls of the birds coming from the trees.

The guards who'd tracked them down and followed them inside the restaurant sat at a nearby table and looked far more relaxed than they had before as they ate a meal as well. She guessed their good mood was because they could charge the meal to Hanran Fattal.

"What was that screen I saw when we were in the alley?" She kept her voice low, because Rina Fattal would sure know what it was.

"When the Cores took control of all the independent businesses six months ago, they fired everyone, and each day, whoever wants work has to go stand in front of the screen and see what jobs are available that day."

"They turned everyone in gen-pop into a casual worker?"

"And they offer a rate of pay that's just short of nothing."

She could see even talking about it was making him angry.

"Even the little they offer is enough to cause near riots as people vie for the jobs, and sometimes it ends with the guards firing their weapons into the crowd." His jaw clenched, and then he leaned back in his chair and scooped up more food.

"What about the Cores businesses? Are the workers there still full-time employees."

He gave a nod. "Wouldn't do to have strangers come in every day. They vet their workers and they pay them more than they're giving the others. Most of the permanent workers can afford to live in Dar Raca itself. Everyone else has been forced into the forests."

He hesitated, as if to say something else, and she waited him out.

"The thing is, one of the resistance members worked for the independent contractor that was paid to get the screen up and running. She's set things up so that every day, she adds some extra workers to the schedule. Not enough to make them suspicious, but more than they actually asked for."

She grinned. "Now that sounds similar to something we were doing on Garmen. Tipping the scales in our favor."

He mirrored her smile and when she bit into a tiny pastry, his gaze moved to her mouth before lifting up to meet hers again.

It felt as if the air between them was full of static, and it was only when someone left the restaurant, banging the door behind them, that he looked away and went back to scooping up tender strips of meat with thin, aromatic bread.

"You're a good kisser," she said.

He choked, and then flashed another look at her, and she guessed he was wondering how much of it had been real, how much of it was for show.

Theoretically it was all for show, because they wouldn't have been locked together, tasting each other, if they hadn't needed to look like lovers. But that wasn't to say she hadn't enjoyed the hell out of it.

"I'd do it again, given the chance. Without an audience."

He paused, a sliver of meat pinched between bread just short of his lips. "Is that so?" His face was completely serious.

Little crackles of desire ran up her arms, and her blood seemed to slow, running thick and heavy in her veins.

He frowned at her and she sucked in a breath.

Since she'd met him, that face had made her want to do the verbal equivalent of mussing his hair, and she gave in to temptation again.

"Oh, yes." She drew the words out.

He had difficulty swallowing his mouthful, his gaze lifting to meet hers.

"I got the sense you wouldn't say no, either." She grinned at him.

He shook his head, put both hands on the table beside his empty plate, and leaned back.

"Full?"

"Yes." He looked over at her plate. "You haven't finished."

"I can put away a lot, but not this much. Even Fluffy's defeated." She'd been secretly passing Fluffy tidbits throughout the meal, and the talu was now curled up, asleep, in the bag.

Dee tilted the plate to him in an unspoken offer, but he shook his head with regret.

"Can't." He eyed the food, though. "Feels wrong to leave it, but I just can't."

"The staff won't let it go to waste." Of that, she was sure. When they'd first sat down, she saw their server's surprise at the sight of Sebastian.

He'd recognized him.

If he was part of the resistance, she bet the leftover food would find its way to the mouths of those who needed it.

Sebastian had said nothing about the server, although Dee was sure the recognition was mutual.

He leaned across the table, took her hands in his own, and she leant forward, so their faces were so close together, she could see the warm gold flecked through his dark brown eyes.

They were focused and all business now.

"Time to pay and run," he murmured. "Give me some ports and while I settle the bill, you get out the door and get out of here. I'll block them, give you some time. They're only interested in you. Hide, and then come back here in an hour. I'll be waiting."

She nodded, reached into the bag's side pocket and pulled out a heap of ports, dropped them into his hand.

She stayed seated as he stood and moved to the counter.

The guards watched him, but they didn't look worried. They were drinking something cold in tall glasses, and went back to their conversation almost immediately.

Dee pivoted on her chair, angling for the door, and then ran for it, pushing her way out of the cool interior into the hot, humid night. She jumped the steps, darted across the street, and dived into the unlit alleyway between two buildings.

She was two steps in, in total darkness, when an arm hooked around her throat, throwing her feet out from under her and choking her. She could hear Fluffy's high pitched screech of anger as her bag banged against her attacker's arm, and then, from the corner of her eye, she saw the blinking lights of a laz as it pressed against her forehead.

She went still.

"Now, I'm not supposed to hurt you," the guard said, his voice regretful. "But I am to ensure you obey orders. It seems your daddy knows you all too well."

THIRTEEN

HE AND GERT pretended not to know each other as Sebastian paid the bill.

He handed over more ports than necessary for the meal, and Gert slipped the extras into a pocket as they chatted easily.

He heard the door close as Dee slipped out, but he didn't look around, and Gert's gaze didn't lift.

The guards noticed, though.

One gave a shout, and Sebastian did react to that, turning toward them, stepping in their way. "What is it?" he made his voice sound concerned.

Both guards were on their feet, and the one closest to him tried to shove him aside.

He was ready for it, though, bracing himself and then pretending to stagger even more into their path.

"Out of the fucking way."

He was shoved at again, managed to stick out a foot and trip one of them, but the guard didn't go down, he stumbled a few steps, and then they were out.

"They didn't pay." Gert looked worried for the first time.

He'd be blamed for it. That's how it worked here.

Sebastian tossed a couple more ports at him to compensate, and then headed for the door himself.

Just in case they got her. Although he had the sense she could really move if she wanted to.

The guards stood in the middle of road, looking around wildly, and Sebastian felt a sense of satisfaction.

He watched them for a few moments, then turned away from them and began walking down the street.

"Hey!" One of the guards spotted him. "Where'd she go?"

He raised his hands. "I'm the hired help, she doesn't tell me what she's going to do. She tells me what *I'm* going to do."

The guard turned away from him in disgust, but the other one took a step closer to him. "I don't like you."

The feeling's mutual.

He'd seen guards like this when he'd been a guard on the pipelines himself. He knew how to push their buttons, and equally, how to deescalate.

He shrugged in response, half-turned away, and felt the punch of a laz hit him in his upper right shoulder.

Pain lanced through him and he crumpled to the ground and lay on his side, trying to breathe.

"Shit, Bauer. You shouldn't have done that."

That he could hear what was being said was a good sign, but he couldn't move.

"Accidental discharge," Bauer said, and there was a smirk to his voice.

"Your funeral. We're looking for the daughter of Hanran Fattal. He hears there was an accidental discharge near her, you are done for."

He didn't see Bauer's reaction to that, but the silence said everything it needed to.

The asshole was nervous now.

"Got her."

From his position on the floor he saw both sets of boots turn back to the street.

"Be careful with her." There was relief and worry in the guard's voice. "You don't want to explain any bruising."

"Nah, we're good. Right, princess?"

"What have you done to my bodyguard?" Dee kept her voice steady. Cold as ice.

Just hearing that she was all right loosened the tight grip fear had on his chest.

"Just a little accidental discharge on the lowest stun. He'll be up and moving in ten minutes or so."

"Well then, I'd watch my back if I were you." Dee said the words calmly. "No telling what kind of consequences there could be for accidents like that."

"Enough of this. Your daddy is waiting."

Sebastian couldn't see the bastard who was speaking, but he had the sense he had Dee in some kind of tight grip.

"Bring my bodyguard along."

"We're not carrying him. He's a big boy. He can make his way back to the Tree when he's ready. *If* your father wants him back."

Sebastian guessed they'd make sure he was blacklisted. Especially Bauer.

He might not like to have to come face-to-face with Sebastian on a level playing field.

But that didn't matter now, because they were taking Dee away. And she'd be facing Hanran Fattal in a couple of hours.

Alone.

The one thing he'd promised her wouldn't happen.

———

DEE OPTED to keep things low key. No sense causing a fuss when the last thing she wanted was more eyes on her than she had already.

It meant pretending she didn't care about Sebastian, lying like a felled tree on the strip of green grass in front of the restaurant, but that couldn't be helped.

The guards didn't seem to expect much of a reaction from her about that, anyway. But that was Cores guards for you. Seemed like the Garmen and Lassian versions were similar.

At least Sebastian knew someone in the restaurant. She hoped they'd help him if they could.

The guards boxed her in as they walked, and when they got to the big central building, the Tree, it was alive with light, music and people, and she was even more grateful to be hidden from view.

She wasn't short, but the three men were all taller than she was, and they shielded her well.

As they took her up the lift toward the suite she'd been in earlier, she wondered why Hanran Fattal was so eager to see his daughter tonight.

She was starting to form a nasty suspicion Rina Fattal might have been more than just a spoiled daughter going where her whim led her.

It had occurred to her that perhaps Rina Fattal was on the Felicitos Deck for a reason other than a jaunt.

And Hanran Fattal was looking for an update.

She suppressed a shiver.

One of the guards opened the door to the apartment and stepped inside with her, and the other two took up position outside.

She tilted her head to look at the one who'd entered the apartment with her, standing with feet planted apart, saying nothing.

"Don't mind me." It was Travi, the one who'd grabbed her in the alley. "I've got orders to make sure you're ready on time. Long as you're working toward that, I'll leave you alone."

She considered him for a long moment. "I'll let my father know how dedicated you were about it." She made it sound like a threat, and it was obviously a pretty good one because he paled a little.

"No disrespect intended." He turned his back on her, walked to the window and stood looking out.

She turned away herself, walking into the big bedroom, and closed and locked the door.

She set her bag on the bed and opened it, scooping Fluffy out and crooning to her as she tried to soothe her.

After her initial shriek of rage, the talu had gone still, and Dee had been afraid she was hurt, but she seemed all right, arching under Dee's hand, and curling up under Dee's chin when Dee lifted her close.

"They are nasty thugs." She turned to look at the door as she spoke. "We are going to have to get away from them, first chance we get."

She walked into the bathroom, ran a sink of warm water for Fluffy, and then stepped into a hot shower.

As she rubbed cleanser through her hair, she wondered how Sebastian was doing. Whether he was on his feet.

And hoped he would take the chance he'd been given to get out. He needed to run and make a new plan to bring down the Cores and the Caruso.

No matter what, she didn't see how he could get into the function she was being dragged to. Which meant he couldn't help her now.

She was on her own.

She was used to working as a team, had done so for a long time, but she could go solo if she had to.

Guess that time had come.

FOURTEEN

"YOU ALL RIGHT?" Gert crouched beside him, a cup of water in his hand.

Sebastian levered up on his elbows, and took the water, gulped it down in a few swallows. He nodded, and then dragged himself to his feet. "I'll live."

He felt better as he stood, and the water helped, too. "Can I get more water?"

Gert disappeared, and when he came back, Sebastian had worked out most of the kinks.

He drank the water, handed the cup back, and then leaned in close. "Get word to headquarters that I'm going back to the Tree. I'll be in touch when I get Dee out."

He didn't wait for a response, he started walking back into the center of Dar Raca. Every minute that ticked by was important.

He shook off the tightness in his muscles as he walked, until he was able to jog, and then run.

He had to slow down, though, when he reached the central ring of Dar Raca, and could no longer use the back alleys.

A running man wearing black tended to attract all the wrong attention.

He got to the end of the last curve of buildings before the wide landscaped park around the Tree. The elevated rail was a few blocks to his left, and a hover traveled on it--silent and all lit up.

He eyed the security arrangements. It was something he'd done before many times, but he'd never judged the risk of getting caught worth the dubious benefit of getting inside.

Things were different now.

Getting in was imperative.

There were Cores guards at the street entrance, and groups of two wandered the park. He wanted to swear, because the security looked even tighter than when he'd last assessed it.

And then he went still. Because coming out of the Tree, hurrying along a path to Sebastian's right, was Peyt. The asshole from the lift earlier this afternoon.

Sebastian took a chance and went back a few steps so he could follow the narrow lane behind the building to his right. He reached the other end in time to see Peyt had just passed him, and was heading deliberately for one of the lower, smaller versions of the Tree that were dotted around Dar Raca. The preferred living quarters of the Cores execs.

He fell into step behind him, pleased there were so many people around, both coming and going from the Tree.

Peyt didn't look back, he was talking on his comm. As he ran his finger through the lock on the door, Sebastian stepped up to him, slung an arm around his shoulder and jammed his laz into his side with a smile.

"Your apartment. Now."

Peyt's hand curled tight around the door he'd pushed open.

"Ever been hit by laz fire?" Sebastian asked him, conversationally. "I have. Just today, in fact. I'll be happy to give you your own taste of how unpleasant it is."

Peyt dropped his hand, pushed his way through with his shoulder. He said nothing as Sebastian dropped his arm but kept close to his side, laz still touching his shirt.

They stepped into a lift.

Peyt hesitated, then touched the button for the third floor.

"So, you went back to the Tree looking for Rina, even though you know she isn't really Rina, and when she didn't answer the door, you hung around waiting for her to return." Sebastian kept his tone conversational.

Peyt glanced at him, eyes jumping from the laz to the door, as if working out what chance he had to outrun it when they reached their floor.

"And unfortunately, your skulking didn't pay off, because when she did come back, it was with three guards, and they've taken up position in front of her door, so you have no way to approach her." He charged the laz, letting the hum fill the silence, and he felt Peyt slump a little in defeat as the door pivoted open.

"So what if I did?"

"No reason, just working out how you came to be there when you did. What was the next plan? To find her at the function?"

"Again, so what if it was? It's got nothing to do with you." Peyt hesitated as they stepped out into a foyer. It was a circular space, similar to the one in the Tree, but smaller, and it only had two doors off it.

"Oh, it has a lot to do with me."

Peyt took a step toward the door to the left, and then stopped. "I don't know who she is, or what your game is, but I intend to find out. And I don't think you're going to stop me."

He tried to twist away, and Sebastian shot him, the laz flaring against his ribs. He grabbed Peyt as he fell, and then hefted him to the door, swiping his finger through the lock. He shouldered his way in to the apartment and tossed Peyt onto the ground, looking around as the door closed behind them.

That had gone better than he'd thought it might. No witnesses. No one else home.

The interior was poorly lit, and when he raised the lights, he found himself in a spare, surprisingly tasteful space.

He crouched beside Peyt and went through his pockets, giving a satisfied grunt when he found the thin card he knew was the key to getting into most Cores functions.

The resistance had managed to get their hands on a few of these through the years, but they were always cancelled when the exec realized it was missing, so it had limited, usually one-time usefulness.

That was fine with him. One time was all he needed.

And Peyt wasn't going to be raising the alarm any time soon.

He straightened, then studied the unconscious man lying at his feet.

They were a similar size, although Sebastian was a little taller, and a lot leaner.

He walked into the bedroom and found something in a dark purple that looked like the kind of outfit a Cores exec's son would wear to a Cores function and put it on.

He searched for and found a small bag, put his black clothes inside it, and all the ports he could find lying around the place.

He looked longingly at the comm station tucked away in a small alcove, but he didn't have time to access interplanetary comms now. Then he decided there was no reason he and Dee couldn't come back here if they made it out safely.

It was the perfect place to hunker down for a bit.

He cut the straps off a couple of bags and tied Peyt up. He wasn't able to change the locks--high-level tamper-proofing, probably--so he left the door closed but unlocked when he stepped back out.

It was time to crash a party.

THE NOISE COMING from the function swelled and crashed over Dee as she walked toward it, tightly surrounded by Hanran Fattal's guards.

They kept darting quick, shocked looks at her, and she didn't know whether to count that a success or a failure.

Rina Fattal had a lot of strange clothes, and that worked out, because Dee needed to distract people from her face. She'd picked the most outrageous outfit in Rina's massive wardrobe.

She tugged a little at the strip of cloth over one breast, making sure it was securely in place.

The dress looked like a complex effort to tie her up, the thin straps twisting and crossing, knotting and trussing her in a weave that actually covered her fairly well, but gave the impression of near nakedness.

The problem had been the shoes. She wanted something she could run in, so she'd chosen black boots that laced up to just below her knees, the most practical pair Rina owned, and judging from the wide-eyed stares of Travi and his two friends, it was a look that worked.

She rarely wore makeup in her role on Leo Gaudier's top security team, but she wasn't completely incapable. She'd gone wild tonight, making herself look as different as she could, and she left her hair down, all the better to fall across her face and hide her features if necessary.

It was the best she could do.

As Travi opened the door and stepped aside for her, her heart jumped in her chest, and she had to hope her best would be good enough.

She stepped into a crowded room that was circled on three sides by second floor balconies.

They were still in the Tree, and this was obviously a Cores gathering place, people laughing and talking at volume, at ease as they ate expensive delicacies and drank fine wine.

She knew Sebastian would probably have a hard time keeping it together here, because to look at the guests, you wouldn't think there was a crisis beyond the walls.

People without any hope of relief.

She realized after a few steps that the three guards were no longer behind her.

Either they'd been stopped at the door, or they considered their duty done.

She edged her way through the crowd, getting a little deeper into the room, and glad for once that she was of medium height.

She was invisible here, surrounded by taller men and women.

Fluffy had gone very still on her shoulder, and Dee guessed it was a defensive mechanism in the face of too many people. The talu had made herself completely invisible.

"Sorry," she murmured. "I don't want to be here, either."

Hopefully she could remedy that right away.

She wormed her way through the packed space, heading for the opposite side of the room.

When she made it across, she grabbed a door just before it closed, slipping through it into a room that was green and lush, full of exotic plants and vibrantly colored flowers.

She looked up, saw the ceiling was made of glass, and then down when she realized even the floor was made of some kind of springy ground covering that released a delicate scent as she walked.

Fluffy chittered in her ear, and Dee smiled as she tilted her head to try and see her little sidekick. The talu's eyes were open, taking it all in.

A woman stepped out of a door to Dee's left, showing a bathroom beyond before it swung closed.

"Do you know if there is an exit here?" Dee asked her as the woman headed back toward the main hall.

"Just the way you came in, and I think from the second floor." The woman's gaze flicked over her, noted the outrageous outfit, and then moved on.

"Well, damn." Dee stood for a moment to get over her disappointment. She was not near an exit.

She steeled herself to go back out, pushing the door only partway open and edging through cautiously, her gaze on what she could see of the entrances on the other side of the room.

There were a few men and women in black uniforms flanking the doors.

She looked up, and while there were guards above on the balcony, she could only see the one pair. She could always come back down if it didn't work out.

She worked her way along the wall to the stairs, and then hesitated when she saw how few people were above.

She'd stand out up there, if anyone happened to look up, but it might also mean there would be less trouble making it to an exit.

Just look like you know where you're going, what you're doing.

Finkle, the head of Leo's security, had drummed it into her when she'd first joined the company. It was the best strategy she had right now.

She centered herself, blew out a breath, and sauntered up the stairs, keeping her gaze raised as she climbed. None of the people chatting quietly in small groups as they leaned against the balustrades turned in her direction or seemed to notice her, and as she reached the top, she felt a little easing off of the tension that had gripped her.

She guessed the exits were on the same side as the doors she'd used to get into the function, so she started strolling toward it.

"Ah, there you are. I'm glad you came straight up."

Dee carried on walking, but looked over her shoulder, letting her hair fall across her lower face.

A man dressed in a black suit, not a guard uniform, had stepped out from one of the two corridors she'd seen that led deeper into the building, and he wasn't even looking at her, his head was down as he tapped something on a screen.

"I've let your father know you're here."

Her throat tightened and she turned back, kept walking.

"Rina. No games." The man's voice was exasperated. "Enough of pissing your father off. He's lost patience."

She risked another look back, saw he'd turned, was walking away, sure she would come to heel.

That would be a no.

She broke into a light jog, aware that the dress wasn't designed for anything even slightly strenuous. Bits were slipping their moorings, and she had to ignore it.

She made it across the landing, her hand closed around the door handle, and she pulled it toward herself.

A wall of three guards stood in front of her, blocking her way.

She considered them for a moment.

At this point, she did not have anything to lose.

One of them flicked something at her, and a thin, glowing blue cord wound around her wrist.

It tightened, suddenly painful, burning her like acid.

Electric shackles.

She'd heard about them. Never seen them. Never knew they hurt so much.

The pain seemed to freeze her in place.

"Thank you. I'll take it from here." The man in the black suit leaned past her, hand out, and the guard handed him the end of the shackle.

"If you can't come when you're asked nicely," Black Suit said into her ear, still standing behind her, "you force me to not be nice." He made a tsking sound with his tongue, leaned a little closer, and moved the strap over her left shoulder, so it covered her breast a little more modestly.

Her neck was stiff, her body in a sort of rigor, but if she could, she would have turned and snarled at him.

He walked away, towing her, and she was forced to follow, her feet stumbling.

He was so sure she was Rina, he hadn't looked closely at her, preferring to treat her with dismissive contempt.

That surely couldn't last too much longer.

On her right shoulder, Fluffy chittered quietly into her ear, and Dee realized she'd forgotten the talu was even there. Her brain only had room to deal with the pain.

It didn't even seem to originate at her wrist, it gripped her whole body, vibrating her bones, scraping her nerve endings.

She stumbled as Black Suit seemed to speed up a little, and she caught sight of a man walking up the same staircase she'd used earlier.

His eyes widened at the sight of her, and she nearly fell as she saw it was Sebastian dressed in Cores exec formalwear.

"Too fast for you?" Black Suit barely glanced back. "That would be a first, wouldn't it, Rina?"

She could only guess Rina Fattal had humiliated this man, given the glee he seemed to feel at her entrapment and powerlessness.

He stopped beside a door, touched the little box that the electric shackle was attached to, and while her body shuddered at the relief of being released, he opened the door and shoved her inside, closing it behind her.

She sensed he hadn't stepped into the room with her, but she couldn't turn to look, and didn't care enough as she gasped for breath.

She staggered back, fetched up against the wall, and bent over, lowering her head as she tried to get herself back under control.

She didn't know how long it took, but she finally felt calm enough to look up.

She had to do it carefully and slowly, because Fluffy had been forced to scrabble onto her upper back when she'd bent over, and she felt her claws grip the elastic straps of her dress as she clambered back onto her shoulder.

She was in a large room with couches and a low table to one side. It was decorated with an abundance of plants, and there was a desk set beside a pair of double doors.

No one sat there, but she guessed an administrative assistant or some kind of office manager usually occupied the spot.

She had no doubt Hanran Fattal's office was on the other side of the double doors.

She also had no doubt that Black Suit was standing in the corridor blocking her exit, electric shackles at the ready.

Sebastian was out there, too.

The longer she stayed in this room, the longer he had to find a way to help her. She had nothing to lose by waiting it out.

She forced herself to walk toward the couches, and sank down onto one.

She'd thought Sebastian would have taken off as soon as he'd shaken off the laz hit, but he was here, blending in.

He'd come back for her.

It was what she'd expect from her team on Garmen. Every single one of them had her back, and she had theirs, but Sebastian had bigger problems, and her safety had to rank right at the bottom of his list.

Fluffy leapt from her shoulder into her lap, and she stroked her, scratching under her chin and behind her ears.

A faint sound caught her attention, and she realized it was an electronic beep coming from the desk.

A comm station.

She rose up and moved to the desk, set Fluffy down on it, and realized as she drew the screen toward her that her hands were shaking.

She entered the code to hail Gaudier Transport, tapping the table with a finger nail as she waited for the interplanetary comms to connect.

The door behind her opened, and she froze, head whipping around to look.

A man was just visible, hand on the handle, his body angled back into the room beyond.

"You are putting us all at risk, Hanran." As he spoke, his hand tightened on the handle in a white-knuckled grip.

"The Verdant String has chosen to pull back. Either we take this opportunity the Caruso are offering us, or we fade away to obscurity. How long do you think the gen-pop will let us starve them out when we can't afford to pay the guards anymore? When it becomes clear we're on our own?" The man who answered, Dee assumed it was Hanran Fattal, spoke calmly in the face of his colleague's agitation.

"That's the only reason any of us are considering it at all. But there's still a chance we can make things right again with the VSC. We haven't tried every avenue." The man opened the door a little wider, but he was still turned away from her, looking into the room.

"The Caruso are standing by, Nasta. They're not going to be

patient for too much longer. Either we give them the signal that we want to do business, or they'll go look for opportunities elsewhere. Don't forget, the same deal is on the table for Garmen. They could get the jump on us with this."

"What worries me is that they'll get impatient, but they won't move on, they'll just take over. They're not known for accepting the answer 'no'." Nasta released the door handle, took a step backward, so he was almost touching her.

Dee could hear the scrape of a chair, as Hanran Fattal presumably got up from his desk.

"We've got a backup plan for that."

"Really?" Noam snorted. "We're really saying that if the Caruso break their word, we'll go running straight to Bodivas for help? How do you think that'll work out?"

"Bodivas may not like us." She could almost hear the shrug in Hanran's voice. "But they'll like the idea of a Caruso base right in their backyard even less."

"What's to say Bodivas won't humor us any longer. What's to say they won't decide to make us a vassal?"

"Well, which is it, Nasta? Are you afraid of the Caruso, or are you afraid of the Bodivas?" There was a hint of contempt in Hanran Fattal's tone.

"I'm unhappy we're even in this situation. Whatever you involved us in, that thing on Cepi and the shitshow on Parn, has left us with no good choices as far as I'm concerned."

"I wasn't the only one involved in that decision." Hanran Fattal was almost directly in front of Nasta, now. Dee could just see one of his arms.

"No. But you sold it to us. And let's face it, it's been an absolute disaster."

"Everyone had the same information I did. Everyone chose to get involved. Do I regret our participation? Yes. But I find it very self-serving that you're suddenly pointing the finger at me, as if we didn't all have equal votes."

Nasta took a deep breath. "You're right. We do have equal votes, and we'll be considering our options a lot more carefully this time, to avoid finding ourself in a situation where there's no good outcome."

"Don't take too long, or we could find ourselves with no allies at all." Hanran stepped closer, and Dee spun on the chair, hunching over the comm unit, so her hair fell around her face.

"We've got until the end of the week, and we'll take it." Nasta turned and took a step into the room, and Dee sensed him check his step as he noticed her, and then moved past, ignoring her as he strode out of the room.

"There you are."

Dee waited for the door to close behind Nasta, enjoying the flash of surprise on Black Suit's face as he realized Hanran Fattal had been in a meeting.

"You wanted to talk to me?" She spoke as if her throat was hoarse.

"You know damn well I do. It was supposed to be a there and back, Rina, but you took your damn time. And then I got word the resistance was going to try and kidnap you, so I had to take steps."

Now that was something Sebastian would like to know.

Someone had shared the resistance's plans for Rina Fattal with the Cores. There was a traitor.

"Steps." She said the word sarcastically. "You sicced the Caruso on me."

"You're lucky they're indulging me at the moment, because they know I'm the one pushing their cause here. Otherwise, they wouldn't give me the time of day."

"Lucky me." She kept her voice dry.

"Where's Voy?"

She was silent, wondering who Voy could be. "Your goons wouldn't let him come in with me."

"What's wrong with your voice?" His hand came down on her shoulder and he turned her in the chair.

She stood, pushing at him, and he was so surprised he stepped back, giving her room to escape and move to the other side of the desk.

She saw the slow change on his face, from irritation to suspicion.

"You're not my daughter."

"No." She forced her hands still, and studied the top Cores exec.

He had that dead, pitiless look in his eyes she'd seen before, both on the faces of the opportunist criminals who preyed on the people of Tether Town, the city at the foot of Felicitos, and on the faces of the Cores execs who stole from the same people in a less violent way, but on a far grander scale.

She hated that look.

"Well, who are you, then?" The snap in his voice had her tensing her muscles.

"It doesn't matter. I was mistaken for your daughter on Garmen and brought here against my will. I've been trying to escape ever since."

"And where *is* my daughter?" He sounded a little panicked. A little angry. "And her bodyguard, Voy?"

She didn't like Hanran Fattal, but she didn't want to have to tell him she thought his daughter was dead. And Voy along with her.

"I can only imagine she's still on Garmen."

"If she was still on Garmen, I would have heard from her. Rina is nothing if not quick to bleat for help when she's inconvenienced. And Voy would make sure to get in touch."

Dee rubbed her palms against her thighs. "Things were . . . chaotic . . . when I left. It is likely they can't contact you."

He tilted his head. "Chaotic?"

Could he really not know? Or was he bluffing?

"The Caruso tried to take Felicitos. The Cores fought back, and then Arkhoran Special Forces arrived and took control."

He was silent for a long beat. "I don't like liars."

She didn't know how to read him. The dead eyes gave nothing away.

"I'm not lying. Contact the Garmen Cores. Ask someone who's still alive what's going on there."

He stared at her, as the hairs on the back of her neck prickled. This man was unpredictable, and she couldn't get a sense of him.

He didn't want to believe her. That was obvious.

Fluffy made a chirping sound and she bent to scoop her up.

"You have the talu?" For a moment, the dead eyes held a spark of life.

"She was in your daughter's suite on the cruiser."

His eyes narrowed, she guessed because it was so difficult to make Fluffy out. "At least she did her damn job. Give it to me." He held out a hand.

Dee stroked Fluffy's head. "No."

Hanran Fattal took a step closer and touched something on the lapel of his jacket. "Gorshra, step into my office."

Dee turned as the door opened to reveal Black Suit.

As Black Suit swung the door wide, his gaze flicking between her and Fattal, Sebastian loomed behind him and struck him in the neck with the blade of his hand.

Black Suit stumbled, his hand going to his throat as he tried to breathe, and Sebastian shoved him hard, so he fell forward, arms flailing, making Hanran Fattal jump back.

Sebastian kicked Gorshra as he hit the floor to roll him clear of the door, and then pulled it closed behind him.

For a single moment, everyone was still and silent.

Dee's gaze flicked to Sebastian, but he was focused on Hanran Fattal and she turned her head to see.

The Cores exec was holding a laz in his hand.

"Gorshra, get up. Take the talu." Hanran's hand shook a little. "You get back." He waved the laz at Sebastian, who raised both hands, and shuffled back a little. He'd said nothing since he'd come at Gorshra like a shadow prowler, the feared predator of the mountains where she'd grown up.

She took a step away from Gorshra.

"You stay still." Hanran swung the laz in her direction.

Gorshra groaned as he struggled to his feet, but as soon as he was standing, he lunged for her, hands like claws, groping wildly for where he guessed Fluffy was.

Dee flinched, tried to step to the side, but Gorshra must have grabbed onto some of Fluffy's fur. He lifted a fisted hand, and she heard the talu screech in fury.

Fluffy writhed wildly in his grip and Gorshra made a sound of pain. He flung her away from him, tossing her at Hanran Fattal, and the talu twisted in the air before colliding with the Cores exec, lunging at Hanran's face.

He raised his hands, batting her off him.

It was hard to make her out, but Dee saw her land hard on the desk. She gave a keening cry, and Dee scooped her up again.

It had taken five seconds, maybe less, but as she tucked Fluffy protectively under her arm, Gorshra collapsed, his whole body shaking, and his feet began drumming on the ground.

He was making a strange, choking sound, and when Dee took a step to the side, she saw foam on his lips.

"You didn't milk it?" Hanran Fattal's face was white, and he stumbled back, lifting up his thumb to stare at it. It was bleeding. He fumbled for his lapel again. "Help. I need help."

Then he sat down suddenly on the ground, and started to laugh, a mad, hysterical sound that disturbed her to the core.

He started to rock from side to side.

"You know what's going on?" She all but whispered it to Sebastian.

He'd stepped forward and was crouched down beside Gorshra, who had stopped moving, and pulled out the electrified shackle and the laz from the small of his back. "No." He put a hand to Gorshra's neck. "He's dead."

He rose up, pocketing the two items, his gaze on Hanran Fattal, now giggling strangely to himself. "We have to go." He grabbed Fattal's laz, and then made for the door.

She followed. There was no doubt if Hanran Fattal had managed to thumb on his comm unit, there would be guards on the way.

They stepped out, looking both ways, and then started down the passageway.

"You should leave the talu here." Sebastian kept his voice low.

"She only bit them because they hurt her." She thought about

Gorshra. Dead in less than five seconds. Whatever venom must be in Fluffy's bite, it was not as strong for the second dose because Hanran looked as if he would live.

They came to the deep balcony, but no one was coming up the stairs from the function room below. The few people who had been up here earlier were also gone.

She hooked her arm through Sebastian's and slowed her step, forcing him to do the same.

They walked toward the door she'd been caught at earlier, as if enjoying the evening.

"They wanted Fluffy. Badly. I won't leave her because then they'll have what they want, and because . . . I just don't want to."

Sebastian handed her one of the weapons he'd just stolen. "I was afraid you'd say that."

FIFTEEN

THEY EACH HAD A LAZ.

Sebastian noted the easy way Dee handled hers, as if she was very familiar with it. She'd told him there was most likely three guards waiting for them on the other side of the door. It didn't seem to worry her, though. She moved with a predatory focus that made the hair on the back of his neck rise up.

It felt a little too good.

She opened the door a crack, the laz hidden against her thigh, then leaned forward with a flirtatious smile on her face as she swung her laz up and shot. As the guards beyond gave a shout of surprise, she stepped to the side, pushing the door open for him to get a clear shot.

She'd already shot a second time by the time he'd taken the third guard.

They lay crumpled in a heap and not one to waste resources, he bent to collect their weapons.

"There might be cameras here so we better hurry." She headed for the end of the passageway and he caught sight of the curve of one glorious ass cheek as the straps that made up her ridiculous dress parted as she jogged away.

"Sebastian, come on." She glanced over her shoulder and glared at him, and he stumbled into a run.

"You are not an inventory manager." He kept his voice low as he caught up to her.

She gave a little twist of her lips. "Well, no. But no time to talk about it now."

She ran down the spiral staircase to the side of the lift, and then pointed to what looked like a service entrance.

It's the way out he'd have chosen. He followed her down a narrow, ill-lit corridor, catching a glimpse of Fluffy's eyes as they peered at him from Dee's shoulder.

He stared back, and the talu turned away from him, tucking herself under Dee's hair, which swung in a dark, glossy wave to her shoulder blades.

He thought back to Gorshra's nasty end, and Hanran Fattal, rocking in madness above them.

Where the hell did Rina Fattal get the little creature, and why?

He had a strong feeling they should release it into the wilds of the forest around Dar Raca, but Dee wasn't going to go for that. Not unless Fluffy went voluntarily.

A man pushed through the door ahead of them with his shoulder, holding a tray in his hands, his face in profile.

Dee gasped, and then she stopped, her body tense, her laz lifting.

Sebastian did the same.

The man stepped all the way through, turning to face them, and then the door swung silently shut behind him.

Karr.

There was a look on his face that told Sebastian he had not planned on this meeting.

"Oh, shit, right?" Dee said to him, a sharpness to her tone.

He blinked at that.

Then he glanced at the closed door behind him. "I have to go." He lifted the tray in his hands, his expression nervous. "I need to keep cover. I'll meet you later."

Before Sebastian could ask him where, the door swung open again, and another server pushed her way through.

She frowned at the little gathering, and Karr straightened up.

"You've come down the service entrance, but there is an exit through the door." He gave a deferential bow, and walked away.

The woman gave them a surreptitious look as she hurried past.

"I need to go after him." Sebastian bent to whisper the words.

"No." She gave a firm shake of her head.

"I know we should stick together, but in this suit, they won't stop me. Hide outside and wait for me, or you can--"

She pressed two fingers to his lips to stop him talking. "Hanran Fattal knew that the resistance planned to kidnap Rina, that's why he was so eager to get her back to Lassa."

Sebastian took a step back. "Hanran knew what we planned?"

She tilted her head up to him, so he was looking right into her warm golden eyes. "Yes. And unless you know what Karr is doing here, I'd say he's the one who told him."

That made it even more vital to follow him.

"I stole this suit from Peyt, that idiot from the lift earlier today. He's in the first smaller Tree building you come to when you leave the Tree from the main entrance. Get up to the third floor, the door on the left. I left it unlocked and Peyt tied up."

"Why?"

"Because he has a full-function comm unit."

Her eyes widened, and he didn't know why he felt a quick spike of regret at giving her a chance to speak to Leo Gaudier again.

She gave a nod. "Good luck then. And don't turn your back on Karr."

She turned to walk away.

"Wait." He reached out, gripped her arm, and the warmth of her skin and the spicy scent of her perfume made him want to get even closer. He drew in a deep breath. "Go to Sootko's after you've contacted your boss, it's the restaurant we ate at earlier. I'll be there in an hour. If I don't make it in time, the waiter who works there, Gert, will get you out of Dar Raca, and I'll find you at the resistance head-quarters."

Her brows drew down and she shook her head. "I don't like that idea, so be sure to be there in an hour."

She turned and walked away, and he noticed the straps across her buttocks had shifted out of place again.

He thought less of himself, but he watched her until she disappeared out of the door.

THE DRESS HAD TO GO.

Dee stepped out into the warm, humid evening air, and ducked behind a big bush planted up against the wall. She fought her way out of her clothes and then pulled on the sleek, stretchy pants and shirt she'd stuffed into her bag.

When she was ready, she hesitated.

She'd made the choice to get to a comms unit, but she felt uneasy with Sebastian still inside the Tree.

There was only so far his disguise would take him, and if Karr was a traitor, then he could easily sell Sebastian out to the Cores.

She didn't want to leave him in there alone.

She leaned back against the wall, and closed her eyes, listening to Fluffy scratching around on the ground at her feet.

Aside from the quick, sudden flare of lust she felt every time she looked at him, Sebastian had come through for her, and she always paid her debts.

But he was also a big boy. He ran the Lassian resistance, and he couldn't have gotten there without being able to take care of himself.

She would have to trust him to know what he was doing.

And she *did* need to contact Leo.

She pushed away from the wall, put her hand down for Fluffy to climb onto, and walked away, keeping to the shadows.

This was a crazy place, she decided, as she headed for the smaller Tree where Peyt lived.

She was used to Tether Town, a dank, damp, run-down huddle of houses below Felicitos, which was as magnificent and sleek as Tether Town was downtrodden and rough.

Dar Raca looked like a Verdant String city, all smooth pathways, recessed lighting, and the crisp, white towers that echoed the trees in the forest around it.

There were no shanties in sight.

The Cores had made a small town just for themselves, walled and pristine because they didn't have a Felicitos in which to live, high above the gen-pop.

They'd made sure the gen-pop lived out of sight.

She could tell some of the people hurrying by, heads down, were gen-pop. They had a pinched look about them and clothes that looked even worse that the usual attire in Tether Town.

As she got closer to Peyt's building, she slowed down, watching carefully for any sign of trouble, and noting that the two people who'd entered as she approached both used the laslock on the main door.

She wouldn't be able to get in.

She kept walking up to the door.

She didn't have time for an elaborate plan, the clock was ticking, and she still had to get to Sootko's to meet Sebastian.

She stood right in front of the door, fiddling with her bag, as if looking for something, and Fluffy hissed quietly in her ear as someone approached from behind her.

It was a man.

He pushed past her impatiently, flicking his finger through the lock and stalking into the building, and Dee smiled as she stepped after him, letting the door slide closed behind her and giving the man a moment to get into the lift on his own.

When she got to the third floor, she moved more cautiously, keeping to the wall as she reached the circular foyer and studied the door on the left.

She opened it, and sagged with relief when it gave beneath her hand. But when she stepped into the apartment, she saw the cut straps lying in a jumble on the floor and froze.

Peyt wasn't there.

She drew her laz and put Fluffy on the counter before she moved quietly into the bedroom.

He wasn't there, either.

She returned to the living area, and her gaze locked on the comm unit.

She would have to be very, very quick.

She thought back to Hanran Fattal's office, and hoped that the request for contact she'd sent to Leo on Fattal's assistant's comm unit had expired before Hanran Fattal's guards arrived to help him.

With luck, they wouldn't even check it, given the state their boss had been in.

Before she started, though, she found a saucer in the kitchen and poured some water in it for Fluffy before turning to the desk.

She didn't dare sit, she leaned over the table and tapped in the request.

It seemed to take forever.

She'd had very little experience with interplanetary comms. Like Lassa, the Garmen Cores cut off all gen-pop access to it a few years ago, but she understood the technical issues. She just didn't have time for them.

"Dee?" Finkle peered out at her.

She leaned in, so relieved to see him looking his usual grim self she felt a little weak in the knees. "Fink. I've got to be quick."

"Where are you?"

"In Dar Raca, but the plan is to get away as soon as possible."

"You still with Sebastian Xian?"

She nodded. "He's not with me now, but we're meeting up in less than an hour. What do you have for me?"

"Our Arkhoran friends have told us that a Bodivas ship will reach Lassa in a day's time. They need coordinates to pick you up."

She lifted her hands in frustration. "I can't say where I'll be. Somewhere close to Dar Raca, is my guess, in the forests that surround the city. I took a chance trying to reach out to you because there was a comm unit available, but I'll have to try again in a few days time."

"I don't like it." Finkle scowled at her. "We've been vetting the people the Arkhorans have rounded up who went floating off the Deck when Sofie cut off the grav generator. We're checking everyone before we allow them back on Garmen, and one of them is Vur, the captain of Ruanne's trader who you were going to meet on the Deck before the Caruso attacked."

"What did he have to say?" She risked perching on the edge of the chair to get closer to the screen.

"He admitted that Ruanne disappeared, is probably dead, and they've been working for the Cores for the last six months. He also said they believed their every move was being watched, and when the Arkhorans checked, there were hidden scanners, cameras and trackers on their ship. The cameras were recording, and then transmitting the footage whenever they got near a signal booster."

"Did anyone in Ruanne's group give the Cores information on our operation? Is that why the Garmen Cores started coming down hard on us? Because their attacks definitely ramped up in the last six months."

Finkle gave her a rare smile. "Interestingly, he wasn't too keen to answer that question, until he realized the Cores were no longer in charge, and then the floodgates opened. Yes, a few of Ruanne's crew thought the information would give them some extra privileges."

Dee sighed. "That explains so much--"

Fluffy chittered, and Dee just made her out, up on her hind legs, looking at the door.

"Got to go."

"Wait--" Fink so rarely raised his voice, she stopped.

"Just be careful. None of Ruanne's people can be trusted now, and you were our main liaison with them. Be careful if you bump into any of them."

She gave a nod. "I'll try to get in touch later." She shut down the comm on Fink's worried face, and had taken two steps to scoop up Fluffy when the door opened.

She and Peyt stared at each other for a beat.

Behind him was another man, mouth agape.

"Hope you don't mind, the door was open," Dee said. She nodded down to Fluffy as if in invitation, careful to keep her laz tucked between her hand and her body as her arm cradled the talu close to her chest. "You seemed to be interested in my pet, so I thought you wouldn't mind a visit."

"Not at all." Peyt stepped inside, his expression hard to read. He turned to the man behind him. "Thanks for all your help, Henri, I'd still be lying tied up on the floor without you."

"Is that a talu?" Henri followed Peyt in, despite him already swinging the door shut. He pushed it aside.

"Are you a friend of Peyt's?" Dee asked.

"I'm his neighbor. I just took him to the med techs for a checkup." Henri stared at Fluffy with a look that made Dee want to turn and hide her. He walked past Peyt, and Dee saw Peyt's lips thin as he realized Henri wasn't going to leave.

"How does it work?" Henri reached out a hand to Fluffy, then dropped it.

Dee thought back to what had happened to Gorshra and Hanran Fattal. *Very dangerously.*

She remembered Fattal asking if Dee had milked Fluffy, the fear stark on his face.

She knew there were reptiles that had to be milked of their venom to make them safer, so perhaps the method of obtaining a drug-fueled trip that wouldn't kill you was to take a safe amount of the milked venom. She couldn't think anyone would actually want to be bitten by Fluffy.

"Let me see it." Peyt shouldered his way past his neighbor. "I can barely make it out. I'd heard they were practically invisible, and I thought that was an exaggeration, but if anything, it's an understatement."

Dee bristled at his use of the word 'it' and at his creepy enthusiasm.

"She doesn't like to be grabbed." She took a step back.

"A female." Henri breathed it out. "I've heard they're more potent than the males."

Dee was watching Peyt, and she saw his face hardened.

"I'll give you a piece of this, Henri. I owe you. But go back to your apartment, get into something comfortable, and when we've milked the talu, I'll bring some over to you."

Henri didn't like that, but Dee could see him thinking it through.

"It'll be better if you're in your own bed, right?" Peyt asked.

He nodded reluctantly. "You won't freeze me out?"

"As I said, I owe you."

Henri gave a last look at Fluffy and then turned and walked out.

"Interesting how you think you can decide who will and won't have a 'piece' of this," Dee said as soon as the door closed.

"You're the one in my apartment without an invitation." Peyt slid his hands into his pockets. "Who are you, anyway? Why would Rina need a body double?"

Dee had been wondering how to explain the meeting in the lift, and she kept her face blank as he handed her a reason for free. Of course Peyt would think Hanran Fattal knew she wasn't Rina, that he was in on the deception. Why else would his own guards be escorting her?

"I am not authorized to say." She sent him a bland smile.

He smiled back, cajoling. "I won't tell."

She laughed at that, and saw his face close down in thwarted anger.

"You tell Hanran Fattal that one of the guards protecting you followed me and attacked me in my apartment. That's why I owe Henri a favor--his guard left me tied up here, and Henri heard me shouting and came to investigate."

"Which guard?"

"The big one who looks like he skipped a few too many meals."

She lifted a shoulder. "Nothing to do with me. I'm not in charge. What he does off-shift is his business."

Her lack of sympathy obviously enraged him.

"I'll tell Hanran Fattal myself, then. And while I'm at it, I could let him know you're moonlighting on the side, selling hits from Rina's talu."

"Go ahead." She kept the bland grin on her face. "What's your position in the Cores, anyway? Someone's son? An actual exec with a job?"

His lips narrowed to a thin line and he looked away. He was backing down, she realized in astonishment. He couldn't be anyone with real power, and it seemed he wasn't prepared to associate himself with wanting talu venom. So there had to be some taboo to it.

"How do you milk it?" he asked, standing a little straighter, his gaze shifting to Fluffy. "And how much do you want for it?"

"How much do you have?" She hadn't trusted him before, but something in his manner and the way he moved told her he was going to attack. She turned to put Fluffy on the counter, out of harm's way.

"Not enough for the going rate--"

She spun to face him as he came toward her, saw his arm was lifted up and back to strike. The calm she always felt before a violent confrontation settled on her, and she lifted the laz she held against her thigh, and shot him.

He collapsed with an expression of shock on his face, jerked once and then went limp.

She stood over him, looking down at him for a moment.

She forced herself to do this every time she had someone at her feet who she'd had some hand in putting there. Sometimes, like now, they were just unconscious, sometimes, they were dead.

Garmen had been a place of kill or be killed for too long, but she tried to hang onto her soul by acknowledging what she had done, and memorizing each face.

It helped that she'd been part of a tight-knit team on Garmen. The sense of purpose helped.

As she stared down at Peyt, she realized she felt the same here on Lassa. She was not sorry for this. Peyt would have at the very least hurt her and taken Fluffy. And he was part of the Cores.

She only had to bring up Sebastian's gaunt face to shrug off any lingering sense of guilt.

"Let's go before Henri decides he's waited long enough and comes back over." She picked Fluffy up again, reached for her bag, and she was out the door.

She'd wasted a lot of time here, and she still had to get over to Sootko's, the restaurant where they'd eaten dinner earlier.

She just hoped Sebastian would be there.

And if he wasn't . . . she rubbed a hand against her sternum. If he wasn't, she would have to go back into the Tree to find him.

SIXTEEN

WHEN HE GOT BACK into the hall, Karr had disappeared. Sebastian's gaze flicked to the staircase, but there was no sign of Karr making his way up to the floor above.

He moved through the crowd, growing rowdier now as the night wore on, and saw several other men and women dressed in the same dull gray Karr had been wearing, circulating with trays.

He could sense a few people turning to look at him, and guessed he stood out as being someone they didn't recognize.

He would need to make this fast, before someone stopped him and challenged his right to be here.

He caught a glimpse of sandy brown hair that looked like Karr's, and turned in that direction, and then relaxed a little when he saw Karr standing beside the bar at the back of the room, talking to the bartender.

Their conversation did not look happy.

He moved out of the flow of the crowd and watched.

The two were constantly interrupted as they tried to speak to each other, the bartender having to stop to serve drinks, and more than one person coming up to help themselves from Karr's tray.

The men and women present either worked in management for

the Core Companies, or owned a piece of them. They dressed too garishly and laughed too loudly, and he fought to keep his lip from curling and his hands from fisting.

He needed to find out what was going on and get back to Dee. He didn't like the fact that she'd had to go off without him, and as he moved back into the flow of the crowd and made his way around to approach Karr from behind, he tamped down real anger at his teammate for forcing him to follow him and leave Dee on her own.

She didn't know Dar Raca. She was vulnerable out there.

As he stepped right up behind Karr, he turned his body to the side, trying to keep them unaware of him for as long as possible.

"I can't talk to you here." The bartender was saying as he shot Karr a furious look.

"Then you should have met up with me earlier, instead of dodging me." Karr pro-offered the tray to someone who approached with a fake smile.

"Can I help you?"

The bartender had spotted Sebastian, was looking straight at him, and so he stepped around Karr, and then leaned against the bar.

"Yes, you can."

Karr was staring at him, eyes wide. "I thought . . ."

"You thought wrong." Sebastian kept his face relaxed. "You can get me some water," he said to the bartender. He leaned forward, and plucked a savory pastry from Karr's tray.

"Karr?" The bartender was looking between them, unbridled panic on his face.

"Calm down, Frino. This is Sebastian." Karr grimaced.

Frino blinked. "The leader--" He shut his mouth with a snap.

"So." Sebastian took the water Frino handed him, and took a sip. Propped himself up against the bar with an elbow. "What's happening?"

"I thought I could trust you." Frino was staring at Karr, and Sebastian read pure terror on his face.

"Karr's told me nothing, which is why I'm asking. I saw him come in here, and I followed him." Sebastian glanced at the bartender, and saw him take a deep breath, and relax his features.

"Well, I can't help you. I've got to go." Frino nodded to a woman approaching them, dressed in the same gray outfit. "My shift is over."

Karr leaned over the bar, his hand gripping Frino's forearm. "Good, you can come with us right now."

Frino hesitated, then gave a nod.

"After you." Sebastian wasn't going to go ahead and lose either of them.

Karr gave him a narrow-eyed look, and started to move back through the crowd, empty tray tucked against his side. Frino mumbled something to the woman as she reached the bar, tossed a cloth at her, and then edged past Sebastian and followed Karr through the crowd, an empty jug of water in his hand.

Sebastian strolled after them, making sure not to jostle anyone, or give them any cause to notice him.

Frino disappeared through the service door behind Karr, and Sebastian stepped through it less than twenty seconds afterward.

Karr lay slumped against the wall, blood oozing from a head wound.

"Hit me." He blinked, eyes unfocused. "With water jug."

Sebastian slid an arm under Karr's, braced himself, and heaved, lifting him to his feet.

Karr shook his head, then groaned, clutching his temples.

"We're going to walk nice and slow." Sebastian tried to keep his voice soothing as he maneuvered Karr down the passage. They were exposed here. And if Frino was a traitor, they could expect Cores guards at any time. It took maybe half a minute, although it felt infinitely longer, but they reached the far door, and Sebastian angled himself so his shoulder nudged the door open.

Beyond was a second passageway to the left, down which he could hear the sound of voices and the clang of pots and dishes. Directly in front of him was an exit.

He half dragged Karr through it, and stepped into the humid air of the night.

"You able to keep walking?" he asked Karr. He could see people using the main entrance into the Tree to his right, but none were looking this way.

Karr nodded, taking more of his own weight, and they moved around the building, heading toward the more downtrodden end of town.

The thought of going to Sootko's again sent a shiver through him, but he couldn't decide if it was the laz hit, or the kiss he'd shared with Dee before that that had set his senses buzzing.

Karr stumbled in the poor lighting, and the wrench to his shoulder brought Sebastian back to the present.

"You going to tell me what this is about?"

Karr didn't answer. Instead, he shuffled to the first wall they came to and bent his head down. After he caught his breath, he looked up.

"Frino's an informant. An old friend I grew up with. He told me something before we left to follow Rina Fattal. Something about the Caruso." Karr's eyes caught the light filtering down from the higher levels of the Tree and they glinted in the darkness as he turned to Sebastian. "I didn't believe him and I didn't say anything, because I didn't want to look like I gave any credence to it."

Sebastian let his head fall back against the smooth surface behind him. "So when the Caruso attacked on the Deck?"

"I was shocked, but it was Garmen, not Lassa."

"And when Dee told us the Caruso had plans to do the same on Lassa?"

Karr raised his own head and straightened a little. "I didn't want to believe her. And I felt guilty and angry at myself for not speaking up."

Sebastian turned to look over at him. "And what does Frino say now?"

"Now, he says it was all a mistake, that he doesn't know anything, it was just a rumor he'd heard and he can't remember where." Karr rubbed at his eyes.

"Did you tell him you've seen proof?"

"Yes." Karr slowly pushed away from the wall. "And he didn't want to speak to me, and then, the moment my back was turned, he hit me over the head and ran."

"How deep is his connection to the resistance?" Sebastian hadn't recognized him, but then, he couldn't know everyone. And he'd only just stepped into the leadership role. Or had it thrust at him.

Karr raised his shoulders. "He's sympathetic. Gives us information when he can. He doesn't come to meetings, though. He works a lot to support his family."

Somewhere nearby, a peet-mee began its hiss and snap in the darkness, and was joined by another, and then another.

Sebastian pushed away from the wall. Dee was waiting. "Can you walk? If not, I'm going to have to leave you here to meet up with Dee."

"I can walk." Karr fell into step, although his stride was not as quick as usual. "Where are we going?"

"Sootko's." He hoped she was already there.

"That's where I tried to track Frino down earlier." Karr looked at him with surprise.

"When?" A sudden chill seemed to dance down his spine.

"About an hour before I saw you."

So, after he had been shot there by Hanran Fattal's guards.

"Gert is Frino's friend. They grew up together." Karr touched the back of his head with careful fingers. "I tried to get a message to Frino through Gert."

A whisper of worry stirred in Sebastian's gut.

"Gert knows you're with the resistance."

Karr nodded. "He wouldn't help me. Said he'd pass the message on to Frino if he saw him, but he wouldn't tell me where I could track Frino down."

"How did you find him, then?"

"I always knew where he worked. I followed him the day he told me about the Caruso."

Sebastian lifted his brows. "So you took it seriously enough to follow him."

Karr looked away. "You don't need to tell me I mishandled this, I already know."

Mishandled was an understatement. "I saw Gert myself this evening. He was cooperative. I told Dee he'd help her if something went wrong and I wasn't able to meet her."

Karr shrugged. "Maybe. She's a stranger, and there is no mercy from the Cores these days. No one wants to take too many risks. He might turn her away."

"He saw us together. He knows she's safe."

Karr shrugged again, and Sebastian sped up.

He took a side alley, leaving Karr to struggle on behind him. It ran toward the street that Sootko's was in, and would spit him out on the main street directly opposite the restaurant.

He slowed as he reached the end of the narrow walk way, keeping to the deep shadows.

All three moons were shining, and they lit the street in front of him in pale silver.

There was a light on in Sootko's, but he couldn't make out the interior.

Despite the late hour, people were still walking around Dar Raca. A few passed him as he stood watching for any sign of danger, two couples talking quietly together, three gen-pop workers in their gray uniforms walking together as if for safety, heading for the gate out to the dark forest, and the homes tucked out of sight.

He stepped into the weak moonlight and crossed the road, aware that Karr was just behind him.

He ran lightly up the steps to the door, over the spot where he'd been shot with a laz, and put his hand on the door to push it open.

He was the one carrying a laz now.

SEVENTEEN

"YOU'RE REALLY FROM GARMEN? I thought you were Lassian Cores."

Gert set a glass of water in front of her, and Dee noticed a faint tremor to his hand.

"That was an elaborate ruse. I grew up in Phansi, the mining town on Garmen." She set her bag carefully on the counter. She'd thrown out the dress so that Fluffy could fit inside.

Given the strange reactions most people had to the talu, she'd decided it was better if she was out of sight. Safer for everyone, too.

Gert wiped down the counter, looking at some people eating at a table in the corner, and his hand clenched into a fist around the cloth he was using.

She leaned forward. "What's wrong?"

His gaze jerked up to hers, startled. "Nothing. How did you get here? I heard things were the same on Garmen as they are here. You aren't allowed to leave."

She propped her elbows on the counter, but before she could answer, the couple who'd been sitting nearby got up to make payment.

Dee noticed it was in ports, not transfer.

The same was mostly true on Garmen. Or had been until now. Portable credits had been the currency of the gen-pop. Almost no one had been wealthy enough to enter the credit transfer system. And the Cores had liked to keep it that way.

The couple left, and Dee glanced at the table of four men Gert had been eyeing earlier. They were the only customers left.

"Are you afraid of them?" she asked. Her laz dug into the small of her back, but she didn't touch it or give any indication it was there.

Gert shook his head, but he wouldn't meet her gaze. "Why are you back here?"

"It's a long story. Sebastian is meeting me here soon." She sipped at the iced water. "When do you close?"

"When the last person leaves." There was an undercurrent of bitterness to that statement.

She understood it.

"When those men leave, I'm happy to wait outside for Sebastian if he isn't here by then. You can close up."

Again, Gert sent her a startled look. "Thanks." He looked over her shoulder and went still. His expression was guilty.

Ah. Now she got it.

She shook her head at herself.

She was usually the most cynical of her colleagues. She was teased about it, because she almost always suspected the worst.

And here she was, surrounded.

In her defense, it had been a very long day.

She turned on the stool she was sitting on, leaning so her back rested against the counter behind her, her arms propping her up. Her hand dangling nice and close to where her laz was tucked into the back of her pants.

"Friends of yours, Gert?" she asked.

"Yes." He moved from around the counter to form a neat ring around her.

"And how can I help you?"

Her words seemed to surprise them.

They were all clearly gen-pop. Not guards, just men who scraped by in the cut-throat world of the Breakaway planets.

They looked less starved than Sebastian and his team did, but they were all lean, their bodies honed and muscular from hard work.

Dee looked them over with a professional eye. She couldn't take all five of them. Even with the laz. Unless she was extremely lucky and they didn't have much training when it came to fighting.

One of them moved, a nervous, agitated gesture, and she decided maybe they weren't as much of a threat at they appeared.

"How *could* you help us?" The one to the far left of her, the tallest one, asked.

She shrugged. "I don't know. That's why I asked. I'm no enemy of the gen-pop of Lassa. I'm gen-pop myself, from Garmen."

The man looked over at Gert and he shrugged.

"She was dressed like a Cores brat earlier, but she was with Sebastian, so she could be telling the truth."

"Sebastian?"

"New leader of the resistance." Gert wet his lips nervously.

"Him?" One of the men in the middle rounded on Gert. "The one who replaced Vahn?"

Gert nodded.

"I thought he'd disappeared, too?" There was distrust in the tone. "I heard he hasn't been seen for almost a month."

"He was off on a mission. I don't know what he was doing or where he was going, but he came back with her in tow." Gert nodded toward Dee.

"He went to Garmen?" The tall man's voice was incredulous.

"He did." Dee closed her hand around the laz. "How I came back to Lassa with him is a long story, but suffice to say, I'm not in any way sympathetic to the Cores."

"So where is Sebastian?" The tall one narrowed his eyes at her. "What are you doing running around Dar Raca pretending to be a Cores brat?"

"It doesn't sound like you're involved in the resistance, so I'd rather not say." She gave him a polite smile.

"I'm not involved, because more than one friend of mine who has helped them in the last few months has disappeared or been hurt. If you want a Cores target on your back, help the resistance. That's how it seems to work now. So if you've been running around playing games with the resistance, you're putting your life at risk. If you're from Garmen, what's happening here isn't your fight. I can't understand what you're even doing here."

She sighed. "As I said, it's a long story. Let's get to your interest in me. You were already here when I walked in, and I didn't know I was coming here until an hour ago, so this isn't specifically about me. What's going on?"

They were silent for a long beat.

"Gert indicated you might have some ports to spare." The tall man's voice bobbed a little.

Dee put her other elbow on the counter, drawing her laz out of her pants as she shifted position. She stared at each of them in a long, slow sweep. "So you're oppos." She looked over at Gert. "And so are you, presumably."

They stiffened at the accusation.

"We're starving, is what we are. And you don't belong here." The tall one shot a look at the others.

"You didn't know that when you approached me. You were going to try to rob me, regardless." Her quiet words seemed to fill the space.

"Gert told us you were Cores."

Dee tipped her head. That was fair enough.

Gert moved restlessly. "She's connected to Sebastian, so maybe this isn't a good idea."

"It was you who pointed her out." The man next to him grabbed his shoulder. "Now, no matter what happens, we're marked."

"Not if you genuinely thought I was Cores," Dee said, raising a shoulder. "No one could blame you for that. I was pretending to be Cores earlier, I admit that."

"All very civil," the man in the middle said, his eyes so dark Dee couldn't tell their color. "But I still have a family to feed."

"You looked like you were having a very nice meal just five minutes ago. Where was your family then?"

Her words seemed to incense him.

"Listen you--"

The door swung open. "Careful now."

Sebastian stepped inside and the door swung closed behind him. The laz in his hand was steady. "I'm extremely fond of Dee, and I take personal exception to any insult to her."

Dee used the distraction, as they all looked over their shoulders or turned toward Sebastian, to draw her feet up onto her stool, and then hop up onto the counter.

Her movement as she straightened had them turning back, and she saw the surprise on their faces as they took in her stance, and the laz she had pointed at them. She couldn't help but smile.

"Nice to see you, Sebastian."

He sent her a look that she couldn't decipher.

"It's just a robbery, from what I can gather, and not a very good one, at that. If they were professionals, they'd have had at least one person watching the door. Gert here let them know I had ports that they could liberate."

"Is that so?" Sebastian flicked his gaze to Gert. "So this doesn't have anything to do with your friend Frino?"

Gert went still. "What about Frino?"

Sebastian angled slightly toward the door as it opened, but it was Karr who stumbled in, mouth agape.

She gave him a cool look, but he was more interested in the men in front of her.

Sebastian seemed to give him a signal, because he closed his mouth with a snap and took up position by the door. He was injured, though, Dee could see it in the way he moved.

His eyes looked like they weren't working properly, so she guessed concussion.

Still, pale faced and slightly swaying, he barred the way out.

"You ready to go?" Sebastian asked.

"Oh, yes." She bent to the side, grabbed up her bag, which she saw one of the men eye wistfully, and she walked to the far end of the counter, out of reach of anyone who might decide to lunge at her, and dropped down to the floor.

Fluffy stuck her head out, but Dee hoped no one noticed her as she slung the straps over her shoulder.

She kept close to the wall as she walked to the door, and Karr opened it up for her.

Sebastian walked slowly backward, his laz lazily moving from side to side.

"Sebastian . . . I'm sorry." Gert lifted his hands in distress. "I thought she really was Cores at first."

Sebastian had reached the door, and he took over from Karr, holding it open as he stood in the doorway. "I'm sorry, too. Don't come near her again."

He stepped back, letting the door swing shut.

The night was still warm, the air was heavy with the scent of the forest and seemed almost silky against her skin.

"You all right?" Sebastian was watching her with hooded eyes.

She nodded.

"Then let's disappear."

EIGHTEEN

THEY WEREN'T FOLLOWED.

Sebastian kept careful watch behind them as Karr stumbled ahead, leading them to a ramshackle building at the edge of Dar Raca, built no more than an arm-width from the smooth, white wall.

There was no way he was taking the risk of going through the gate to the informal settlements outside the city. Fortunately, there was another way out.

Karr and then Dee stepped through the slightly crooked doors into the lobby, and somewhere above them a child began to cry.

Dee glanced up the stairs and then to the closed doors of the lift. In all the time Sebastian had been coming here, he'd never seen them open.

The child's crying stopped abruptly, and Dee turned to look at him, eyes full of questions.

"This way." He opened a door beside the lift, and the cool, musty smell of underground wafted up the stairwell. "We can use the old drainage tunnels to get out of town."

Dee stepped through without hesitation and disappeared into the dark.

Sebastian followed with Karr, keeping an eye on him as he struggled not to stumble.

"He needs a med tech."

Dee was standing at the bottom, waiting. The only light was what filtered down from beneath the door above them, making it almost impossible to see anything, but he guessed she could hear Karr's shuffles and groans.

"He'll get help." They had a med tech at resistance headquarters, but Sasha hardly ever had all the supplies and equipment she needed. They would have to make do.

Dee stepped up beside Karr and got her shoulder beneath his. Sebastian was struck at how naturally she did it. She'd been cool and calm in Sootko's, too, even though until he'd arrived she'd been completely outnumbered.

The way she'd jumped up onto the counter the moment she'd had the chance had been smooth and professional.

She was a professional.

And she was watching him while she supported Karr's weight, waiting for him to explain how they would be getting out of the dark, dank basement.

He slid the false wall aside, and a stream of cool, moist air flooded the room. He stepped through into the old drainage tunnel and helped Dee get Karr through the rough doorway before he closed it behind them.

"What happened back at the Tree?" Dee shifted her bag as they started walking, supporting Karr's weight as he stumbled through the shallow water on the tunnel floor.

Sebastian heard Fluffy chirp. He'd almost forgotten about the talu, but the reminder focused his mind. She was too dangerous to forget about.

"Karr was trying to question an informant who'd told him about the Caruso forming an alliance with the Cores before we left to kidnap Rina Fattal. He agreed to leave the Tree with us and talk, but instead, he hit Karr on the back of the head and disappeared."

"What does that mean?" In the almost pitch darkness, her voice bounced softly around him.

"It means we have people keeping secrets. If Frino knew about the Caruso, and he's a resistance informant, why didn't I know about it?"

"Why didn't Karr tell you?" She didn't take an accusatory tone, but he could sense her distrust of his friend.

Karr made a weak sound at her words. "Can still hear," he mumbled. "Didn't believe Frino, that's why." His words slurred toward the end.

She made a sound of disgust.

Sebastian said nothing but he agreed with her. Karr's judgment was now in question. When he recovered, Sebastian would have to have a hard talk with him about what else Karr hadn't believed.

Dee shifted, trying to get a better hold on Karr, and her arm pressed against his on Karr's back. He could smell the sweet perfume of her, even over the cold stone smell of the tunnel.

Everything in him went tight. He cleared his throat.

"What happened at Peyt's? Did you manage to get in touch with Garmen?"

"I got hold of one of my colleagues. Finkle says a Bodivas ship will be here by tomorrow. I'll have to get in touch when they arrive, give them a location to fetch me."

It was good that she had a way off planet.

He *was* glad about that.

"Did your colleague say what the Bodivas are planning to do?" If Bodivas had not even had ships in the area already, and were only sending one now, it seemed they'd washed their hands of Lassa.

Bodivas hadn't done anything to help when the Cores started taking back every business on the planet and beggaring their own people. And the Verdant String Coalition planet had to know about it. There was no way there weren't Bodivas spies here.

He didn't understand how they could be blind to the danger of the Caruso setting up a base so close to their own planet. Even if they didn't care about the gen-pop of Lassa, surely it was in their own interests to keep the Caruso's influence at bay?

"No. But if they do what the Arkhoran have done on Garmen, they'll be taking control of Lassa."

"The Arkhorans acted because the Caruso attacked, though. And it sounds as if your boss was already in talks with them. They knew how serious things were ahead of time."

She lifted the shoulder not under Karr's armpit. "The Bodivas must know things are likely to get just as serious here. Especially after what the Caruso tried in Garmen."

"According to the terms of the non-interference agreement, I don't think they can do more than hover off-planet, unless the Caruso actually attack."

"Which is why the Caruso are keeping a low profile." Dee trailed off, and then suddenly tapped his shoulder in a quick, hard warning.

He realized Fluffy was growling, a low, quiet sound that was only just audible.

They stopped, and even Karr was silent as he strained to see ahead in the dark.

"Taken a wrong turn?" The voice that called out from the pitch black up ahead was strong and female.

Sebastian relaxed. "Seems not."

"Sebastian?" A light snapped on, and a figure strode forward, a metal pole just visible in the glow.

"Hello, Mona." He squinted a bit as she reached them and then she lifted the light up above her head so that it illuminated everyone.

She had her hair braided back in intricate patterns and she visibly startled at the sight of Dee. He saw the moment she realized Karr was injured.

"We need to get him to Sasha," Sebastian told her.

She spent one more beat looking at them in shock and surprise, and then gave a sharp nod and turned on her heel. "I'll go ahead, get a stretcher ready."

She disappeared into the darkness, taking the light with her.

After so long in the dark, it was a relief.

"Resistance sentry?" Dee asked.

"Yes. We've taken over all the passageways and hiding places. Even the ones that used to be for the smugglers and criminals."

"They fight you for control?" she asked, and he could hear genuine curiosity in her tone.

"A few did." He didn't elaborate, but even though he didn't regret the hard line they'd taken with the oppos and criminals who'd tried to stand in their way, he didn't revel in it, either.

"That was our job . . . my job . . . in Tether Town." She spoke quietly, as if making a confession.

"You weren't in the resistance, though?" He frowned.

"No. Leo tried to join up with them. It didn't work out, we later discovered that was because the resistance leader was a traitor in the Cores pay. So we went our own way for a long time, cleaning up the streets, dispensing justice, until Leo's . . ." She tailed off, as if struggling to come up with a word. ". . . Leo's partner, Sofie, connected us to the resistance again."

"Leo is involved with her, romantically?" Sebastian tried to keep his interest from showing.

"Oh, yes."

He could hear the smile in her voice.

"Leo is completely gone over her. It was alarming to watch at first, when we didn't know if we could trust her, but now that we do, it's more funny. And sweet."

He cleared his throat, but before he could respond, he heard the sound of water splashing up ahead, and then two men loomed out of the dark, carrying a stretcher between them.

Karr was almost completely unconscious, barely able to keep his feet under him, and he heard Dee groan in relief as they stepped in to take him.

"Sebastian." Millo, one of the stretcher bearers nodded to him. "Welcome back."

Sebastian nodded, but he stood with Dee as she massaged her shoulder, taking a moment to catch her breath as they jogged away with Karr.

"You should have told me you needed to rest." There was more light here, they were close to where the tunnel opened into the rough enclosure they'd built around it to disguise their comings and goings, and he guessed someone had set up a light to make the rest of the journey easier.

He could just make her out in the light that danced on the thin layer of water at their feet, and reflected upward.

Dee flashed him a tired smile. "I would have said if I couldn't go on." She arched her back, groaning, and then reached out and patted his shoulder. "I don't know about you, but I'm ready for this day to end."

He was on board with that.

NINETEEN

LASSIAN RESISTANCE DIDN'T KNOW what to do with her.

Dee tried to keep her sense of humor, but the last two days had come with very little sleep and a lot of unpleasantness. She was losing her tolerance.

"Just a place to sleep. That's all I ask." She was talking to Mona, who was sizing her up with eyes fringed with lashes so thick, Dee couldn't work out if they were natural or not.

"Sebastian's hut?" Mona's tone was difficult to analyze.

"If it has a spare bed in it that's free, that sounds good."

Mona sucked in a breath. "Come on then."

Dee followed her, trying to work out the layout around her in the darkness.

There were trees looming all around, and the ground they were walking on was a thick carpet of old leaves that was slightly slippery underfoot.

Huts and shacks were on either side of the path, using the tree trunks as part of their structures. Most of them were quiet, but there were a few with lights shining under the doors, or from badly fitted window screens.

Some of them were up on stilts, sitting higher off the ground, amongst the thick branches of the trees.

She stumbled, and forced her eyes back onto the path. Mona had a light, but she wasn't walking slowly, and Dee realized she'd fallen behind.

Fluffy chirped, and Dee widened the neck of her bag so the talu could scramble out and up her arm, to hide under her hair.

"What's that?" Mona stopped and turned back, eyes narrowed.

Dee shrugged. She didn't have the energy to explain Fluffy right now, and Mona clearly couldn't see the talu.

"Well," she gestured to a small square shack that seemed to have been built against the trunk of a tall tree. "This is Sebastian's place." Mona stood to one side, and Dee pushed on the door and stepped into a stark space that looked as though no one lived in it.

Mona leaned against the doorframe. "There's a couch that should be big enough for you." Her expression softened a little. "Thank you for helping Karr."

Then she was gone, the door closing behind her.

Dee stared at it for a moment, then shuffled toward the couch. She sat down, undid her laces and pushed off her boots, and then lifted Fluffy off her shoulder and set her down on the arm of the couch. "Don't bite anyone, okay?" Her words came out slurred, and she gave up, laying down her head and lifting her feet.

She was done.

SHE WOKE UP FEELING HOT.

That's because someone had put a blanket over her, Dee realized. And slid a pillow under her head.

It sent a cold chill through her.

She should have woken up for something like that.

She had always been a light sleeper. Her sleeping through someone coming in, let alone rearranging her while she slept, made her stomach cramp.

She moved her head, and a light weight landed on her chest.

"What were you doing?" she asked Fluffy. "Watching me from the back of the couch so you could pounce the moment I opened my eyes?"

Fluffy chirped back, and Dee struggled up on her elbows, trying to gauge the time.

Light streamed in, green and dim, from a long, narrow window behind her. She picked Fluffy up and threw off the blanket, got her first good look at her surroundings.

Sebastian's jacket hung on a hook behind the front door, and she guessed it was him who'd tried to make her more comfortable in the night. A door stood ajar to her right, and she caught a glimpse of a basic bathroom.

Yay.

After she and Fluffy had both washed up, she in the shower, and Fluffy in the sink, in water that was cold, but clear and refreshing, she stepped out to find Sebastian awake and staring down into a cup of jah.

The counter he was leaning on separated the kitchen from the rest of the room, and behind him, she noticed a sink and a cooker, with the window set above them.

He looked up as she emerged. "I'm sorry you had cold water. I can heat it, but it takes an hour at least to pump the water through the pipes at the top of the tree, and this early in the morning, it would only be lukewarm, at best." His voice was rough, and he looked exhausted.

She shook her head. "I don't mind it cold. I'm from Garmen, remember? Cold and wet is what we know."

He stared at her, letting the moment stretch out just a little too long, and then turned away, pulling out a second cup and setting it under his jah machine.

It was the only new item in the house, she realized. The man had his priorities straight.

He handed her the cup, and she took a deep gulp of the hot

liquid. Her eyes watered a bit at the burn in her throat as she swallowed, but she didn't care.

"What time did you come in?" she asked when she could finally speak.

He cleared his throat. "An hour after you." His gaze moved to the blanket. "You should have taken the bed."

She grinned at him. "My guess is I'm a better fit for the couch than you are. And I honestly was too tired to care where I laid my head."

"I noticed." He took a sip of jah himself, and at last she saw a little spark in his eyes as his lips twitched.

She lifted her shoulders. "It's been a wild, wild time. Better than being shot dead by the Caruso on the Felicitos Deck, but still, I needed to recharge."

Her response had the opposite effect than she intended. The spark in his eyes died. "I'm sorry about that. About everything." He set his cup down, and then glanced across as Fluffy scrabbled up the side of the counter. "We should have taken you back."

"I thought so at the time." She leaned against the counter with her hip. "But my guess is the Caruso were watching the ship, and I don't think they'd have let you turn around anyway."

He conceded that with a nod.

"I play high stakes games all the time," she told him. "I go up against the Cores every day. Your Cores may have a slightly different flavor, but I'm not exactly out of my depth."

"I'd be dead without you, so I can't disagree." He gripped the edge of the counter with both hands.

He looked like a man with a huge weight on his shoulders. He wore a short sleeved shirt, and she could see the corded muscles in his arms flex as he bent his head.

"You didn't have a good meeting last night?" she asked softly.

He laughed on an exhale and shook his head, and she moved around the counter, past him, and set her empty cup in the sink.

When she turned, he was right in front of her, leaning back with arms crossed over a muscled chest.

Her heart leapt into her throat, so that she actually felt a vein throb there.

He was coiled power, and she wanted him.

Really wanted him.

He watched her, and the silence spun out, building between them like a massive static charge.

When they came together, it would be explosive.

She jolted at the thought, because there was no doubt in her mind. They would come together.

She didn't know who moved first.

Maybe him.

Maybe he started to push away from the counter before she stepped forward, but it didn't matter.

She met him halfway in a clash of lips and a clutch of hands, their bodies flush against each other, every touch like a lick of lightning against her skin.

She tipped back her head, and his teeth grazed the side of her throat as his hands slid under the thin fabric of her shirt.

She groaned as he cupped her breasts, her own hands sliding down the loose waist of his pants. She gave a hum of delight in finding he was wearing nothing beneath them, and the sound seemed to snap something in him.

He hauled her up on the counter's edge, stepped between her thighs. "I want you." His voice was hoarse.

"I want you." She used her position to unsnap the fastening on the top of his trousers.

They fell to the ground immediately, and she had just a moment to feel a stab of anger that he'd gone hungry, that he was too thin, before he was lifting her up with one arm, and tugging down her own pants with the other.

She helped him, wriggling until she was naked from the waist down and they were both panting.

"I'm not going to survive this." He rested his forehead against hers, suddenly slowing things down, his fingers gently rubbing between her legs in a slow, almost languid pattern.

It had been a long time for her, and she went from highly aroused to orgasmic in moments, shuddering in his arms as she came with an incoherent cry.

He swore as he lifted her a little higher, and she held his gaze from beneath heavy lids as he thrust into her.

He braced one hand behind her on the wall, and she could see the sweat beading on his forehead as he looked down at where their bodies were joined, his face almost grim with concentration.

And then he started to move, and she stopped thinking at all.

TWENTY

SEBASTIAN MANAGED to get them to his bed.

He didn't know how, because he didn't think he'd walk again.

They'd fallen together, and her laughter had loosened something so tight and hard in his chest he hadn't even realized it was there.

He felt like he was breathing easy for the first time in longer than he could remember.

He rose up over her, pulling her tight black shirt over her head and then nuzzling his way down her body. Her laughter turned to a soft moan, but even as she arched under him, someone started pounding on the door.

They both froze, and then Dee sent him a pained grin.

"Looks like the fun is over."

He closed his eyes, fists clenched beside her head, and she lifted up and touched her lips gently to his.

"We'll find time later," she whispered, and he opened his eyes, looked down into a warm golden brown gaze filled with wry humor.

The pounding started up again, and with a low curse he levered himself off the bed, and walked through into the living area, scooping up Dee's pants as he buttoned up his own.

She was standing by the door of his bedroom to take them from him, top back on, naked from the waist down.

He felt his legs go a little weak as he pulled her to him, and then took a deep breath, inhaling her scent, before he pushed her gently away and closed the door to give her privacy.

Fluffy hissed from the counter, and while he couldn't see her properly, he guessed she was looking at the front door.

"Sebastian!"

He sighed as he pulled the door open.

Koan was almost hopping from foot to foot in agitation, and behind him Mona, Karr and Luschka stood together in a tight little group.

Koan blew out a breath of relief at the sight of him. "Good. We need to talk. What took you so long?"

Sebastian let his gaze move over the group. Karr looked pale, but much better than he had last night.

He stepped back to let them in.

"This couldn't wait until I came into headquarters?"

Koan walked into the room, then went still as Dee stepped out of his bedroom.

Fully dressed and in the presence of strangers, she looked her usual sleek, dangerous self.

Her hair was loose, swinging over her shoulders, but the black outfit she'd taken from Rina Fattal's things made her look anything but soft.

"The Garmen woman," Koan said.

Dee inclined her head. "The Garmen woman."

Fluffy took that moment to leap from the counter into Dee's arms, and she caught her, then lifted her in what was becoming a practiced move onto her shoulder.

"I knew I heard something last night." Mona stared at the talu. "What is it?"

"It's called a talu." Dee watched them carefully, and Sebastian realized she was trying to see who reacted, who knew what a talu was.

No one said anything.

"It was in Rina Fattal's suite on the pleasure cruiser." Karr flicked a hand in Fluffy's direction. "It's attached itself to Dee."

"You sure she really isn't Rina Fattal?" Koan asked.

Dee lifted an eyebrow at him and said nothing.

"I'm sure." Sebastian's tone was short. "What was so urgent, Koan?"

He moved behind the counter. If he couldn't have more time in bed with Dee, he needed more jah.

Laschka cleared her throat. "Maybe if . . . Dee could give us a bit of privacy?"

Sebastian handed Dee a cup of jah, and then turned to get his own. "Dee stays."

He heard Koan's shocked grunt. "This is important, Seb. We've got to continue last night's discussion--"

"Dee stays. If it comes down to it, she's the only one here I know I can trust." Sebastian braced his hands on the counter. "I was completely behind the plan to kidnap Rina Fattal, but someone knew the Caruso were involved. Even one of our low-level informants in town knew, but for some reason, that wasn't passed on to me."

Karr winced and looked away.

"I don't just mean you, Karr. Someone told Frino about the Caruso. So that makes me wonder. Who thought it would be a good idea for me to be off-planet on a risky trip while the Caruso made themselves at home at the Cores' hover base? When I asked that question last night, all I got back were blank stares."

Mona sucked in a breath. "That's not fair. With Suski and Darren away, we don't have all the information, and there have always been a few Caruso ships coming in to the hover port. The Cores do carry out some trade with them."

"Not a warship though," Karr said.

"No." Mona glanced at Koan. "Wasn't Huti watching--?"

"Huti's missing." Koan clenched his fists at his side. "He never came to our last meeting, and I admit, I didn't think anything of it. I assumed he had nothing to pass on, but I asked around after our meeting last night, and no one's seen him in two weeks."

"An informant reporting in from one of the most sensitive areas of Cores control never turned up for a debrief, and you didn't follow up?" Sebastian stared at Koan in disbelief. He'd been in charge of the resistance in the far-flung pipeline communities around Dar Raca until six months ago, so he'd never worked closely with Koan until he was voted in by the resistance members as leader after Vahn disappeared, but since he'd stepped into the role, he'd sensed some simmering resentment from the burly lieutenant.

If that resentment had led Koan to disregard vital signs of danger, he was done. Sebastian wanted him out.

Koan's gaze snagged on his, and the smaller man took an actual step backward.

"Things were shook up after Vahn disappeared. People started to think we were finished. That there was no hope left. I thought Huti might be one of them. That he'd given up his duties to focus on putting food in his children's mouths." Koan narrowed his eyes accusingly. "All I remember is that you were as eager as anyone to take the risk of grabbing Rina Fattal."

"That's because it seemed like the last chance we had." Sebastian watched him, didn't like what he saw.

Laschka cleared her throat. "If grabbing Rina *was* the last chance we had, then what do we do now?"

There was silence for a long beat.

"I'm not giving up," Sebastian said at last. "But we have no resources left. I spent the last of my personal ports and whatever was left in the resistance coffers on hiring the ship we used to follow Rina Fattal. We're going to have to get creative."

A pall seemed to settle on them all.

"What do we do about Frino?" Karr asked.

"Hunt him down." Sebastian was tired of playing nice with people who were supposed to be his allies.

"We need to tread carefully, Seb. Things aren't like they used to be. People are living too close to the edge." Laschka waved her hands.

"Asking them to put themselves even more at risk has to be done with a bit of finesse."

"Asking them to help us save them and their families, you mean?" Sebastian kept his voice low. "Either everyone's with us, or we give up now. When the Caruso finally take over, we won't be dealing with a group like the Cores that at least has to pretend to treat us like we matter so the VSC will keep doing business with them. When the Caruso take control then everyone on Lassa will either be useful, or a nuisance. And they will rid themselves of any nuisance very quickly."

"You can't know that for sure, that the Caruso are going to take over." Koan's mouth was a thin, sulky line.

"They certainly tried oh Garmen. They attacked the Cores openly on the Deck of Felicitos." Sebastian straighten up. "It was a surprise attack, and the Cores guards fought the Caruso in front of us."

"It's true." Karr slid his hands into his pants pockets and hunched his shoulders. "The Cores have finally let greed interfere with their own sense of self-preservation."

There was a light knock at the door, and a young woman Sebastian didn't recognize leaned in. "Gert's at headquarters, wanting to spcak to Sebastian." She looked them all over with bright interest.

Sebastian wondered if he'd ever looked that young and enthusiastic.

"What's that about?" Laschka asked, and he turned to find her watching him with a considering expression.

Might have had something to do with the way his fists clenched at the sound of Gert's name.

"He and some friends tried to rob Dee last night." Sebastian glanced over at her, remembering how the four men had hemmed her in, and the cool way she'd faced them down.

She lifted a shoulder. "They thought I was a Cores brat. It was no big deal."

"It's a big deal to me. Gert knew you were with me." He looked up at the messenger. "Tell him I'm coming."

He leaned over and kissed her on the temple, unwilling to leave without some acknowledgment that he was barely able to keep his hands off her.

She looked up at him, face serious, and brushed her own kiss on his cheek, sliding her arm around his waist and drawing him in for a quick, tight hug.

"I'll see you for lunch." He glanced at the cooler, realized there was nothing inside it. "We'll probably have to go shopping first."

Then, unwilling to lose a chance to talk to Gert, he forced his legs to move, jogging out the door.

Karr fell in beside him, but the others followed more slowly.

He'd seen the looks as he'd kissed Dee, and he knew they didn't know what to make of it.

Truth was, he didn't know what to make of it himself. But there was no way he was giving it up.

TWENTY-ONE

SEBASTIAN LEFT with a crowd on his heels, but Laschka stayed behind.

Dee watched her turn with the group and then slow walk to the door. She stopped, one hand braced on the door frame.

Dee took the last sip of her jah, one leg crossed over the other as she leaned back against the counter and waited.

"You and Sebastian seem close." Laschka kept her voice even as she pinned Dee with a hard stare.

Dee said nothing. She put down her mug and the silence stretched out between them.

Laschka made a sound of frustration. "I'm watching you." She pointed a finger at Dee then stepped away from the door and closed it with a bang.

Dee lifted Fluffy from her shoulder and scratched the top of her head. "I don't know about you, but I think she's suspicious of me."

She herself had been very suspicious of Leo's girlfriend, Sofie, so she understood the instinct.

She sighed, and then put a hand to her stomach as it grumbled.

"I can't wait for lunch." She rounded the counter, opened the cooler, and found it empty. Sebastian had not been lying about needing to shop.

"Let's do some exploring." She lifted Fluffy into the bag, sliding a few of Rina Fattal's ports into an outside pocket before she stepped out of the house.

She had been too tired, and it had been too dark, for her to work out the lay of the land last night. Now she stood in Sebastian's doorway and found herself on a twisting thoroughfare that wound its way through the forest. Huts and shanties were set right on the road or just beyond it, nestled beneath trees so big, she gawked in wonder at them.

This was nothing like the low, thorny scrub of Garmen.

The path was well-worn, although unpaved, and a spluttering, battered hover coughed its way past her, going slowly as it passed pedestrians.

Most of the people were headed to the right, the same direction Sebastian had gone with his entourage.

She had a vague memory from last night of stumbling out of the rough shack built over the tunnel entrance into a central square, with actual buildings, rather than makeshift wooden huts, and the massive screen that she'd caught a glimpse of from the alley in Dar Raca had dominated the skyline.

She sniffed the air and headed in that direction herself, certain she could smell some open-fire cooking.

The road meandered, and she turned a corner to find the number of buildings on either side of the road had increased. They stretched back from the path, two, three, even four structures deep rather than the single line of dwellings that was the pattern where Sebastian had his house.

The sound of a chair scraping back caught her attention, and she peered down a narrow pathway to find a tiny square set behind the first row of houses, and people sitting hunched over small tables with steaming bowls in front of them.

A group of ragged children stood watching as those seated at the tables ate in quick, almost guilty bites.

She sniffed the air again and walked cautiously down the narrow path.

The people in the square looked up at her, and some continued to stare, but most went back to the hot porridge in the bowls in front of them.

It was like they'd been broken.

She'd seen defeat like this on the faces of some of the inhabitants of Tether Town, especially if they were the victims of the oppos, the opportunistic criminals who grabbed what they could from people who couldn't afford to lose anything. But that was individuals.

It seemed to her that that broken spirit hung over everyone here.

Quietly, she found a free table and sat, and the children's attention focused on her. It made her heart squeeze tight in her chest.

She didn't know the dishes of Lassa, and last night, Sebastian had ordered the food in the restaurant, but she didn't have to make a decision, she found.

A young girl came out with a bowl and set it in front of her, hand out for a port. Dee pulled out all the ports she had.

"How much to feed the children?" she asked.

The girl turned and looked at the crowd.

"If you buy them breakfast, they'll be here all the time, hoping."

"How much?"

The girl sighed. Named a price.

Dee looked at the ports she'd taken out, handed most of them over.

The girl took them, turned to the children, and made a gesture. They moved hesitantly toward her, and then looked at Dee, shocked, when she murmured something to them.

They followed her inside, absolutely quiet.

Dee looked at the food in front of her, but now she had to force herself to dip a spoon in to what looked like cooked grains. Her stomach felt full of rocks.

This place was so wrong, she wanted to rage.

She swallowed her first bite and found it was thick and rich, nutty with a slightly sweet aftertaste.

There was no saucer or small bowl for Fluffy, and the serving girl was busy feeding innocent children, so she scooped Fluffy out of the pack, put her on the table and then put some of the food into the palm of her left hand, and held it out like a bowl.

She ate her own food with the ticklish rasp of Fluffy's tongue on her skin, and it comforted her. Helped calm her rage.

About halfway through her meal, everyone seemed to get to their feet, as if on a schedule, and more than one lifted their faces upward, over the low roofs.

Dee looked herself, and saw the big screen that sat on the Dar Raca city wall had lit up.

They were about to announce how many were needed to work for today.

People moved quickly, and while they'd eaten together peacefully enough, no one looked at anyone else as they disappeared down the pathway toward the big square.

The door to the kitchen, which had been open before, was now closed, and there was a silence to the place that disturbed her.

She hadn't seen the children leave, but they'd possibly used another entrance.

She felt invisible eyes on her and shivered.

She got up, put Fluffy back in her pack, and then took the narrow alley back to the road, stepping out into the main street with a sense of relief.

A crowd was gathering in the square, and she hesitated, not wanting to get caught up in what was obviously the push and shove as people vied for a job.

"Dee!"

The voice came from the almost impenetrable gloom of what seemed more like a thin gap between two buildings than an alleyway.

She turned, unwilling to step closer, and tried to work out why the voice was so familiar.

Darkness suddenly surrounded her as a dank, black sack was shoved over her head from behind.

She fought, but whoever had her was huge, his arms like steel bands around her as he clamped her arms to her sides and lifted her off her feet.

He carried her into the narrow alley in just a few steps, she could tell because what little light had come through the rough-woven sack disappeared, and it felt like only moments later a door banged open. She threw her body wildly and her head hit something hard before she was deposited on her back on the ground.

Bright lights danced in front of her closed eyes and she breathed through the pain and nausea and then started coughing as the musty smell of the bag caught the back of her throat. She could hear Fluffy's outrage from her pack, which was still looped over her arm.

"What's this?" A man's deep voice sounded by her ear, and before she could say anything, before she could work out if she wanted to say anything, she heard him cry out in pain.

She ripped the sack off her head, and struggled up on her arms, taking in a simple, clean and well-lit room, a man lying on his side choking, and a woman crouched next to him, face white with fear.

"What's happening to him?" The woman tried to lift his head.

Dee stared at her. "Jamari."

She turned more fully to Dee. "What. Is. Happening?"

Dee looked at the man with regret. "He's been bitten by a talu. I honestly don't know what that means for him, or what talu poison does, or if it can be countered."

"A talu?" Jamari's eyes were huge in her face as Fluffy wriggled free of the bag and jumped into Dee's arms. "Then Paka's dead."

PAKA WAS HEAVY.

Dee worked that out first hand as she helped Jamari lift him up onto the bed in the corner of the room.

They propped him up with pillows and then Jamari trickled water down his throat.

He swallowed reflexively. His skin was a warm brown, but now it had a yellow tinge to it, and white foam had dried around his mouth.

145

He looked bad.

Dee had tried to put Fluffy on the table in the middle of the room to help Jamari lift Paka, but she'd refused to let go of Dee, and so she ended up clinging to Dee's shoulder as they moved him, chirping from her perch like she was scolding him.

Dee stood back as Jamari fussed over the big man, and lifted Fluffy off her shoulder and held her close. The talu curled up under her chin, and Dee soothed her with long, gentle strokes, to calm her shivers.

"Get that thing out of here." Jamari's eyes were slits.

Dee shrugged, and walked to pick up her bag, and gently placed Fluffy inside. "Don't blame the talu. You hurt and frightened her. You hurt and frightened *me*." She walked to the door. "If you'd called me over and spoken to me like a normal person, this wouldn't have happened. Instead, you got Paka to abduct me. What the hell, Jamari?" She opened the door.

Jamari's face crumpled, as if she'd been deflated. "I'm sorry." She pressed her fingers against closed eyes. "Sorry. Don't go."

Dee hesitated. Jamari was one of Ruanne's best trader captains. And Finkle had warned her they were all working for the Cores now, willingly or not. But something was going on here, and she did feel bad about Paka's fate.

Maybe she should learn how to milk the venom from a talu.

"What are you doing here?" Jamari got up and ran some water from the sink over a cloth in her hand, then walked back and wiped the thin line of white foam from around Paka's mouth.

"It's a long story. It wasn't by choice. But since I've gotten here, I've learned you lied to me six months ago when I spoke to you on the Deck."

Jamari winced as she wiped Paka's face in slow, gentle strokes. "I didn't lie, I swear. Ruanne disappeared while I was piloting the trader back to Lassa. Or, that's when I found out about it, anyway. Cores guards were waiting for us when we landed and took everything we had in the hold." She folded the damp cloth over and pressed it gently against Paka's forehead.

"Do you know what happened to Ruanne?" Dee closed the door and set her bag on the table.

Jamari shook her head. "She could be dead. They could be holding her prisoner. I don't know. They corralled everyone from the trader together, marched us into the hover port, and set about embedding a tracker into everyone's upper arm."

"What?" That wasn't something Finkle had passed on from the trader captain he and Leo had in custody.

"They started at one end of the group, and there was a lot of objections to it, as you can imagine. All the guards moved forward to deal with the resistance. I was near the back because I was the last one out of the trader. The door behind me, the one we'd all come through, hadn't closed properly because there were bags in the way, and I just squeezed out and then walked away."

"Did they try to find you?"

Jamari nodded. "I've had to keep away from the markets and public places. Paka's the one who goes out. I sometimes risk it, but always with some kind of disguise. Some of my old crew wouldn't go running to the Cores if they saw me, but a few would. Especially if they'd been offered a reward for it. I can't trust anyone."

Fluffy poked her head out of the bag, and Dee put out an arm for her to climb up.

"Where did you get a talu?" Jamari asked. "I've never seen one until today, and I had no idea they were so tiny."

"Tiny and cute." Dee chucked Fluffy under the chin, and she chirped back. "She was in Rina Fattal's living quarters on the Verden, the pleasure cruiser Rina was using."

Jamari stared at her. "What the hell were you doing in Rina Fattal's living quarters?"

"Hiding from a Caruso attack. I was on the Deck to speak to your colleague Vur, to warn him we'd heard the Caruso were about to attack Lassa, so he could pass the message on to Ruanne. While I was looking for him, the Caruso attacked Garmen instead. They were shooting at everyone on the Deck."

Jamari sucked in a breath. "What happened?"

"I took cover in the first open door I found, which just happened to be Rina Fattal's ship."

"What happened to Rina?"

Dee's lips twisted. "Dead."

Jamari's eyes were saucers. "And how did you get here?"

"The Lassian resistance were on the ship as well. They'd planned to kidnap Rina and they took off with me, thinking I was her. By the time I convinced them I wasn't who they were after, the Caruso had swept down on us, and the only way any of us got out of that alive was by me pretending to be Rina. It seems her father was eager to get her back, and the Caruso obviously have some deal with him."

"He wasn't eager to get her back. It was the talu." Jamari was still sitting on the edge of the bed, but now her hands were braced at her sides, clenched tight. "They're so rare. What's a bet Rina was on the Deck to acquire one in an illegal trade?"

Dee nodded. "Could be. She might have gotten Fluffy earlier and then stepped out to look at the view. She was killed on her way back to the ship."

Paka made a choking sound, and Jamari rolled him onto his side.

He started breathing a little better.

"Do you know what's happening to him?" Dee asked.

Jamari tipped her head from side to side. "Sort of. I've heard rumors about talu venom out on the trade routes. There are some places where anything goes, you know? Word is talu poison is lethal in large doses, a psychedelic drug in much smaller doses, and a truth serum in tiny amounts." She glanced at Fluffy. "I'm betting Hanran Fattal wanted her for the truth serum abilities, and Rina Fattal was probably keen to indulge in the psychedelic ones."

Dee pulled out a chair and sat. "Truth serum?"

"The VSC won't allow anything like that to be produced. It's a massive violation of the rights of the individual, but I'm sure some groups illegally try to produce it in a lab. Nothing apparently beats talu venom, though. It's got a reputation as the most reliable product."

"So that's why that horrible man was so determined to take you from me." Dee rubbed Fluffy's head.

"Who tried to take her? Where have you even been, if the Caruso took Rina Fattal's ship?"

"They escorted us to the Cores hover base, but as I say, they thought I was Rina, and I played that role until I could get away. Hanran Fattal and one of his guards got me into Fattal's office first, though, and when they realized I wasn't Rina, they tried to grab Fluffy. She bit them both. The guard was bitten first, and he died almost immediately. Hanran Fattal got very strange after he was bitten, but if the poison has psychedelic properties, that would explain it." She kissed the top of Fluffy's head. "I think Paka is probably lucky she already bit two people within the last day. And he's so big, he might be able to take a dose that would kill someone smaller."

Jamari turned and looked down at Paka, and threaded her fingers in his hair, pushing it back from his forehead. "I shouldn't have asked Paka to grab you like that. He told me we should just ask you in, but when we saw you eating breakfast, I wanted to know what was going on. I didn't want to risk you calling out my name or running away to talk to the resistance. It's my fault Paka is lying here."

"Why are you afraid of the resistance?"

"Because they're compromised. Vahn, the leader, disappeared around four months after Ruanne, and since then, some of their informants have disappeared as well. Just gone. Their families are desperate to know what's happened to them, but they're afraid if they make too much of a fuss, they'll be next. Paka keeps his ear to the ground about it."

"The Cores knew about the plan to kidnap Rina Fattal, and that's why the Caruso were sent to escort her home, so I know there's a mole in the resistance. The team who were supposed to grab Rina Fattal would have been killed by the Caruso if I hadn't pretended to be Rina, and convinced the Caruso that they were my regular crew."

"But you just said the Caruso killed her."

Dee nodded. "They were killing anyone who moved. It was completely indiscriminate. From what was said when they caught up with the pleasure cruiser, they didn't know Rina was on the Deck. They were angry at her for not letting them know her whereabouts."

"You think Hanran Fattal sent her to get the talu in secret?" Jamari looked up from Paka.

Dee shrugged. "He didn't like hearing the Caruso had attacked the Garmen Cores on the Felicitos Deck, that's for sure." She stood up and walked to the tiny, dusty window and leaned against the wall beside it, looking out onto the dark alleyway. "Just like on Garmen, the Caruso and the Cores are playing each other, each thinking they can cooperate while it suits them, and then turn on the other and get the upper-hand when it doesn't."

"Jamari." Paka's voice was weak but audible.

"You're okay, sweetness." She cupped his cheek.

"No, I'm not okay. I feel strange." He stared up at her.

"You have some venom in your system, but I think you'll be all right."

He didn't look as if he understood her.

"What can I get you?" Jamari smoothed the damp cloth over his brow again.

"Nothing. You're the most important thing in my life."

From the look on Jamari's face, that was news to her.

Dee guessed talu venom really was a good truth serum.

Jamari squeezed her eyes shut, then opened them again. "Shh. Just rest. You need to rest." She kissed his forehead, and he sighed deeply and closed his eyes again.

Dee had to fight not to laugh at the panic she saw on Jamari's face. They exchanged a look, and Jamari pointed a warning finger at her.

"Not a word."

Dee pretended to seal her mouth closed, and turned back to the window.

Someone ran past the front of the alley, on the main road, and she could hear shouting.

She frowned. "What's the time?"

"I'd guess just before midday."

"I have to go. I'm meeting someone, and they'll get worried if I don't show up." Dee put Fluffy back in the pack and hitched it over her shoulder.

"Who're you meeting?" Jamari stood up.

"Sebastian Xian. The new leader of the resistance."

Jamari's mouth fell open. "Dee, that's not safe."

Dee closed her hand over the door handle. "Too late for that warning, Jamari. Way, way too late."

TWENTY-TWO

WHEN DEE REACHED THE STREET, there was no sign of the disturbance she'd heard earlier. She hesitated for a moment in front of a row of stalls with displays of fruit and vegetables, but they were mostly unfamiliar to her, and she chose to head back to Sebastian's place first. She was most likely already late.

His door was open, and she heard raised voices within.

She gave a short knock and stepped inside.

Sebastian was facing the door, and his gaze locked onto her.

Karr stood in front of him, and he turned at the sound of her knock, and she could see relief on his face.

"Sorry I'm late. I got lost." She walked past Karr toward Sebastian, and then stopped beside him, suddenly unsure how to greet him.

He put his hands on her shoulders, his gaze raking her. "You're all right?"

She nodded but he lifted a hand and his finger lingered on the bruise on her temple. Her back was to Karr, so she mouthed 'later' to him, and he frowned but said nothing.

"Word was, someone grabbed you."

She turned as Karr spoke. "Word from who?"

"That's just what I was asking," Sebastian said.

"Someone noticed something. Passed it along." Karr lifted his shoulders. "They didn't leave their name."

"How could they pass it along without revealing who they are?" Dee wondered.

"We have an anonymous voice drop at headquarters." Sebastian slid hands into his pockets. "Out on the pipelines, they'd have come in themselves, told me everything they knew."

"This isn't the pipelines," Karr said.

His words seemed to insert a chill into the conversation.

The silence was broken by a ping of sound coming from Karr's shirt pocket.

He frowned, pulled a small comms unit out. "Yes?" He blinked. "Cores guards, headed this way." His eyes were wild when he looked at Dee. "Looking for you."

"Guards? In the settlement?" Sebastian shook his head. "We'll worry about that later. Let's go." He grabbed her arm, and she ran with him into his bedroom. He scooped up a bag set in a corner, then pulled a lever below the window and a small panel came away, just large enough for them to crawl through.

Dee dived out, with both men right behind her. Sebastian took a few seconds to close the panel back up, and then he took the lead, running through the trees.

Dee realized he was running parallel to the road, back toward headquarters, then he stopped beneath a particularly massive tree, and began climbing it.

It was only when he was halfway up the trunk that she noticed the tiny metal spikes set in a staggered pattern up the side that he was using for foot and hand holds.

She followed him up, and Karr came right behind her.

When she reached the first thick branch, the spikes disappeared, and she had to pull herself up from branch to branch, working harder than Sebastian because she was at least a head shorter than he was.

He looked back more than once to offer her a hand, but she shook her head. She could tell he was in a hurry. He wanted to get up as fast as he could, and she was slowing him down.

She was breathing hard by the time she found him crouched on a small platform set two thirds up the trunk, with a good view of the main pathway.

Fluffy had poked her head out of the pack when they'd started running, and now she wriggled out and chittered as she ran to the end of the branch the platform rested on.

Karr hauled himself up beside her, and forced her to more or less plaster herself to Sebastian's side. His arm came around her and held her close to him.

"Did you see anything?" she asked quietly.

"Not yet." As he answered, a group of four guards came into view. They walked in a line, weapons cradled in their arms.

"What the hell?" Karr breathed it out. "They never come into the settlement."

"Hanran Fattal must be on the mend. And pretty annoyed with me." Dee remembered the cold hatred in his eyes when they'd met before.

When the guards disappeared from view--the trees and other houses shielding them--Sebastian blew out a breath and sat down.

"Guess Hanran Fattal is looking for some payback."

Karr looked sick. "What do we do?"

"They aren't looking for you, so I'd say the best thing to do is leave us with that comm unit and go back. Dee and I will try to keep in range, and you can use it to let us know what's going on."

"Whoever told them where you live will know I'm most likely someone you'll rely on for help." Karr rubbed a hand over his mouth.

"It won't matter if they don't know about this comms unit. I certainly didn't." Sebastian held out his hand, and after a moment of hesitation, Karr handed it over.

"Vavi and I found two in the staff sleeping quarters on the Verden, and we took them. They seem to be set to a specific frequency, so they're only useful to communicate between each other." Karr settled down cross-legged. "We didn't have a chance to tell you about them after the Caruso towed the ship."

"Good thing you had them." Dee meant that. Without the warning, they'd have been in the house when the guards arrived.

"Vavi saw the guards come through the Dar Raca gate, demanding to know where Sebastian lived. Then they asked if anyone had seen Dee."

"Someone told them I was with Sebastian." Dee thought back to what Jamari had told her and knew she was right. The resistance was definitely compromised.

Sebastian nodded, face grim. "So we know we can trust Vavi and you." He looked over at Karr. "Everyone else is suspect."

Karr looked like he wanted to argue, but eventually he gave a tight nod. "I'll go find Vavi right now. We can keep an eye on what's happening. Let you know when it's safe to come back in."

Sebastian didn't answer, and Dee wondered if it was because he didn't want to state the obvious. That until the Cores were defeated, there would be no safe time to come back.

She leaned into him a little, loving the way he wasn't shy about showing he liked having her close. Loving it a lot.

"Did you put this lookout here?" Karr asked, and she could see he was uncomfortable with the way Sebastian was holding her, but unwilling to leave just yet.

"Vahn built it. He showed it to me when I stayed with him a few months before he disappeared." Sebastian went still, and Dee saw why a moment later.

The Core guards were coming back down the pathway, retracing their steps. This time there was one in the lead, one taking up the rear, and two walking side by side in the middle, all with guns raised.

"Not so sure of themselves now?" Dee watched them carefully.

"Maybe they're looking for trouble." Karr's voice cracked.

Dee leaned forward, trying to get a better look. "Doesn't look like they're finding it."

Sebastian shook his head. "They probably won't. But the reason they're walking back a bit more cautiously is they've suddenly remembered there are a lot more people in the settlement than they could deal with if there was a coordinated attack. The people have the numbers. The Cores don't send their guards into the settlement because it reminds people of that fact." He turned to Karr. "Go. Right now. Find out what's going on and let us know."

Karr nodded and then swung off the platform.

Dee could hear him crashing through the branches in his haste to get to the ground, and then he ran off to the right, angling toward the center of the sprawling informal settlement.

"Do you really think we can trust him?" she asked.

Sebastian looked up at her in surprise. "You think there's a chance we can't?"

She shrugged. "I don't know him as well as you, but there are some serious leaks in your organization, and he's someone in the inner circle."

"So's Koan."

Dee sat back, legs crossed, and Fluffy leapt into her lap. "You suspect him?"

"Things he's done have raised a few questions in my mind." He reached out and took her hand, rubbing his thumb over her knuckles in a back and forth motion she suspected he wasn't really aware of. "Now tell me. What happened?" He scooted forward, until his knees were touching hers, and gently stroked his fingers down her bruised temple again.

"I was grabbed off the street. The guy picked me up and ran with me down a narrow alley and into a room."

He went absolutely still.

"Fluffy squirmed out of the pack and bit him, and Paka went down like a felled tree."

"You know his name? That's good." He said it like a promise.

"No." She shook her head. "Paka didn't even want to grab me. That was Jamari's idea. And she is truly sorry she chose that route." Dee thought back to Jamari leaning over Paka on the bed, face white with fear. "Believe me. She's sorry."

"Jamari? Where do I know that name?"

"She used to captain one of Ruanne's traders. I've met her a couple of times up on the Deck of Felicitos. She recognized me, and wanted to find out what was going on. But she didn't know if she could trust me, so she persuaded Paka to scoop me up. If I hadn't been fighting so hard, I wouldn't have knocked into the door frame, and I would be more or less unharmed."

Sebastian gave a tight nod, but she didn't think he was feeling any more forgiving.

"She told me the locals have stopped cooperating with the resistance. A few of them have given up some information, and then they've disappeared. Completely gone. Their families think they were killed because whoever in the resistance is working for the Cores doesn't want them to keep handing over good intel."

"So that's why Frino and Gert were so unwilling to help all of a sudden. They think it'll put a target on their back." Sebastian blew out a frustrated breath.

"What did Gert say when you met him at headquarters?" She suddenly remembered why he'd had to rush off this morning.

"He was nervous that we'd come after him and his friends. He came to explain and apologize, and he did it all in public, in front of the building we use as our headquarters."

"He was protecting himself." She said the words slowly. "He was making it harder for whoever is responsible for the disappearances to target him. By openly admitting you had a grievance against him, and trying to make it up to you, he was hoping to make it difficult to get rid of him without causing more trouble than he was worth."

Sebastian gave a grim nod. "I'm coming to the same conclusion."

She looked at his face--worried, and serious--and didn't even try to curb her instinct. "Gert himself could be the leak, you know." She set Fluffy beside her, and then climbed into his lap, her legs on either side of his hips. "He knew I was with you."

"He could be." Sebastian made a sound that was almost a rumbling purr, pulled her in closer and then kissed her neck.

She felt her heart beat faster, felt her nerve endings fire up, and tilted her head back to give him better access, even as she slid her hands down to rub the erection that had sprung up between them.

He groaned, lifting a little into her touch. "Not here. I'm not the only person who knows about this lookout."

"Hmm." She shouldn't have started anything, but she wanted to wipe away that grim look, before it sank into his soul. "Where do we go, then?"

"There's a place I know of. It's a little further than I'd like to be from the settlement, but no one knows about it."

She rested her forehead on his shoulder, blew out a frustrated breath. "Then let's go."

TWENTY-THREE

SHE WAS like the golden light that spilled over the planet each morning.

Sebastian watched Dee as she carefully made her way through the forest, following the tiny track he'd put them on, and knew without her, he'd be in a far darker place.

Her hair was tied in a tail high on her head, and tendrils stuck to her neck in the steamy heat. She'd pushed the long sleeves of her black shirt up her arms and every now and then, pulled it away from her body.

"I hope we're close." She looked over her shoulder, and he forced himself to concentrate on where they were.

"Not far." He could still feel her hands on him, could still taste the salty sweet of her skin. They couldn't get there soon enough.

The comm set buzzed in his pocket, and he reached out to grab her shoulder to stop her moving ahead.

"Yes," he said, unwilling to identify himself, in case Karr or Vavi were no longer the ones in control of the comm unit.

"It's Vavi. The Cores sent a message. They've got Lucia."

He could barely hear her, and he didn't know if that was because of where she was calling from, or because they'd moved too far away from the settlement.

"What did you say?"

"They've taken Lucia." She sounded like she was breathing heavily. "They say they'll kill her if Dee doesn't give herself up."

Sebastian didn't know if the static was from the comm set, or his ears.

"Did you hear me, Seb?" Her voice cracked. "They'll kill her."

"How did you get the message?" He made his lips move.

"They gave it to one of our informants who works as a cleaner in the Tree. Someone outed her to them, and they told her not to come back once she'd passed on the news."

The world seemed to slow, and get colder. "They give a time limit? A place?"

Dee was watching him, head cocked to one side as she tried to work out the conversation.

The conversation about her being part of a hostage swap.

Rage descended on him for a long beat, and he had to clear his throat. "Repeat that."

"They want her to step into the Tree lobby tomorrow morning or they'll dump Lucia's body outside the Dar Raca gate."

He took a deep, deliberate breath. "Who knows this?"

"Everyone at headquarters." Vavi blew out a breath. "Seb, people here don't know Dee. They'll sell her out in a heartbeat to get Lucia back. Some may already have done it."

"Karr?"

She was silent for so long, he wondered if they'd lost the connection.

"I don't know," she said at last. "He's been friends with Lucia for a long time. He'd give Dee up without thinking twice."

"Where's Karr now?" Might as well know.

"He went to the Tree. Said he wanted to see if he could find where they may be holding her."

Sebastian closed his eyes and gritted his teeth. "Did he take back up?"

"No." She sounded worried.

Which was logical. Because from the Cores perspective, two hostages were always better than one.

Or maybe Karr was going there to tell them what he knew about Dee's whereabouts.

"Tell him to get in touch when he gets back."

"I will." The line crackled a bit more. "Where are you, Sebastian?"

Sebastian cut off the call. Then he dropped the comm set onto the ground and stamped on it.

He looked up, found Dee watching him with wide eyes.

"See a rock anywhere?"

She turned, stepped off the path, and came back with two.

He put the comm set on one, smashed it with the second one.

"Trouble?"

He laughed, a mirthless, bitter sound. "You could say that."

"Someone sell you out?" There was a well of sympathy in her tone.

"You've been there?"

She nodded. "Two of our people were taken by the Cores. Tortured and killed, and their bodies left outside one of Leo's warehouses as a message. We thought the Cores got inside information on who to take."

He picked up the broken comm set and stepped off the path, heading north.

She followed behind him without a single question. Above them, high in the branches, birds called to each other, and he could see the flash of bright yellow and red.

"You find out who it was?" he asked at last.

"Yes."

There was something hard in her voice now.

"You can't just leave it at that."

"It was someone Finkle and I hired. One of the security team."

"I take it he's no longer a problem."

She gave a snort. "Leo and Sofie took him down. From the sounds of it, Sofie stopped him, Leo ended him."

"Why did he do it?" He knew he was stringing this out, but he'd rather not think about the traitors in his own team right now.

"Garmen is a Breakaway planet. Why do you think he did it?"

Sebastian sighed. "Money."

He caught a glimpse of what he'd been looking for.

"Oh." From the surprise and interest in Dee's voice, she'd seen it, too.

Sebastian pushed through the last of the thick foliage, and held it back for Dee to join him on the thin strip bare of all vegetation.

The hum of the track was so low, you could only hear it when you were almost on it, and even then, it was more like a vibration in your bones than something you actually heard.

The pillars holding the track up were at least a story and a half high. The hum swelled, Sebastian wound his arm back, and as a hover, piled with supplies, ran past, he threw the comm set up to it.

It made a ting as it landed inside, and then the hum settled to a quieter level as the vehicle disappeared toward Dar Raca.

When he turned, he saw Dee watching him with eyes that told him she knew something was very wrong.

"We're not that far from where I was originally taking us. Do you mind if we don't talk about it for a bit?"

She hesitated, then nodded. She stepped back the way they'd come, holding the foliage back for him this time, and he felt a surge of gratitude to her, just to have some time to think.

To find a way out of this.

He led the way, and it seemed the roof of the hut he was looking for came up sooner than he was ready for.

The sound of water grew louder as they got closer, and he gave a grunt of approval as he turned the last corner and stepped into the clearing. There had obviously been enough rain deeper in the forest to keep the waterfall flowing.

"Oh, yes please." Dee crowded behind him, and then pushed past, carefully setting down her pack and Fluffy, and then pulling her shirt off.

She bent, unclipped her boots, and then wriggled out of her

pants, leaving them in a pile. She walked naked up to the river bank, stepping into the shallow pool that curved around the dilapidated hut. She looked over her shoulder at him and smiled, then walked across to duck down under the low waterfall that cascaded over the rocks on the opposite side.

She gave a tiny squeak as the water hit her, and he guessed it was a bit colder than she'd thought it would be.

She eventually dropped into a crouch, so that the water poured over her head as well, tilting her head back so it hit her face.

By the time she pushed her hair back and stepped away, wading through the shin high water back to the bank, he had had the sense to get out of his own clothes.

She trailed a hand down his arm as he passed her, then stood watching him as he had watched her.

It made him harder than he ever remembered being.

When he had rubbed the sweat off himself, and turned back, he found she'd perched herself on a smooth rock a little way upstream, lying back on her elbows.

"I checked. There's no decent bed in that hut."

He walked toward her. "That's disappointing. But this will do just fine."

IT HAD BEEN MORE than just fine.

It had been wild, and fast, and urgent.

Dee stretched, liking the feel of Sebastian's wet, taut skin against hers. She didn't want to break the mood. Didn't want to end this moment, but . . .

"What's the problem?"

He sucked in a breath. Closed his eyes.

She waited him out.

It was bad, whatever it was. He had made love to her like she was about to be ripped from his arms.

"They took Lucia."

She thought back to Lucia of the solemn face, and no bullshit. She had seemed to be the closest team member to Sebastian when they'd taken Dee hostage on the Verden. "For what reason?"

"To swap for another hostage."

He could barely say the words.

And it became as crystal clear as the water flowing around her. "To swap for me."

"Yes." Sebastian sat up, taking her with him. He lifted her, arranging her on his lap, and she leaned forward to rest her head against his shoulder.

His big hands settled on her back, rubbed up and down.

"So, they picked Lucia at random, or because she's your closest friend?"

He stiffened. "My closest friend?"

"Well, isn't she?" She leaned back to look him in the eye.

"I hadn't thought of it, but . . . yes." He narrowed his eyes. "We worked together for years on the pipelines. I'd trust her before I trusted anyone else."

"So they conveniently get rid of your closest ally and the one person you'd most likely trade for your new lover in one neat step."

He stared at her. "Whoever gave the Cores that bit of inside information had better be enjoying whatever they got for it, because they won't be enjoying it for long."

She didn't respond.

"Hey." He gripped her shoulders and shook her gently. "Hey! There is no way I'm giving you up to them. No way."

She let out a slow breath. "So what's the plan?"

"I'll go back. Tell them you were picked up by the Bodivas warship that's coming for you. I can't give up what I don't have. Whoever gave Lucia's name to the Cores did it because they see her as a weak spot for me, but she's worth nothing if I don't have what they're looking for."

"If she's worth nothing, they won't simply give her back." He must know this as well as she did. "They'll kill her first."

In her experience, the Cores never passed up on an opportunity

164

to remind the gen-pop that they couldn't win. Without constant rein-forcement, they might just forget and do something risky.

Like remember they were many and the Cores were few.

"I can't give you up. I don't have a right to, anyway." He gestured to his pack, lying on the river bank. "This isn't your battle. I dragged you into it, and I'll get you out. I've got a location device in my pack. You take it, hike as far as you can, and then in a day's time, activate it for an hour or so. If I haven't given the frequency to your friends on Garmen by then, wait another day, activate it again."

The sun had set swiftly, painting the sky with oranges and reds so deep and vivid, Dee lifted her head and tipped it back to take it all in. The cool blues, lavenders and pinks of Garmen were beautiful in their own way, but this was bold and striking. Gorgeous beyond words.

The air had cooled, too, just enough to make her perfectly comfortable in her own skin.

"What are you thinking?" Sebastian was watching her with his dark eyes, thick eyelashes clumped together from the water, and she felt her heart lurch in her chest.

"That this is a beautiful place."

Something crashed through bushes on the other side of the stream and then hooted, the sound so loud and aggressive Dee froze, her gaze snapping to the quivering undergrowth.

"A fintel." Sebastian turned to look as well, but she relaxed a little at his calm demeanor, even as she caught a glimpse of a mottled brown and green coat, and then heard another ear-splitting hoot.

"They're rare." Sebastian's lips twisted with regret. "Or at least, around the settlement in Dar Raca they are. With jobs and money so scarce, they've been hunted out."

The fintel gave another hoot and Fluffy scrambled up from the water onto the rock and jumped onto Dee, climbing up her arm to dig sharp claws into her shoulder and hiss at the invisible fintel.

"Ow." Dee tried to pry the claws out of her skin, and saw pin pricks of blood all the way up her arm and a scratch on her shoulder. "This is the downside of being naked."

Sebastian shot her a grin while the little talu focused in the direction of the hooting noise, fangs bared and growling softly. Dee's lips twitched because her fur was soaking wet and it made her look even tinier than she was.

"That was probably our signal to get going." Sebastian lifted Dee up, muscles standing out in his arms, and set her down in the stream beside the rock, then stood himself.

She wondered if he thought things were settled.

She hadn't agreed to his plan, did not intend to walk off into the forest and leave him to deal with the mess.

Time was wasting, though. Especially if Lucia was being held by the Cores.

Dee climbed back onto the bank and started picking up her clothes, scattered in a trail from the path to the stream.

They were sweaty and dirty, but she didn't have much choice but to put them back on.

She lifted her shirt, and then choked out a scream as a large, flying insect, wings clacking, flew up into her face.

Fluffy leapt from her shoulder with a primal scream, and when she landed on the ground, she had the insect struggling feebly in her mouth. It was almost a third of the talu's size.

"Good girl." Dee crouched beside her and gave the top of her head a scratch.

When she turned, she saw Sebastian watching her with amusement. He was back in his pants, but his chest was bare, and she spent a moment enjoying the view.

"It's harmless," he said, tipping his head to where Fluffy was happily eating her kill.

Dee laughed. "It surprised me more than anything. Although it's given me a moment of sympathy for Leo's girlfriend, Sofie. We were traveling out of Tether Town, and she picked up a rock with a grass spider on it. I never heard anyone scream like that when she realized what was sitting on her hand."

"Are they dangerous?"

"Most poisonous spider on Garmen." Dee felt her world tip a

little as she finished speaking, and she wondered how she could have forgotten what was attached to this memory. How she could have gone into this territory so easily.

"What is it?" Sebastian crouched beside her, and she realized she was still naked, holding her clothes in a tight grip in front of her.

She shook her head. "I'd forgotten for a moment what came next."

"What did come next?" He took her clothes from her, shook out her top to make sure there was nothing else hiding in its folds, and then slid it over her head, dressing her like a child.

"Sofie picked up that rock because we were under attack. Being stalked by a traitor." She stood and took her underwear and pants from him, bent to pull them on.

"You killed him?"

She pressed her lips together in a parody of a smile. "It was either him, or one of our group. And yes. I was the one to do it."

She sat down beside her boots, and concentrated on pulling on her socks.

"I'm glad you got him before he got you." Sebastian sat down beside her. "And I know for a fact that if it had been the other way around, he would not be spending even a moment worrying about the morality of what he did."

She drew in a deep breath, tipped back her head to catch the last of the spectacular sunset, and then nodded.

"Sometimes it weighs on me, though."

"I can see." He ran a finger down her cheek. "When you want someone to carry that for you, just shout."

She looked over at him, momentarily lost for words. "That's the nicest offer I've ever had, but it doesn't work like that."

He sent her a crooked grin. "Maybe not. But I'm also available as a distraction."

She leaned in to him, kissing him in a long, slow exploration. "Your application has been successful," she whispered as she drew back.

TWENTY-FOUR

THEY SAT TOGETHER, shoulders and thighs brushing as they ate the energy bars Sebastian had pulled out of his emergency pack.

Even though he was angry with her, he still liked being close.

She thought that was just about the sweetest thing she'd ever had in a lover.

"You can be angry," she said, then tried to gnaw on the corner of one of the bars, "but it won't change things."

"I wish you'd reconsider." He snapped a piece off his own bar. "If you get hurt or captured . . ."

"Then I'll face the consequences of my own decisions." She wasn't particularly brave, but there was no way she could leave Sebastian to deal with the Cores and be swooped up to safety by the Bodivas military.

If they were even in a position to save her anyway.

After a long moment of silence, he sighed, and gave a tiny nod.

She ran a hand down his arm, and twined her fingers with his. "If we need a place to hide in the settlement that the resistance doesn't know about, I think Jamari and Paka would help us."

"I thought you said Fluffy bit Paka. Isn't he dead?" Sebastian turned to her.

"She put him on his back, but he's really big, and Fluffy had already bitten Hanran and his guard by then, so she wasn't at a lethal level. He'll live. Jamari says Hanran Fattal probably sent Rina out to buy Fluffy because he needed the truth out of someone."

Sebastian let go of her hand. "The truth?"

"Seems a talu's venom is a truth serum in tiny doses, a psychedelic drug in slightly larger doses, and a lethal poison after that."

"Fluffy is a walking truth serum factory?" He stared at the talu with sudden interest.

Dee shrugged. "That's what Jamari's heard, and she's traveled a lot for Ruanne. She says the word is that a talu's venom is the most reliable truth serum to be found."

"And Hanran Fattal was after it." Sebastian nodded thoughtfully. "He sent his daughter out to get it. I know she was a drug user. She must have had some connections if it's also a drug."

"And the way Peyt and his friend next door were acting suddenly makes a lot more sense." Dee's jaw was getting tired, but she needed the calories, so she kept chewing.

Sebastian frowned at her. "Peyt and his friend?"

"When they caught me in his apartment."

He came up off the ground, crouching in front of her. "What?"

"Didn't I tell you?" So much had happened, she couldn't remember.

"No." Temper snapped in his voice.

She grinned. "No harm done. I stunned him with a laz and Fluffy and I got out of there."

"So how do you extract the venom?" He was looking at Fluffy with a lot more warmth than he had before.

"Uh, uh." She tucked Fluffy under her arm. "I'm not hurting her, and I'm not scaring her."

"I've heard the med techs out in the deep forest collect snake venom in a cup to send to the labs to create antivenom." Sebastian dug in his pack and came up with a long insulated bottle with a small lid. He took the lid off and handed it to her. "That looks about the right size."

Dee took it reluctantly, holding it out in front of her. Fluffy squirmed out from under her arm into her lap and then lifted up toward the lid. Curious, Dee lowered it, and the talu grasped it with both front claws and bit down on the rim. Then she dropped down and chittered expectantly.

Dee peered into the lid, saw a small amount of clear, viscous liquid at the bottom.

"I think she wants a treat," Sebastian said, voice dry.

"Yes." Dee took the piece of energy bar he handed her, keeping a firm hold on the lid. "I have a feeling she's done this before."

Sebastian pushed up into a crouch, watching Fluffy nibble on her reward. "The one thing I'd like to know, given the evidence is mounting up that Hanran Fattal wanted Fluffy for her venom, is who does he want to get the truth out of?"

SEBASTIAN HOPED the person Fattal was holding was his friend, the former resistance leader, Vahn.

Dee could see it in his face before he'd packed everything up and started leading them back toward Dar Raca.

He set a punishing pace.

"If it is Vahn they're guarding down that passage, it's not your fault he's there." She spoke as he waited for her, holding a branch to one side so she could climb over a fallen tree trunk.

Sebastian narrowed his eyes at her. "I should have known he wasn't dead. That they'd want to get him to tell them who our spies are."

"Except someone's already giving them that information."

She stopped beside him, and he let the branch go with a vicious snap.

"It isn't Vahn giving that information. He'd rather die."

"I'm sure you're right." She didn't touch him, or soften her voice, she simply stood in front of him until he looked at her. "They wouldn't need the truth serum if they'd already got him to talk. And Jamari says the people disappearing are those who reported information to resistance headquarters. It's most likely someone there who's passing on information.

"And you need to make some room for the possibility that it's Ruanne they're holding, not Vahn. Because I'm betting she'd be just as disinclined to talk to the Cores, and that she'd have a lot of knowledge in that wily, clever brain of hers that they'd like to know about her trade routes and her trading partners."

He nodded. "Or it's someone else altogether. They've had Vahn more than two months, and they've had Ruanne just under six. I don't know that the Cores are able to look after prisoners for that long."

His words sent a chill through her, because they were true. The Garmen Cores never bothered to keep prisoners longer than a few days, after which they threw them away, broken beyond all saving.

"I'll be happy if we just get Lucia back," she said.

Sebastian nodded, and then pulled her close, kissing her forehead and then her lips. "We will."

THERE WAS no one stationed at his house.

Sebastian had no plans on going in, but he was interested to see who might be waiting there.

After ten minutes, he withdrew, feeling his way in the shadowed dark of the forest until he reached the spot where he'd left Dee.

She wasn't there, and he knew a moment of panic before she stepped out from the other side of the tree.

"See anyone?" she asked.

"No." He swung the pack she held out to him over his shoulder, and then pulled her close, holding her face in his hands and kissing her. He seemed unable to help himself.

"What's that for?" she asked as he drew back, and he liked that she sounded breathless.

"Do I need a reason?"

She laughed softly. "No. No, you don't."

She slid her arm around his waist and kissed the side of his jaw, and then stepped back.

"How do you not have a lover already?" He hadn't meant to say it, but it had been something he'd been mulling almost since he'd met her. "Are the men on Garmen idiots?"

She gave an indelicate snort. "For a long time, at least the last eighteen months, but probably longer, I've worked in an environment of extreme suspicion. The Cores were out to get us, and we were out to get them, and I took no one, not a single person, at face value. Especially if they weren't part of my team."

"And those on your team?"

"My colleagues were out of bounds as far as I was concerned. Before I was promoted, I didn't feel strongly enough about anyone to risk the problems that would come up if things went bad." She shrugged. "And when it became my team to command, I obviously couldn't go there. I was their boss."

"Lucky, lucky me."

She looked over at him sharply, almost as if she suspected he was joking.

He stepped into her space, loosely looping his arms around her waist. "I don't know how long we have together. I don't know if you'll be leaving when this is over, or whether we'll even make it, but I want you to know when I say I feel lucky, I mean it.

"I don't remember a time when I wasn't fighting what seems to be a never-ending battle. I was close to going under when I met you, and you've reminded me that there are some good things to be found. That there are some truly beautiful things in this world, and while I'm sorry I involved you in this mess, I'll never be sorry I met you."

She put her hands on his chest, and ran them upward, hooking them behind his neck. "You are--"

He froze, brought a finger to her lips, then lifted her in his arms and stepped silently up against the tree.

He set her down when they on the other side of the thick trunk, and then he edged back around, crouching low.

The sound he'd heard came again, the snap of twigs and crackle of leaves underfoot.

Dee crouched beside him.

"Anything?" someone asked softly.

"I thought I heard talking, but it might have been a bird." As the second person spoke, a bird did call, although the cack, cack was muted.

Sebastian felt a cold chill as he recognized both voices.

"The comm unit is still out of range, so either Sebastian isn't coming or the comm set is broken. We're wasting our time." Laschka kept her voice low.

"You think Sebastian would leave Lucia in Cores hands and do nothing? You think he's that far gone on this Garmen woman?"

Laschka shuffled. Sighed. "I don't know, Darren. But no matter what he thinks about it, he doesn't own her. You think he'll force Dee to give up her life for someone she barely knows?"

"If it's a choice between Lucia, who's been part of the team for years, and some woman he's just met--"

Sebastian heard them move away.

"As far as I know, the resistance doesn't own people, or force them to do things they don't want to do." Laschka's voice was faint.

"Then best I resign from the resistance." Darren's voice was cold as he followed her down the path.

He sensed Dee relax, then blow out a breath.

"He'd grab me and haul me off to the Tree in a heartbeat, wouldn't he?"

Sebastian felt the icy hand of rage caress his neck. "Looks like it."

"And it puts you in a difficult position." She had twisted, so her back was against the tree trunk, and she was sitting on the ground. She looked up at him, a thin beam of moonlight making her eyes gleam. "You'd be better off walking in to headquarters and telling them you gave me the choice and I decided to head deeper into the forest and see if the Bodivas would rescue me."

He crouched beside her, considering it. "And what would you really be doing?"

"Finding a way into the Tree without being seen, and looking for Lucia, and whoever else they may have in there."

"And what good would it do for me to be in headquarters? I won't be popular for letting you go." By the sound of it, Darren might try to murder him for that alone.

She paused. Frowned. "I don't know. Try to renegotiate with the Cores by telling them I'm gone?"

"That sounds like a losing proposition." He caught her hair between his fingers, and let it slide, cool and smooth, between them.

"Because they'll kill Lucia."

He nodded. "Why not? If they don't have any chance of getting you, then killing her will damage me in the eyes of most of the resistance. They'd still be racking up a win, even if it's not the one they were after."

"The trouble is, I don't think I *am* who they're after. Hanran Fattal wants Fluffy, although I'm sure he'd like to see me suffer because I'm guessing he didn't like being helpless and off his head in front of his loyal soldiers."

"Why didn't he say so, then? Why not just say they want Fluffy? Theoretically, that'd be a much easier choice for us to make." His lips twitched at the look on her face. "I said 'theoretically'."

"You're right. So if they don't want to admit they want her, then it's because Hanran Fattal wants to hide the fact that he's procured a talu. He doesn't want others to know he has access to a truth serum. And I don't think the psychedelic properties are well regarded, either. Peyt wasn't at all eager to go to Hanran Fattal and admit to negotiating with me for the venom. He threatened to, but when I challenged him on it, he backed down."

Sebastian slid her hair behind her ear, frowning. There was more to the incident in Peyt's apartment than she was telling, but he'd been the one to suggest she go there, so there was no one to feel angry with, no one to blame, but himself. "You could be right. He might want to use it on his fellow Cores execs. He might not have Vahn or Ruanne prisoner at all."

The thought wasn't acceptable to him, and he shook it off.

"We can infiltrate the Tree together if you think it's a better idea." She lifted her hands. "See if we can get Lucia out. But if we can't get to her, I can still meet him as promised, and when he realizes Fluffy isn't with me, we can negotiate."

"But you don't want to negotiate," Sebastian reminded her.

"No. But I'm prepared to talk a good game to get Lucia out alive." She let her cheek rest in his palm.

The cack, cack of a night caller broke the moment, and they both rose to their feet.

"The night is wasting," she said, quietly.

He could do nothing but nod in response.

TWENTY-FIVE

DEE KNOCKED SOFTLY on Jamari's door, and felt a quick rush of relief when she opened it.

There was a dim light on inside, and it was absolutely dark in the settlement's back alleys, so she couldn't read the trader captain's expression, but after a moment Jamari stepped back, allowing them entry.

No one said anything until the door was closed.

"How's Paka?" Dee asked.

"Fine." She looked over at the bed, and Dee just made out the outline of Paka's massive form under the covers.

"This your resistance leader?" Jamari asked, looking Sebastian up and down.

Dee nodded. "This is Sebastian."

After a moment's hesitation, Jamari gave the Bodivas greeting Dee had seen before, a clenched fist held out and then covered with the other hand.

Sebastian watched her, and then returned the gesture.

"Are you both originally from Bodivas?" she asked. No one, unless they were under the age of sixteen, had been born on either of the Breakaway planets.

They both nodded.

"And you?" Jamari asked.

"Arkhor." Dee shrugged as she said it, to deflect any comments. She'd been ten years old when her parents had brought her to Garmen, but she knew from every interaction she'd had since then that Arkhorans were considered the pushy, aggressive ones in the Verdant String.

"Explains a few things," Jamari said, and Dee gave her the same cold stare she'd perfected as a comeback for any Arkhoran remarks.

She could barely remember Arkhor. Now, since the Arkhorans had taken control of Garmen, she supposed she could go back there. See what it was like.

If she got off Lassa alive.

Sebastian shifted beside her, and she had to push away the suspicion that she didn't want to get off Lassa. Or, not without Sebastian.

Or Fluffy.

"What are you doing here in the middle of the night?" Jamari asked.

"You didn't hear about the Cores guards coming for her?" Sebastian asked, and suspicion laced his voice.

"I haven't stepped outside since Dee's talu bit Paka. I haven't dared leave him." She shot Dee a look. "The Cores came for you?"

"More like for Fluffy, but yes."

At the mention of the talu, Jamari focused on her pack. "So why aren't you far, far away?"

"They took one of my people hostage in exchange for Dee." Sebastian leaned back against the wall, arms crossed.

"You're going to hand yourself over?" Jamari's voice was hushed with shock.

"Not if I can help it. We're going to see if we can find her, and whoever else they're holding, and get them out." Dee put her pack on the table, and Fluffy popped her head out. She held out her hand and the talu scrambled up into her palm. She reached into the bag with her other hand for the small cup Sebastian had given her.

Fluffy happily grabbed it with both front paws and bit down, and Sebastian stepped forward, ready with a treat for her.

The talu sat on the table, eyes bright and inquisitive, nibbling the piece of energy bar.

It soothed Dee's conscience a bit. Fluffy didn't seem to be nervous or hurt by the milking.

She poured the venom into the small vial Sebastian had found in his med kit for her, and when she screwed the lid on, she saw Jamari watching her with interest.

"Things have changed in the hours since I last saw you."

Dee nodded. "It turns out Fluffy's an old hand at being milked."

Jamari focused back on the talu. "They're rare. I don't even want to think about how much Rina Fattal must have paid for her. But it makes sense that she was well looked after." She glanced at Paka, and then back. "So what's the plan?"

"This isn't your fight, Jamari." Dee lifted her hands. "We just wanted a quiet place to milk Fluffy one last time, and hopefully to borrow some clean clothes."

Jamari looked at Paka again. "This is more my fight than yours, Garmen Girl. I've been living in a self-imposed prison cell for the last six months. My lover nearly died today because I'm so desperate to get out, and none of us can live a normal life with what's going on. Don't tell me it's not my fight."

"What aid are you prepared to offer?" Sebastian asked.

"I can get you some maintenance uniforms. My neighbors are a couple who are two of the lucky ones with Cores jobs. They're cleaners--not of the Tree itself, one of the smaller Trees, but I think the cleaning uniform is the same. I'm also prepared to keep your talu here, if you want me to, and I can start to spread the word about the Caruso."

Jamari's lips thinned. "Most of the settlement may be suspicious of the resistance now, but they know having the Caruso here is a bridge too far. It's either stand up now, or get crushed."

"You think they'll understand that?" Sebastian's voice sounded skeptical.

Jamari lifted her hands, palms out. "If they don't, they're doomed."

FLUFFY HAD NOT GONE HAPPILY into the box Jamari had found to keep her in. Dee ended up with another scratch, this one from her elbow to her inner wrist, as Fluffy tried to cling to her as she put her inside, but eventually, the lid was closed.

Once it was, the talu kept trying to fit her nose through one of the holes Sebastian had cut out for her to breathe, and whimpered pitifully.

Dee crouched beside the box and crooned to her a bit, and after a bit more chirping, she went quiet, settling into the blanket Jamari had put inside for her to cuddle in.

"She's probably tired," Jamari said. "My guess is you haven't had much down time."

Dee's mind jumped to the rock pool in the forest, and she glanced up at Sebastian just as he looked her way, and blushed.

From the tiny smile on his lips, he realized where her thoughts had gone.

Dee cleared her throat and tugged at the jacket of her cleaning uniform. It was short on her and too wide, but not so bad that it would draw attention.

The worst part was the wig Jamari had lent her. Jamari'd been using it to go outside unseen, and the warm honey brown of it was certainly different to Dee's natural color, but the humid air and heat made her scalp prickle with sweat, and her fingers twitched with her need to scratch beneath it.

Sebastian looked as ridiculous. The pants ended above his ankles, but his ankle-height boots helped. And in the end they settled on him tying the jacket around his waist, as if he was too hot to wear it, because the arms ended halfway to his elbows.

"Good luck." Jamari pulled Dee into a quick hug before they

stepped out into the night. It was after midnight, and the three crescent moons lined up like the fingernails of a celestial hand.

Sebastian led her through back ways and side routes, slipping between huts and shacks built among trees. Even though the branches overhead often blocked out the faint moonlight, a few people were still awake, and the light spilling from poorly sealed doors and windows helped light the way.

The buzz from the pipelines and the hover track was like a tiny stone in her shoe, rubbing at her, just out of reach, and mostly drowned out by the soft sound of the birds and the whine of the insects.

She'd been focused on the members of the resistance when she'd emerged from the tunnel with Karr and Sebastian the night before, so she didn't recognize the entrance to the rough enclosure until Sebastian leaned against a tree trunk, lifted a finger to his lips and then pointed.

She focused, and was just able to make out the shape of the sentry standing guard beside it.

It was hard to believe only a day had passed since she'd last been here.

She tried to shake off the sudden exhaustion that gripped her. There was no time for it now.

Now she was oriented, she realized the poles she was looking at were the legs of the massive screen that sat on the Dar Raca wall.

"What do we do?" She breathed the words directly into Sebastian's ear, and he was so warm, and so solid, she wanted to rest her head on his shoulder and close her eyes.

"We need a distraction." Sebastian pulled his laz from his pocket. "Or I'll have to shoot him in the back." He seemed at ease with the decision.

The door to the enclosure faced away from the square, and it was dark enough that if they shot the guard, no one would notice unless they were looking for him.

The few buildings nearby looked old, as if they'd been built when Lassa was first established as a Breakaway, before the Cores realized they could get away with doing nothing for the workers who came to find their fortunes--dupes who believed the stories that they could make a fortune if they were willing to take risks and work hard--when the Cores never had any intention of letting anyone have access to the wealth they saw as their personal spoils.

Her parents had been two of those dupes, so she didn't judge. Although, by the looks of things, the Cores on Garmen had been forced to concede more than the Cores on Lassa. The nature of the mineral wealth must have had an effect on what was possible for them to get away with.

But that was beside the point. While the entrance to the tunnel was closer to the trees, and not as much out in the open, it was still going to be hard to approach the guard without being seen long before they reached him.

"I'll walk up to him, shoot when I'm close enough." Sebastian had obviously come to the same conclusion.

"I'll do it. You have to live with everyone here afterward." Dee pulled her own laz from the back of her pants.

But before they could decide which of them would go, the guard straightened up and stuck his head into the enclosure, laz out.

Someone spoke to him in low tones from within, and then stepped out into the open.

"Karr." Sebastian's voice was soft and thoughtful.

"Well, Vavi said he'd been to the Tree to try and work out where Lucia was being held."

Karr was wearing a similar uniform to their own, which confirmed what Vavi had told them, as well.

The two men stood close together, speaking quietly, and then they both strode off in the direction of the resistance headquarters, a run-down building on the far corner of the square. With its washing lines strung between the windows, it looked like an apartment block, hiding in plain sight of the Cores.

There was a light shining from the second floor, and another on the ground floor, and both men were dark shapes against the light as they moved away.

Sebastian motioned to Dee to go first, and she ran as fast as she could. She darted through the enclosure opening, crouched down and pulled the lid off the tunnel entrance as silently as she could.

She glanced up as Sebastian loomed in the doorway, saw he was covering her, his laz pointed toward headquarters.

"Get in," she whispered.

He nodded as she started climbing down, but didn't turn.

She shimmied down the ladder, and then stood to one side, laz raised at an angle as he climbed down after her, just in case someone noticed them or it was a trap.

He stopped, leaned out, and started dragging the lid back in place, and she heard a shout, then his name.

She thought he was going to call back, but instead he finished pulling the tunnel lid over the hole, and then dropped down beside her.

"Run."

TWENTY-SIX

WITH LUCK, Lasanai, who'd been guarding the tunnel entrance, had only seen him and not Dee.

And even that was not good.

Lasanai would run back to headquarters to ask what to do, and whoever was betraying them to the Cores would most likely hear about it.

Depending on how quickly the traitor was able to communicate to the Cores, that meant someone could be waiting for them at the other end.

If the spy had told the Cores about the tunnel.

He could see how a traitor might not want to give up too much. Especially if they used the tunnel themselves.

Sebastian's attention shifted to what was happening behind him.

For the last minute, he'd heard the faint splash of boots running through shallow water as someone chased them down.

Lasanai must have called in some help.

That it was Sebastian's own people was no longer relevant. Especially given Darren's comments about Dee.

They'd have to go through Sebastian first before they got her.

The ground started to slant upward a little, and he breathed out in relief as he saw the hidden entrance.

He put on a burst of speed to grab Dee's shoulder as she ran past it.

"We're there?" Her voice was a breathy whisper.

He pointed and she sagged against him, sucking in a deep breath. "Yay."

He couldn't help giving her a quick hug, his lips touching the strange synthetic hair of her wig before he pressed his hand against the door.

"You go high, I'll go low," she said, and he nodded, shoved at the door with his shoulder, laz lifted, and Dee spun past him, crouched low.

There was no one on the other side.

Dee followed close behind him as he negotiated the stacks of boxes in the basement and then hit the stairs.

It was almost completely dark, but he'd been through here enough times in the last few months that he knew the way.

The apartment block was silent now, unlike when they'd come through the night before, but when he stepped into the empty, foul-smelling foyer he moved cautiously.

In case there were Cores guards waiting for them to come through the door, he moved silently to the narrow window beside the front entrance. It had been smashed out long ago, and tiny, jagged pieces of flexiclear were still lodged in the frame.

Dee crept up behind him, keeping low, her laz pointed toward the basement door in case whoever had been following them in the tunnel burst through.

He could see nothing at first except a few lights shining in some of the buildings that lined the road.

The lights illuminated parts of the street, but nothing moved.

Then the whole landscape lightened as clouds parted to reveal the three moons.

They were only in crescent, but the combined light of all three produced a faint illumination.

A man stepped out of the shadows, heading directly for their building, and Sebastian went very still as he watched him.

Then he moved back, taking care to keep hidden, and pulled Dee with him as he ran down the narrow passage to the left of where they'd come up from the basement, and then came to a stop halfway along.

"What's going on?" Dee set her lips against his ear to whisper her question.

"Darren, one of my lieutenants, one of the people who was in the forest earlier this evening, talking about us to Laschka, is out there. He's waiting for us. Or me, at least." He crouched down, and she joined him.

He pointed to the gaping hole in the wall. "I noticed this some time ago. Someone kicked out the wall at floor level." He lay flat, measuring the chances of him fitting through, but he could see there was no way. "I think you'll just make it."

She lay down beside him, swung her legs, and slid out, hanging for a moment with torso on the floor, legs dangling out, and then she dropped the short distance into the back alley.

The jagged wood caught on her wig, and he carefully untangled it.

"So you go out the front, I surprise them from the side?"

He was face to face with her, him lying with his head poking out, she standing outside the building, looking up. "Maybe. But I'd rather they don't know you're here at all. That's our one advantage. Whatever you do, don't attack or engage them. Work through the back alleys, get in position so you can be hidden but still see what's happening. If Darren lets me go on my way, wait for me to come to you. If things get ugly, or if he's not alone and I'm not able to safely leave, hide out until I can find you."

"And Lucia?" she asked the one question he didn't know how to answer.

"The last thing Darren should want is to put Lucia in more danger. If I explain to him--"

"And if he's your leak?"

Again, he had no answer. "I don't want you to go into the Tree by yourself."

She said nothing, but she reached out and squeezed his hand. He reached down to cup her face with his hands, boosted himself forward, and gave her a fierce, hard kiss.

They both heard the sound of a door closing in the foyer. Someone was coming up from the basement.

Sebastian slid back and rose up into a crouch. "Go. Hopefully the coast is clear for me."

She nodded and melted into the darkness, and Sebastian stood and walked softly back the way he'd come.

The foyer seemed empty, but he waited a long beat before he made his way back to the narrow window.

Darren was still out there.

Which meant--

"I have a laz trained on you, Sebastian."

When he turned, he saw Karr standing in the basement doorway.

He sighed, straightened up, and made his way through the front entrance and out into the night.

"JUST GOT BACK to Dar Raca, Darren?" Sebastian kept his voice low, running lightly down the steps toward the man he hadn't seen for over a month. The man who'd taken over Sebastian's own territory out among the pipelines when he'd been made the new leader of the resistance.

"I got back shortly after the Cores guards raided your house."

Sebastian looked behind him, saw Karr and Laschka coming up behind him.

"What the hell is going on, Seb?" Darren moved deeper into the shadows, and Sebastian followed.

It wasn't ideal for Dee. She'd find it harder to keep an eye on what was going on, but it was equally dangerous to be out in the open.

"What do you think?"

"You tell me." Darren's voice was low and harsh. "Sneaking out of the settlement into Dar Raca past your own people? What the hell?"

"I'm sorry I didn't do a better job of sneaking, because right now, whoever in the resistance is passing information to the Cores knows I'm on my way in. If I could have done it without being seen, they'd still think I was out in the forest. Now they know I'm here, and so are you."

Darren lifted his chin. "You think there's someone right in the heart of the organization who's betraying us?"

"Yes."

There was utter silence as Darren seemed to absorb that.

"He's right." Laschka had joined them, although Karr stood a little apart, laz in hand, watching the road and the buildings as a lookout.

"Shit. Why didn't you say something?" Darren asked.

Laschka simply stared at him, and eventually he got it.

"You thought it might be *me*?"

"I don't know who it is." Laschka turned to Sebastian. "I'm assuming you don't, either."

Sebastian shook his head. "I do know that my being here, and maybe your being here, too, is most likely known to the Cores by now. And that any hope I had of slipping into the Tree to look for Lucia has gone up in flames."

Darren was silent, and Sebastian saw his jaw was clenched and a tick moved just under his eye. "What proof do you have of this?"

"The fact that the Cores got word that we were going to kidnap Rina Fattal, which would have led to Karr, Vavi, Lucia and myself all being killed if things hadn't gone to hell on Garmen."

Darren stiffened at that.

"And the fact that the Caruso have set up a little base at the Cores hoverport, and I, as resistance leader, didn't know anything about it." He didn't look in Karr's direction.

"And the fact that the one person I really trust--the one person--Lucia, was the one who was taken today. Only someone in the inner circle of the resistance could have chosen such a perfect hostage."

Darren blew out a breath. "Look, Seb--"

He had had enough of this shit. "No, you look. I'm going to need you to fall back and let me get on with my plan."

"Where is Dee?" Karr had drifted closer.

"I didn't even tell her about Lucia." He lied with no qualms. Someone on his team was a traitor, and until he knew who it was, he'd protect Dee any way he could. "I gave her coordinates and told her to head out."

"Why would you do that?" Darren's eyes were narrowed.

"Because she's only here because we fucked up. She has nothing to do with this. It isn't her fight, and I refuse to put her in harm's way any more."

"And Lucia?" Karr asked softly.

"Lucia is our problem. And I was on my way to solve it until you got in my way."

"This isn't a dictatorship," Laschka said, and for the first time, he could hear anger in her voice. "We all care for Lucia, and we all want to rescue her. You said it yourself, it's our problem. Ours, not yours. You need to let us help."

He was quiet, thinking it through. "First, we need to get away from here."

"Where are we going to go?"

"Nowhere we usually go, that's for sure." Sebastian glanced down the street, but if Dee was watching them, he had no idea where she was.

"And then?"

"Then I come up with a plan. And no one--and I mean no one--goes anywhere on their own while they're with me. I want eyes on all of you all the time."

"Well, I guess that tells us where we stand." Darren glared at him.

"Good. I want no misunderstandings. There's something toxic in the resistance, and I plan to drain it. And I refuse to worry about turning my back on any of you while I work on trying to rescue Lucia."

"If you'd just come into headquarters instead of treating us like the enemy, you'd have heard my report." Karr looked sick. "I went to the Tree earlier, to find out where they're holding her."

"And?"

"And I couldn't even get inside. The keycard I was lent didn't work, and I just managed to get out of there. Three guards came out after I ran it through the reader on the door. They're watching every entrance." He hunched his shoulders. "Rescuing her is impossible. We need to give them what they want."

"We don't *have* what they want." Lashcka's voice trembled.

"No." And he'd make sure it stayed that way. "Even if Dee was here, we wouldn't be giving her up."

"Yes, we would, Sebastian." Karr shot him an angry look. "If I had to use my laz on you myself, we'd be giving her up."

Sebastian turned away from him in disgust. Dee needed to stay far away from him. From them all.

And once again, it looked like they'd run completely out of options.

He was getting very tired of losing.

TWENTY-SEVEN

OUCH.

Dee leaned back against the wall, far closer to Sebastian and his friends than Sebastian would most likely be happy with.

She hadn't had the best relationship with Karr, but to hear him say he'd hand her over to her death without so much as a wobble in his voice was cold.

Stone cold.

Sebastian had been right to warn her away.

She tuned back into their conversation, and heard them moving away, talking softly about finding cover in the big bushes that grew up against one of the smaller buildings where they'd have a view of the Tree's front entrance.

She waited for them to go, leaning against the the wall, and thinking through her options.

Waiting for Sebastian was going to be an exercise in futility.

He wasn't shaking his crew, and he must know it.

Not without making them suspicious.

And given Karr's pronouncement, she didn't want that. At all.

If she was going to be sacrificed, it would be her choice, not Karr's.

She started moving, more because she didn't think it was a good idea to stay in one place too long than anything else.

She moved slowly and carefully, making sure she wasn't catching up to Sebastian.

She made her way through streets that were starting to become familiar to her after all the running around she'd done in them the last few days.

But when she at last got as far as the Tree, she saw Karr was right. There were guards outside each entrance, something that hadn't been in place before.

And when she hunkered down to watch one at the rear of the building, she saw each person who approached was carefully searched.

That wasn't going to work.

She made her way deeper into streets that ran past the lower, square buildings dotted amongst the more exotic tree like structures, and eventually doubled back to Peyt's building.

She crouched in the ornate bushes outside to think for a bit.

She put her hand down the top of her shirt and drew out the two vials she had nestled under each breast.

Sebastian thought there was only one, but she'd measured out a quarter of the amount in the vial and put it in a second one while she was changing in Jamari's bathroom. She was no martyr, but the state of the bodies of her two colleagues, Sunar and Petro, dumped outside Leo's Tether Town warehouse, was etched in her memory.

She was sure both of them would have sought to end their suffering earlier if they could have. There was no harm in making sure she had a way out on her own terms if she was captured. And it was always good practice to have a backup.

Now she had to make a decision. Because Peyt wouldn't help her without some concrete payoff this time.

Not after their last encounter.

So she had to choose.

Give up her Plan B, or not get in to the Tree at all.

Put like that . . .

She stuffed the fuller vial back down the front of her shirt, and put the other one in one of the many pockets on her maintenance uniform.

She moved to the back of the smaller Tree and watched the rear entrance from the shadows in the rear garden. A man stepped out, but the door swung shut behind him before she was even halfway to it.

She stood out in the open, and then shrugged and moved purposefully to the door. Tried it just in case.

It was locked, and so she leaned against the wall beside it, arms folded, head down, and then slid down to a crouch.

It was still absolutely dark, but she sensed that midnight had come and gone, and they were into the early hours of the morning.

She might be wasting her time here, but then, if she couldn't get into the Tree because of the guards, she might as well waste it here as anywhere.

"Coming in the back doesn't mean they won't hear us entering the apartment." The man who spoke pitched his voice low, and the woman with him murmured an answer Dee couldn't hear, even though they were right beside her.

They either didn't see her, or they noticed the uniform and ignored her.

They pushed the door open, and she grabbed it before it closed, waited a beat for the sound of their footsteps to move away, and then she slipped inside.

She took the backstairs up, and could hear the couple who'd helped her get in still whispering to each other at least a floor above her when she turned onto the third floor.

She made her way to Peyt's little corner, and tried the door.

It seemed as if he'd reset the laslock.

She shrugged, and knocked, making sure her laz was firmly in her grip at her side.

There was a sound from the other side of the door, and it swung open.

Peyt stared at her for a moment, confused, but the moment he realized who she was under the wig, he lunged out, trying to grab her. She danced back, the laz pointed at his chest.

She lifted a finger to her lips, and waved him back inside his apartment.

He shook his head. "Fuck off."

"Either I shoot you, and then explain, or you back up, and I come in and explain without the need for another laz hit."

He looked from the laz to her face, and then threw his hands in the air, turned his back on her and stalked inside his apartment.

She moved carefully after him, letting the door close quietly behind her.

"I am very comfortable with shooting you again," she said to him, conversationally. He was fiddling with something in front of him, blocking it from her view with his body and so she was ready when he turned with a knife in his hand and threw it at her.

His aim was terrible. The knife went high, flying over her shoulder, and she shot him in the arm on a light stun.

His face crumpled as he clutched it to him, making a whining sound as he hunched over.

She stood quietly until he pulled himself up straight. There was fear in his eyes when he looked at her. Fear and hatred.

"What do you want?"

"I want to get into the Tree."

"What's that got to do with me?" He rubbed the arm she'd shot with a trembling hand.

"I want you to get me in."

His gaze jerked to meet hers. "Why would I do that?"

She put her hand in her pocket, and pulled out the vial. "Because if you do, you get this."

He stared at the vial for a long time. "Why can't you get into the Tree by yourself. You're working for Hanran Fattal, aren't you?"

She tilted her head in agreement. "Problem is, I've been a naughty girl. I'm supposed to be back in the apartment he set up for me, pretending to be Rina, and I've been engaged in a bit of private enter-prise instead. And now, they seem to have guards parked at every entrance, and I can hardly go in as myself without Fattal working out I wasn't where I was supposed to be."

"How do you think I can help you?"

"You tell me." She waved the vial from left to right, then slid it into her pocket.

He wet his lips, closed his eyes, and she hoped he was thinking about how to get her into the Tree, rather than fantasizing about getting his hands on talu venom.

"My father has an office in the Tree. He sometimes gets his personal cleaners to clean his office, because he doesn't like how the general maintenance workers do it. You've obviously thought of getting in as a maintenance worker already." His gaze flicked to her ill-fitting uniform.

That sounded like it had potential.

"Keep talking."

He shrugged. "I can take you in, I've done it before when my father's asked me to."

"We get in, and get to the stairwell, and I'll give you the venom." She felt a wave of contempt for him, looking at his pouting, sly face. "If you have any thoughts on turning around and going straight to the guards, be warned they'll want to know why you lied to them to get me in, and when they ask me, I won't be shy in telling them. I don't think Hanran will take well to someone trying to steal his venom. And while that includes me, I'll make sure they know to look at you, too."

His lips twisted. "I won't say anything. I'll be happy to see the back of you."

"The feeling's mutual." She shot him a smile.

"Where is the talu?" Peyt tried to ask the question casually.

"After my little incident with you, I decided it was safest back in my apartment in the Tree." She gave him another sugary smile. "Are you ready to go?"

He sighed and nodded. "Do you know why there are guards at the entrances to the Tree?"

She shook her head. "I don't run in such elevated circles."

He snatched up his comm set at that, and she had the sense that he was angry that neither did he.

TWENTY-EIGHT

SEBASTIAN COULDN'T SHAKE his worry for Dee.

He hoped she was following behind them, but her being on her own and vulnerable made him twitchy and irritable.

The only reason he didn't end the charade and admit that she was in Dar Raca with him was his fear that Karr and Darren would go through with their threats to grab her.

No matter how that ended, whether he killed them first, or they killed him--because it would be over his dead body--there was no way it was better than letting Dee trail them, and stay safe and sound out of sight.

Laschka led the way, moving through dark alleys so that they were approaching the Tree from the back.

When they got a block away, she turned sharply into an even tighter alleyway, and then jumped up, catching the bottom of a ladder, and then disappeared upward into the shadows.

Karr and Darren looked as surprised as he did.

He followed her, climbing for two floors before reaching the flat roof of the building.

Lashcka was waiting for him at the top, crouched behind a large cooling unit.

The Tree rose up in front of her, and when he joined her, he saw they had a view of all the back entrances to the building.

Karr was right. There were guards stationed in front of every single one.

Karr and Darren hunkered down beside them.

"I didn't know about this," Karr said, and Lashcka glanced at him.

"You were off trying to grab Rina Fattal when I found it."

He nodded, and for a moment they were silent, watching the guards joke with each other under the weak light above the entrances.

"What's the plan?"

"I was going to get inside the Tree. But I can see that is close to impossible."

From the front of the Tree, they all heard the hum and scrape of a small hover entering the the atrium.

"Could we get into a hover?" Lashcka asked.

Sebastian shook his head. "We'd have to exit it in the atrium itself, and that would leave us completely exposed. There are guards there, too."

"What's happening there?" Darren pointed, and Sebastian looked over to the entrance on the far left.

He went absolutely still.

"What is it?" Karr's tone was sharp.

He said nothing. Couldn't, even if he wanted to.

It was Peyt and a cleaner.

The woman had her back to them, and her shoulders were a little hunched, her light hair gleaming as it caught the light.

Peyt was speaking to the guards and they stepped aside, let the two in, and then went back to their conversation.

She had done it.

Shit!

He almost rose to his feet, then remembered he needed to keep down.

"Seb. What *is* it?"

He wouldn't tell them a damn thing. He didn't trust them, and he wasn't going to endanger Dee in any way.

But his reaction was too extreme. He had to give them something.

He swallowed. "I know the man who went in there. He and I have had a run-in in the past."

"He's coming back out." Lashcka's words snapped his attention back to the Tree.

"Keep watch here. I'm going to intercept him. See if he can get us in." He was running, bent over, for the ladder, before they could respond.

He heard Darren curse, but he was already halfway down.

He dropped into the alley before the ladder ended, and started to run.

To his relief, he didn't hear footsteps behind him.

DEE RAN up the stairs the moment Peyt snatched the vial from her and pushed back out of the stairwell.

She didn't think he'd risk confessing what he'd done, but if his spite overcame his sense of self-preservation, she was determined to be gone by the time the guards came looking.

She tried to remember which side of the building she and Sebastian had been on when they'd originally seen what they had both recognized as a holding area, and decided she was on the opposite side.

She pushed through the door on the floor below where she suspected Lucia was being held, and stood for a moment in the dim light.

There was no one around, no sounds at all.

She walked to the first maintenance door she saw, slipped inside the tiny space, and sat down heavily on a stool that was tucked against the wall.

She hadn't expected to get inside the Tree; she admitted it to herself. She'd expected the guards to turn them away, or worse.

Now that she had managed it, she had to work out exactly what she was doing here. What she wanted to achieve.

What had driven her so far was that she couldn't let them kill Lucia. And that still held true.

She felt the tension and fear that seemed to be crushing her chest ease a little.

The hard fact was Lucia would be killed if she didn't arrive at the designated time. All other possible scenarios came with a chance they'd make it out alive.

And that was good enough for her.

She'd killed. Over the last eighteen months she killed more than she was comfortable with. And yet, there had been no other way to safeguard the innocent victims in Tether Town.

She could have refused the role Leo had offered her, but it had always come down to the question of why *not* her? Why should she get to keep her hands clean and pass it off on someone else?

And now, she had the chance to save Lucia, and not only was there no reason why it shouldn't be her, it turned out she was the best placed person for the job. Almost no one else could have gotten in. And no one else would have had the venom as a bargaining chip.

Funny, in all the years she'd worked with Leo and Finkle on Garmen, she'd risked her life more times than she could count, and yet never really worried about it.

Now, she was sweating, her heart beating like a trapped bird in her chest.

She didn't have the same safety net here. There was no Leo, no Finkle, to come rescue her.

Sebastian would, though.

The thought steadied her, and yet spiked her heart rate even more. She didn't want Sebastian to put himself in danger for her.

So she had to succeed.

She forced herself to her feet and looked around the tiny space.

A light had come on when she'd stepped inside, and it illuminated a maintenance cart with the usual vacuum and cleaning materials.

She rose up, grabbed hold of the handles, and maneuvered it out of the closet.

She walked the length of the floor, heading for the opposite end, and then called the lift.

When the door pivoted open, she forced herself to move, swinging the cart around so she faced the door again.

The lift rose up one floor.

She took a deep breath as the semi-circular door swung open, but there was no one waiting on the other side.

The foyer the lift opened out into was lit with the same dim lighting on the floor below.

She stepped out, moving much more slowly as she headed for where she thought they were holding Lucia.

When she was a few doors away from the passageway where she'd noticed the guards on her first day here, she heard low voices, and she pushed into the first office she came to, leaving it open and switching on the vacuum.

On Garmen, most of the cleaning was done by automatons, but here it seemed they used the gen-pop. Perhaps because they could get away with barely paying them.

She turned her back to the door, and began running the long, slim head of the device along the floor.

"Hey."

She heard the sharp command, and ignored it.

"Hey!"

She pretended surprise, looking over her shoulder with a frown.

"Who sent you to clean?" The guard leaned in and switched off the vacuum.

She didn't want to talk if she could help it. She knew her accent was different. She tipped her head to the side in silent question.

"I thought they'd fired the cleaner. Wasn't she a resistance snitch?" Another guard peered in over the first guard's massive shoulder.

Dee looked down, avoiding eye contact, and pulled the work schedule off the cart and held it out.

The guard snatched it from her. "This doesn't tell me anything except the offices are supposed to be cleaned." He tossed it back in disgust, and it fluttered to the floor.

Dee made a big deal of bending down to pick it up, and reattaching it to the cart.

"It's not like she could have gotten in without clearance. Fattal's locked this place down." The other guard was already moving away, clearly bored with the whole thing.

The big one stood for a moment. "Finish quickly."

She nodded, eyes still averted.

"And bring us some jah."

The last statement was delivered with a nastiness she took to be his attempt at truly putting her in her place for alarming him.

She nodded again, and stepped out of the room after him.

He had gone to the intersection of the two passageways, and was watching her with hostile eyes.

She hunched over, making herself smaller, and giving herself a tiny limp, and scurried back a few doors to the small kitchen she'd spotted on her way down the wide corridor.

As soon as she was through the door she straightened and smiled.

She needed the venom in case she had to do a swap for Lucia, but there was surely enough in her vial for a small drop each into the guards' jah?

She didn't know what it would do, but there was no harm in trying.

Well. No harm to her.

TWENTY-NINE

SEBASTIAN LEFT the protection of the darker alleyways for the main paths. It was faster.

He also didn't worry that he hadn't sighted Peyt since he'd seen him from the top of the building.

He knew where he was going.

He approached the smaller Tree at a flat out run, taking the steps to the front entrance three at a time as the door swung closed.

He grabbed it just in time.

Peyt was walking ahead of him, and stopped to call the lift.

Sebastian slipped inside the foyer and let the door swish silently closed behind him.

He moved to the right, sliding out of Peyt's line of sight as he turned in the lift to face forward, and as soon as the door had pivoted closed, Sebastian shoved open the door of the stairwell and ran up it, the ill-fitting maintenance jacket tied around his waist flapping behind him.

He assumed the lift had beaten him up, and he was right. When he stepped out, Peyt was ahead of him and he followed him to his apartment.

There was something going on with the man. He seemed

unaware of what was going on around him, his hand shaking a little as he swiped his finger through his laslock and opened the door.

As he stepped through, Sebastian shoved him between the shoulder blades, and caught completely unawares, Peyt fell forward with a shout.

Sebastian pulled the door closed behind him and knelt on Peyt's back.

"Careful, careful! You'll break it." Peyt's words were desperate.

"Break what?" Sebastian had stuffed the restraints he kept in his pack into one of the pockets of his maintenance uniform, and he pulled them out and secured Peyt's hands behind his back.

"You." Peyt twisted his neck to look around and up at him, and then winced as if the movement had pulled a muscle. "Look, I did what that little thief wanted. I got her in, and I expect to keep my payment."

Payment?

Sebastian rolled Peyt onto his side, and began going through his pockets, and pulled out a familiar looking vial.

For a moment he looked at it in shock, until he realized it wasn't even close to as full as the one she'd slipped into her top had been.

He hadn't checked, but it was possible she'd put some of Fluffy's venom into a second vial, and his thoughts stuck on why she would do that.

There weren't many places to go with that information, and not all of them were places he wanted to explore.

"So, she gave you some venom in exchange for getting her in. I'll offer you the same deal. Get me in, too, and I'll give this back to you."

Peyt stared at him for a long beat. "You fucker." He kicked out, overbalancing and then tried to kick out again. "Fucker, fucker, fucker. That is mine!" Snot and tears ran down his face as he squirmed and grunted, trying to get to his feet while trying to kick Sebastian at the same time.

Sebastian put a boot on his shoulder and shoved, so he fell back on his hands and arms.

He looked down at Peyt, at the rage and lack of control, and threw out any thoughts that he'd be cooperative, even with the promise of getting the venom back.

DEE BEGAN CLEANING the next office down, but this time facing the door. Whatever the venom in their jah was going to do, she wanted to see them coming if they went looking for her.

They'd taken the cups with a smirk, and she knew they thought they'd gotten one over her. Mostly likely making jah for the guards wasn't in the cleaner's duties.

She kept her own smirk hidden, and her eyes down.

When she heard a thump over the hum of the vacuum, she kept it running, leaving it in the middle of the room, and stepped out cautiously.

"I don't care what Fattal says, the Caruso are going to gut us all, as soon as there's enough of them in that warehouse at the hover base, and as soon as they've stockpiled enough weapons."

"Why would the Cores be so stupid? They have to know it's a risk, and they must have some plan to keep the Caruso in check."

The two men were facing each other, and one of them thumped the wall with his fist again.

"Careful, Cutter. You're going to force me to tell the boss you're not on board."

"Fuck you, Harv. I'm just stating the obvious. If you can't see it, then you're either stupid or blind. Or both."

Harv lashed out, punching Cutter in the jaw.

He went down, and lay on the ground blinking. "What the hell? You asshole." He pushed himself unsteadily to his feet. His back was to Dee, who was crouched low and peering around the corner, and she saw him reach for his laz.

He brought it out in one smooth move, shooting his colleague full on the chest.

Harv went down and Cutter stood over him, breathing hard. Then his foot went back and he kicked him in the ribs with a grunt of satisfaction.

Dee rose up, stepped into the passageway, and shot him with her laz in the middle of the back.

He fell over his friend, toppling like a tree.

She walked up to them, picking up Cutter's laz to check the settings, and saw he'd used the same one on Harv that she had for him.

Both men would be out for a couple of hours at least.

She slid his laz into one of her pockets, found Harv's and pocketed it, too.

She patted them both down, looking for some kind of access card or key. They surely would have Lucia locked up in some way.

She found nothing, and worried about the time she was taking, she stepped up to the door.

There was no laslock, as if it was a general access space, and she opened it cautiously. It swung open smoothly, and she hesitated in the doorway, looking in.

It had probably at one time been an office, but someone had converted it into a prison and torture chamber.

The floor was smooth and hard, and three cages sat evenly spaced across the far wall.

There was a chair in the middle of the room.

There was something ominous about its placement, and she avoided looking at it.

The faces of her colleagues, Sunar and Petro--not as they'd been before they'd been taken, but after she had found them thrown like refuse outside Leo's Tether Town warehouse--flitted through her mind, and she had to breathe carefully for a moment.

The rustle of fabric snapped her out of it.

Someone was in at least one of the cages.

It was dark in here, particularly where the cages were, but the base level lighting used in the corridors was installed in here, too, and she could just make out someone moving in the cage to the left.

"Lucia?" she whispered.

"Dee?" The voice came from the right, and Dee paused in the middle of the room, mouth open.

"Ruanne?"

Finally she made out a woman crouched against the bars of the cage, hands white-knuckled, hair wild around her face and falling over her shoulders.

Time to be surprised and happy later. "How can I get you out?"

"How did you get in?" The question was asked in a deep, hoarse voice, and Dee spun to look at the middle cage.

A man stared back at her, his face a landscape of fading bruises.

"Vahn?"

He reared back in surprise at that.

"Is Lucia here?" She stepped closer to the third cage.

"She's there, but she's out of it." Ruanne's voice was soft. "She only just got in, and it takes a while for the sedative to work through the system." She spoke without emotion, but Dee thought her voice trembled a little.

An unconscious Lucia wasn't good. "So, back to the original question, how do I get you out of here?"

"You don't. But I do thank you for arriving in such a timely manner."

Dee spun, saw Hanran Fattal, flanked by two guards, standing in the doorway.

It was hard to swallow, but she forced herself to. "Well, then, get your thugs to carry Lucia back to the settlement, now I'm here."

"And why would I do that?" Fattal stepped into the room, and even though the lighting was bad, she could see the fury and hatred glittering in his eyes.

"Because if you don't, the next time you demand an exchange, there won't even be a chance you can get what you want. You either honor the agreement, or you never get cooperation again." She lifted her shoulders in a shrug to emphasize the obviousness of it.

Fattal stared at her for a long time, and instead of frightening her, she found it steadied her nerve.

He was a bully, but he was also the head of the Cores, and he couldn't have gotten to a position like that without being at least somewhat intelligent.

"Take her back while she's still sedated. You can leave her at the gate," Fattal ordered one of the guards behind him, and then walked to Lucia's cage, and swiped his finger through it.

So, a laslock tuned to Hanran Fattal. Probably only him, if she was reading the situation correctly.

He was in total control here.

The guard he'd given the order to stepped inside, picked Lucia up, and hefted her over his shoulder.

When he walked out of the room, he was replaced by another guard.

So, they were nervous of her. Or Fluffy.

She glanced back, saw Ruanne and Vahn were watching her with interest, obviously trying to work out what was going on.

"Where's your little pet?" Hanran asked, and she turned back to face him.

"Well, your thugs tried to grab me in the settlement, forcing me to run into the forest. Fluffy decided she liked the trees better than being with me." She lifted her hands in regret. "Actions have consequences."

He struck her, and she went with it, lifting an arm up and falling to the ground, head bowed. It hurt. It hurt a lot. But she'd minimized the impact by moving back.

She felt hands on her, patting her down and taking all three of her weapons, and then she was lifted up, set in the chair, and her arms pulled viciously back and secured behind her.

"So big and strong. So brave," she murmured to the two guards, and she felt one of them flinch at her words.

She slowly lifted her head to look at Fattal as the guards stepped back.

"I don't need you anymore," Hanran said to them. "Go sort out the two idiots passed out outside."

The guards left, and the door closed behind them.

She looked up, and saw Hanran Fattal watching her again.

207

She wanted--needed--to wipe the smirk off his face.

"Scared they'll hear you talking about the talu?" Dee asked him. "I noticed you called her a pet, rather than saying what she is. Not sure they'd be that comfortable with the notion of your using talu venom, are you? And did they know you were off your head on it two days ago?"

Hanran Fattal bared his teeth. "The purchase of the talu is secret. They didn't need to know."

Most likely, that was true. The less was known about his secret weapon, the better.

"So, what do you want from me?" she asked.

"Obviously, I want the talu. I don't believe you'd have let it run off, and fortunately, I know a way to find out where you've put it."

She went ice cold. If he had found out about Jamari, if Dee had put her in danger--

But Hanran Fattal was suddenly beside her, shoving a hand down her top with hard, rough fingers, and then drawing the vial out with a triumphant grunt. "I think you understand how I'm going to use this against you." He lifted it up to look at it. "We've had you under surveillance since you stepped onto this floor. I'll admit at first we thought you were a cleaner, especially with the change in hair, but fortunately there was a hidden camera in the kitchen, and when I saw you putting something in the guards' jah, I knew it was you." He grabbed her wig and ripped it off her head.

Her stomach plummeted and she had to take a deep breath.

At least she'd gotten Lucia out. That was the only win from this situation.

"You sure you want to waste precious venom on me?" she asked with a croak.

"Oh, I don't think it'll be a waste. I think it'll pay back major dividends if I can get the talu back." He smiled at her, and then took out a slim syringe.

He drew only the tiniest amount of venom into it. "No sense using more than necessary." The look he sent her was pure spite, and then he pushed the needle into her shoulder.

THIRTY

SEBASTIAN WALKED WITH PURPOSE, forcing himself to keep a steady pace rather than run, as every instinct screamed for him to do.

He was in Peyt's clothes again, his new access card in his hand.

There was no way Peyt would have been able to come up with an excuse believable enough to get Sebastian into the Tree in his current state, and Sebastian didn't think he'd do it, anyway.

The Cores brat was no longer thinking logically.

He was approaching the front entrance when he saw a guard carrying something over his shoulder.

It wasn't yet dawn, the lights were still dim and barely lit the path, but he could just make out the shape of a woman.

He slowed, and then stopped, staring at the guard as he walked toward him.

"Cores business," the guard said, his gaze hard.

It was Lucia. Sebastian tried not to let the surprise show on his face. "Where are you taking her?"

"The settlement. Keep quiet about it, if you know what's good for you." The guard passed him, and Sebastian found himself rooted to the spot.

It was hard to breathe.

The only reason they'd let Lucia go was if they had Dee.

He tried to pull his thoughts back, to focus.

He turned to face the Tree.

Started walking toward it again.

He was coming in at an angle to one of the side entrances, and as he approached, a scream sounded from the left. The guards at the door he was heading for turned toward the sound and when it came again, Sebastian hesitated, wondering what could be going on--

"Move." Darren was suddenly beside him. "That's Lashcka giving us a distraction."

Sebastian glanced at him and sped up, trying to keep from looking like he was running, but moving as fast as he could. The guards had taken a few steps toward the sound and Laschka switched to a loud groan, as if she was in severe pain.

"Help." She made the call with a trembling voice.

The guards' backs was turned from the entrance completely, and Sebastian stepped up to the door, tapped Peyt's pass and carefully stepped inside, with Darren right on his heels.

"Lucia is out," Sebastian said, voice almost a whisper.

"I know. Karr's following them. He'll get her when they drop her in the settlement."

"Then what're you still doing here?" He hadn't exactly felt any warmth toward Dee from Darren.

Darren winced as they pushed their way into the stairwell. "That was Dee earlier, in the maintenance uniform, wasn't it? Laschka worked it out."

Sebastian nodded.

"She's obviously in trouble now, all for someone she doesn't know and for a cause that isn't hers. I understand why you didn't tell us she was with you and you had plans to get Lucia out, not after the things I said, and I'm sorry about that." Darren rubbed a hand over the back of his head and ducked his gaze. "I want to help."

Sebastian stopped. Considered.

It would be better to have help in rescuing Dee, but right now, he trusted no one. "Don't make me regret this."

Darren grimaced, and gave a nod.

When they reached the correct floor, Sebastian eased the stair-well door open carefully and then stepped out.

"Surveillance," Darren whispered, and pointed to the tiny black sphere set in each ceiling corner.

That's how they'd gotten to Dee.

"It's not too late to run," he told Darren, but the big man gave a sharp shake of his head.

They moved down the passageway, walking normally, as if they were meant to be there; Sebastian in his Cores brat suit, the shirt sticking to his back with sweat under his jacket from his race up the stairs, and Darren all in black--almost indistinguishable from the guards.

It might be the only way to stay invisible.

Sebastian heard the sound of low-pitched talking, and opened a door and stepped inside.

Darren followed, but Sebastian could see he wasn't happy.

"They'll see that on the feed. It's suspicious that we got out of the way just as someone was coming." His whisper was a hiss in Sebastian's ear.

"I know." He shrugged, and then crouched beside the door, leaving it open a crack. "We could be lucky and they're not looking now they have Dee. Either way, it beats meeting someone face to face right now."

He'd barely finished speaking when the sound of something being dragged became louder.

"We should get some help," a man said, and Sebastian could hear the whine in his voice. The breathlessness, too.

"I don't feel like going to find someone. Last I saw, we were all there was inside. Well, us, Cutter and Harven. Everyone else is guarding doors outside." The second guard sounded pissed off.

The first one made a sound of frustration, and Sebastian heard a thump, as if something had fallen.

He risked looking through the narrow crack, hoping the darkness in the room behind him would keep him invisible, and saw one guard had another under the arms and was pulling him along, and a second stood over another guard who was lying unconscious on the floor.

Darren shifted behind him, silently resting a hand on Sebastian's back so he could look out as well.

"Where do we even take them?" The first guard, who'd dropped his burden, straightened up and arched his back with a groan. "What did that woman put in their jah?"

The second guard straightened as well, letting the man he was dragging's head bounce on the floor. He looked down on him with absolutely no pity. "I don't know, but it's something the boss got really excited about. Anyway, they're out because she hit them with a laz, not because of whatever she put in their drinks. That just made them behave like fucking idiots."

The first guard sighed, and then crouched down to get a grip on his guard again. "If it's just a laz hit, they can recover on the floor of the break room."

"I'd leave them right here if I didn't think the boss would have a problem with it." The second guard grabbed the wrists of his man, instead of under his arms, and started pulling again.

"Good idea."

Sebastian rose as they moved away, Darren stepping back so he could straighten up.

"Hear that? No one is watching the feed. Those two are it." Darren's voice was almost inaudible with relief.

Sebastian smiled, and pulled out his laz. "Not for long."

SHE BRACED HERSELF FOR SOMETHING. A feeling of dizziness, a pounding of her heart, but there was nothing.

She looked up at Hanran Fattal, blinking as she took stock.

Was she simply unaware of the change?

The guards whose drink she'd spiked certainly hadn't realized what was happening to them.

"Where is the talu?" Hanran Fattal had come to stand in front of her, and he grabbed her shoulders.

She felt . . . no compulsion to speak whatsoever.

"In . . ." She wet her lips, pretended some reluctance. "In the forest. I wasn't lying." She blinked again, fluttering her lashes.

"Where in the forest?" He shook her, angry.

"Not far away from the settlement." She squeezed her eyes closed. "Near the house where your guards came looking for me."

"What does it eat?" He shook her again and her eyes flew open.

"Chopped fruit. And energy bars." She made her lips form a thin line.

"I can't believe you let it get away." He shoved at her and the chair tipped back, forcing her to throw herself forward as a counter-balance.

"You're the one who put me on the run." She mumbled it, looking down. "It wouldn't have gotten loose if you hadn't forced me into the forest."

He made a sound of disgust. "Where are you?"

She raised her head slowly, trying to work out what he meant, only to see he'd turned his back on her and was talking into a comm unit.

"Well, get off the front entrance, go buy some fruit and energy bars, and set a trap for . . ." He hesitated. "For a rare animal my daughter bought which has escaped." He spun back to face Dee. "Is it tame?"

She lolled her head, as if it were too heavy for her neck and he stepped up to her and shook her shoulders. "Is it tame?"

"Very . . . tame."

"Kaspar, wait. I'll come down and explain what I want." Hanran Fattal spun on his heel and strode out of the room, slamming the door shut behind him.

Dee waited a beat then slid off the chair, turning as much as the manacles tying her hands to the back of the chair allowed. She lifted her arms and grabbed the top of the chair back as best she could and lifted it, turning toward the wall.

"What are you doing?" Ruanne hissed.

"I thought I'd try break the chair against the wall."

"No!" There was panic in Ruanne's voice, and she saw Vahn move reflexively, too.

"It'll be too loud. Come here, I'll try get you free."

Dee nodded and made her way over to Ruanne, who reached through and grabbed the chair through the bars.

"I see you aren't in fact affected by the talu venom."

Dee tried to shrug. "No. Not sure why."

"Did it scratch you?" Ruanne was right up against the bars now.

"It did." Oh. Well, well. Fluffy carried the antivenom with her. How handy. She shot Ruanne a look. "How did you know about that?"

"I run a shipping company, remember? You hear things. And let me just say that was a good bit of acting." Ruanne's voice purred with approval even as she struggled with the chair back, trying to snap the spoke, but eventually she stepped back.

"I can't break it."

"My turn." Vahn had propped himself up against his own bars with a shoulder and was watching them.

Dee glanced at him, saw he was built similarly to Sebastian. He certainly looked like he had the muscle to do some damage.

"Sure." Her shoulders were on fire from the awkward angle by the time she got to him.

"How did you know who I am?" he asked.

"I'm a friend of Sebastian's." She grunted as he moved the chair, nearly overbalancing.

She managed to look back to see what he was doing, and he had positioned one of the chair legs between the two bars at the corner of the cage.

"Fall over to the right," he said.

She hesitated, but she'd get nowhere chained to a chair, so she centered herself, and then threw herself hard to the right. For a moment, the chair leg held, holding her at an impossible angle--she could feel the strain of it, and then it snapped, and she landed hard on her shoulder.

She went up on her knees with a wince and looked at the damage.

"So now I just have a three legged chair." That had been very painful for no apparent progress.

"Come back here."

She shuffled on her knees, and then managed to get awkwardly to her feet.

"Press the back of the chair to the bars."

She did it, and Ruanne made a sound of approval as Vahn threaded the broken chair leg through the spokes of the chair back.

She got it. But she didn't have to like it.

"Lean forward?" she asked, voice wry.

"Sorry." There was humor in Vahn's tone.

She tipped forward, her arms straining back, her angle easily 45 degrees, with no hands to shoot out to protect her face if she fell.

She could hear Vahn taking strain behind her, and then with a crack, the spoke gave.

She fell, but was able to twist to her side at the last moment.

She lay, panting through the pain, and then forced herself to get up.

With slow, aching movements she got to her knees, hands still behind her but no longer caught in the chair. She sat back and threaded her feet through her arms so her hands were now at the front, not the back.

The feeling of relief, of an increase in control, was almost giddying.

"Now we need Hanran Fattal's finger to open the laslocks," Ruanne said, and Dee decided she was dead serious.

"I don't think that's going to happen, so we need another plan." She glanced at the door. "Let's see if I can open it from the inside."

"Just . . . careful--" Ruanne clutched the bars. "In case there's someone out there on guard."

Dee looked around for her weapons, but they were nowhere to be seen. Most likely the guards had taken them with them.

She saw Vahn was tense, too, standing with his hands in tight fists.

Dee moved to the door, slowly depressing the handle, and felt a shot of adrenalin when it turned silently under her hand. She eased the door open a crack, and then stared in shock for a moment.

"What is it?" Ruanne's voice was hoarse.

Dee let the door swing open completely, her eyes on Sebastian, drinking him in as he strode toward her.

"Looks like we have some help."

THIRTY-ONE

DEE WAS ALIVE, and she was safe.

Sebastian took in the room, the cages, Vahn *and* Ruanne staring at them from behind their bars, and when Darren slipped in behind him and closed the door, he gave in to impulse and drew Dee into his arms.

Her hands were manacled, and he could see the remnants of a wooden chair lying near Vahn's cage, but she rested her head on his chest and when he ran his hands down her back, she seemed completely unharmed.

Vahn caught his eye over Dee's shoulder, and raised his eyebrows in question.

"You'll have time for sweet hellos later." Ruanne rattled her cage.

He brushed a kiss on Dee's forehead and stepped back. "What do we need to open the locks?"

"Hanran Fattal's finger." Ruanne smiled her cutthroat smile. "Please go fetch it for us."

Darren stepped around Sebastian and grasped Vahn's hand, pulling him in for a brief one-armed hug through the bars. "We thought you were dead. You've been here all along?"

"No. We were held in a facility in the forest until a few weeks ago, on one of the pipeline routes. I don't think Fattal told anyone we were still alive, so I guess he was keeping us as backup."

"Backup for what?" Dee stood close enough to Sebastian that her shoulder brushed his, and he slid an arm around her.

"The last couple of weeks, he's been asking me to give up the resistance spies in sensitive Cores operations, and asking Ruanne for her trade routes."

"You think he brought you here because he'd sent Rina to buy a talu and he was hoping to get you to spill your secrets?"

"I think so, but I think he was also planning to use some of the talu venom against the other Cores executives." Ruanne bumped a shoulder against the bars in frustration. "He spoke freely to someone on his comm set a couple of times while he was in here, and now I know it was a talu he was waiting for, some of what he said at the time makes more sense. I think he was planning to slip them some venom in their drinks and find out who was with him, who was against him, and make those against him go away."

"We were hiding the guards we knocked out in an office when Fattal walked past," Darren glanced at Sebastian. "We just let him go."

Sebastian shrugged. "I'm pretty sure he'll be back, and if Ruanne is right, most likely on his own. He wants to control the information, and he doesn't want anyone to understand how he's getting it."

Vahn held his gaze. "Things have been rough, I take it?"

Sebastian gave a nod. "Bit hard to move forward when someone's telling your enemies your every move."

Vahn's lips twisted. "Yes, I discovered the day I was taken that we have a mole. Someone sold me out."

"And from the sounds of it, my own people are spilling my secrets to the Cores every day. Fattal knew way too much about my routes already. He just wanted me to fill him in on the details only I know."

"Not all of your people." Dee straightened. "Jamari escaped and she's in hiding."

Ruanne's face lit up. "You've seen her?"

Dee nodded. "She helped Sebastian and I get in here."

"So what now?" Darren turned to Sebastian.

"One of us goes and gets the feed from this room, which I'm guessing shows both of you getting beaten." Sebastian could see swelling on Vahn's cheek and bruises around his eyes, and even though Ruanne's skin was darker than Vahn's, she had obviously been hit. "Darren and I overheard the guards say there's no one up there at the moment, so now's the time."

"What does it matter that they beat us?" Vahn flexed his hands. "No one will be surprised by that."

"It should matter. The deal every adult who came here fifteen years ago agreed to was that the Cores owned the planet, but that everyone had a chance to make their fortune if they worked hard enough and took advantage of unchartered territory. That isn't what happened, and now, the Cores have reneged on even that original deal. You and Ruanne were our unofficial leaders until six months ago. And since then, everything we have has been taken, or stolen, or ripped from us. We're at a point where if we don't mobilize everyone, and soon, there won't be anything to save. The Caruso won't wait too much longer, and Bodivas has never shown an inclination to help us before. I don't see why they would now."

"How would we show the feed to everyone, though?" Darren frowned.

"The announcement board." Sebastian shrugged.

Dee turned to him with a huge smile. "That would be sweet, sweet irony. Your friend could put it up?"

"I hope so." He sent her a small smile back.

"I'd rather you get Hanran Fattal." Ruanne rattled her cage again.

Darren nodded. "Seb's right, he'll be back, and most likely alone. I can wait here while Sebastian gets the footage."

"Then you need to go now, in case you bump into him and he runs." Vahn's agitation was evident in his jerky movements. "And be careful on your way back."

"I'll come with you as far as the room you left the guards in, see if the keys to my restraints are still on them." Dee tilted her head. "You didn't happen to get back my weapons, did you?"

Sebastian pulled out a spare laz and handed it to her, then gave one each to Ruanne and Vahn.

Ruanne smiled in appreciation, and Vahn gave a sharp nod, then bent his head over the settings immediately.

Sebastian left them to it, going ahead of Dee as they stepped out of the room.

The passageway was still empty, and Sebastian hesitated outside the office where he and Darren had left the guards.

"Go." Dee tapped her bound hands on his chest. "As Ruanne says, there'll be time for sweet hellos later."

He bent and kissed her, hand cupping the back of her head, and then he turned and jogged toward the stairs. If he and Darren had overheard correctly, the control room was on the floor above, and while dawn was still half an hour or so away, someone could come off guard duty from below at any time.

He needed to move.

DEE FOUND the electronic key to the locks in moments, and made her way back to the others as fast as she could.

Darren opened the door cautiously at her knock, and then stepped back to let her into the room. She'd brought the restraints with her, and Ruanne gave a sharp nod of approval when she saw them.

"Pity the chair is smashed, or I'd have liked Hanran Fattal to feel what it's like to be tied to it, getting asked uncomfortable questions."

"You and Ruanne obviously know each other." Darren looked between them.

"Ruanne and my boss on Garmen have entered into a few joint ventures together." Dee kept her answer neutral.

"Who's your boss on Garmen?" Vahn was watching her with eyes that gleamed.

"Leo Gaudier."

Vahn folded his arms, and from the way his eyebrows rose, she guessed he'd heard of Leo. "What are you doing here, then?"

"I was on the Felicitos Deck, trying to pass on some information to the captain of one of Ruanne's traders, when the Caruso, who the Cores were hiding in plain sight in one of their warehouses on the Deck, launched an attack on the Cores and everyone else who happened to be docked there."

"They attacked the Cores, not helped the Cores in an attack?" Darren stared at her, mouth open.

"The Cores already owned the Deck, they hardly needed to kill everyone on it to take control of it." Dee kept her tone neutral. "No, the Caruso must have decided if they took the Deck, they'd have control over Felicitos, and by extension, the whole of Garmen."

"What happened?" Ruanne pressed her face against the bars.

"Leo had someone in his corner who was able to temporarily disable the gravity and environmental generators on the Deck. Everyone not in a ship was sucked into nearspace."

Darren gave a long, low whistle.

"So, you were obviously in a ship." Ruanne was watching her with interest.

"Leo was able to warn me, and hopefully most of the Deck crew, about what was coming, and I got into the first ship I could find with an open door. It just so happened to belong to Rina Fattal."

"You're here by accident?" Vahn couldn't hide his surprise.

"It wasn't in the plan, no."

"And the talu?" Ruanne asked.

"Found her in Rina's suite. She took to me, and I took to her." Dee shrugged. "I didn't know anything about her special abilities until Jamari told me."

"If the Cores learn what happened on Garmen, surely they'll kill this deal with the Caruso?" Darren leaned against the door. "If the Caruso attacked one lot of Core Companies, they'll attack another."

"I already told Hanran Fattal what happened on Garmen. He claimed he didn't believe me."

"What?" Darren straightened up from the wall beside the door, mouth open. "But that's why I came back to Dar Raca from the pipe-lines this morning. The Caruso are already out there. I got word from a source they were diverting the gas at the Sunir extraction point straight onto their own traders. They've built a landing pad there. I managed to get close enough to confirm it was true, but I almost didn't make it back out. They've set up a security perimeter. You're telling me the Cores don't know about this?"

It was Dee's turn to stare. "Hanran Fattal's attitude would suggest that, yes."

As he opened his mouth to respond, the door opened suddenly, and he spun toward it.

Dee stepped closer to the wall, out of the line of sight.

Hanran Fattal stepped in and then jerked back in surprise at the sight of Darren, and there was a flash of laz fire.

Darren fell, holding his side, and Hanran Fattal took a step closer to him, his back to Dee.

She guessed he'd gotten off a lucky shot and he raised his laz again, aiming at Darren's chest.

She shot him at close range in his raised arm, and then stepped right up to Fattal and put her laz against his neck.

"Hold still." She put her hand into his jacket pocket, remembering where he'd put her vial and the tiny syringe he'd used on her, and sure enough, there it was.

"Vahn and Ruanne, could you cover me?"

Vahn was already pointing his laz at Fattal through the bars, and Ruanne did the same.

"Don't move, or they'll shoot you." Dee pocketed her laz and drew a small amount of venom into the syringe, and plunged it into Fattal's neck before putting her laz back in place against his spine.

"Now you're going to open the locks on the cages."

Fattal was shivering, and she didn't know if it was with worry about how much venom she'd given him, or if his reaction to it was that fast. He moved, though, opening the locks, and flinched back when Vahn stepped out.

"Why did you inject me?" He tried to turn his head to look at her.

"Because I want some answers."

She stepped back a little and he moved to the wall and leaned against it, then slid down to sit on the floor.

"On second thoughts, Vahn and Ruanne, you've earned the right to ask the questions."

Ruanne gave her a regal nod, then stepped closer to Fattal. "Where are the Caruso?"

"Some are at the hover base."

"And the others?" Ruanne's voice was sharp.

"The big ships," he seemed to struggle for a moment, and then he shrugged. "The three big warships are hidden on the three moons."

"When are they planning to come down?"

He rubbed his face, scowling. "When I give them the okay. But my fellow execs are cowards. Cowards and idiots."

"Do you know the Caruso are already out by the pipelines, taking gas directly?" Vahn asked. He had crouched down beside Darren, and helped him sit up.

"No." Hanran Fattal pursed his lips. "That's very . . . naughty of them." He waggled a finger, then blinked up at Dee. "If the idiots on the Cores Exec find out about that, they'll say no for sure. And we only have a week left. Just one week."

"One week left until what?" Dee crouched in front of him, grabbed his wrists and clamped them in the manacles.

"The treaty." Vahn rose to his feet, and Dee saw Darren rubbing his side. He looked better, which meant Fattal's hit had been a glancing one. "One week left until the treaty with Bodivas has to be renegotiated."

Hanran Fattal clicked his tongue and pointed a finger at Vahn. "The Bodivas are being pushy. Pushy, pushy, pushy. They have spies. Spies!" He almost shouted the word. "And they told us they know we've taken people's businesses. Broken our agreement with the gen-pop. They're threatening to intervene. To take Lassa away from us."

"Is that so?" Vahn looked like he'd been hit between the eyes.

Dee had the sense from everyone that they thought Bodivas had abandoned them. She'd thought the same way about Arkhor. That they'd left Garmen to rot.

Obviously, that wasn't the case in either situation.

"Yes, it is so." Fattal nodded slowly. "So we looked for new trading partners. Especially after a few missteps with the VSC made them less inclined to deal with us. Now that the Faldine War is over, they aren't as dependent on us for our raw materials, but the Caruso, well, they were willing to buy everything we had to sell, in exchange for a few military bases here." He shrugged. "It's less lucrative than the deal with the VSC, but comes with no strings, no minimum standard of how we treat the gen-pop, and frankly," he glanced at them with a sly smile, "most of the gen-pop won't be needed. The Caruso prefer to work with their own."

"So what are they planning to do with everyone who lives here? Will you let them leave?" Dee wanted him to spell it out. She also hoped Sebastian was still in the control room, and he was getting every word of this.

"Leave?" he laughed. "No, that won't do. Even if we don't have to comply with certain standards, I'm not foolish enough to think the VSC might not feel compelled to act if some people get out with stories of their friends starving and living in squalor."

"If they can't leave, and there's no work for them, what do you think will happen to them?" Ruanne asked.

"Do I look like I care?" He giggled, and then put a hand over his mouth. "They'll die, eventually. The Caruso may pick some off, some will starve." He shrugged. "If they get too difficult, we'll have to do something about it."

"What'll stop the Caruso from doing away with you, especially if they have their own workforce here?" Dee asked.

"Won't happen. As long as I and the other Cores execs are here, and own the resources, the VSC has very little grounds to attack. The Caruso won't harm us. In fact, it's in their interests to make sure no harm comes to us."

"And your guards, your official Core Companies workers?" Dee extended her hands, palms up.

Ruanne shot her a look at that, and gave a faint smile. She had worked out what Dee was doing.

"They're gen-pop, when it comes down to it. They'll have to accept a change in circumstances."

Ruanne gave a decisive nod. "Time's wasting." She grabbed Fattal and shoved him into her cell.

It was more or less meaningless, as he was the key to the laslock, but he sat in a corner obediently enough.

"Stay there." She closed him in.

Vahn opened the office door, and looked down the short passageway, then glanced back at Darren. "You good?"

Darren nodded and limped out, and Dee let Ruanne go next.

She moved as if she was hurt, and Dee guessed the bruises on her face only told part of the story.

She closed the door behind them, and followed as Darren led the way back down the passage to the lift.

"Sebastian is still up there." And she wasn't leaving him. "None of you are in the best shape, so I suggest you go ahead, and I'll get Sebastian, and either catch you up, or see you back at headquarters."

Vahn hesitated, then gave a nod. The lift suddenly hummed to life, and everyone froze for a moment, and then turned to the stairwell door.

They didn't have the run of the place anymore.

THIRTY-TWO

DEE HEARD voices as she leaned against the stairwell door one floor up from where she'd left the others.

Two men, she guessed, exiting the lift.

She swore under her breath, then waited for them to pass, forced herself to count to five, and then opened the door just enough so she could slip through, and stepped out into the foyer.

The men were guards, walking side by side ahead of her, and she eased the door closed silently behind her and followed them.

They stopped outside a set of double doors made of flexiclear, and she could see their demeanor change. They went from relaxed to killers in a blink. One stepped forward, forcing the doors open, and he pulled his laz and fired.

Dee started to run.

The one who'd fired flinched back, holding his shoulder, then collapsed as the doors closed.

The second one stood, perfect shooting stance, she could only assume pointing his laz at Sebastian, but he couldn't fire with the doors closed. He'd need to get closer for them to reopen.

All guard number two needed to do was wait Sebastian out until backup arrived.

At that thought, she moved even faster, but the guard was already on his comm, talking in the coded language of security officers.

She was almost upon him when he realized she was coming, and turned, laz still raised, in her direction.

She'd drawn her own laz, but had it tucked against her left side, and she focused her gaze on the guard who was down. "Is he all right?" She made her voice high-pitched and shocked.

She saw him take in her maintenance uniform, her demeanor, and then turn away from her in dismissal.

"Get off this floor. Now!"

She shot him in the middle of his back and he went down like a felled tree.

She stepped over him, but Sebastian was already at the door, and she realized he must have run toward it the moment he'd seen her.

"Will there ever be time for sweet hellos?" he asked her as he grabbed her hand and started running with her toward the stairwell.

She gasped out a laugh, but didn't get the chance to answer, because the door of the lift began to pivot and they both dived through the door at the same time.

He gestured her ahead of him, and she went because there was no time to argue.

When she reached the next floor, she left the stairwell and ran, heading for the other side of the building.

"Good idea." Sebastian caught up with her, although he kept glancing back.

"I think whoever was in the lift probably went to help their friends first. If we're lucky."

It seemed like they hadn't been followed. But the guards could see where they where through the feed . . . "Are the cameras still working?"

Sebastian shook his head. "All destroyed."

She grinned at him as they burst into the foyer at the far end of the passage, and dived through the door.

"The others?" he asked as they started taking the stairs, two, sometimes three at a time.

"Headed back to headquarters." She barely had the breath to answer.

They reached the bottom without meeting anyone else, and she took a moment to catch her breath before she stepped out into the small hallway that led to the side entrance. They both knew there was most likely two guards outside the door in front of them.

"You go first," Sebastian said. "I'll wait. If there's trouble, or they get suspicious, they'll bring you back in this way."

"And then?"

"And then I'll be waiting for them." He gave her a smile and she saw the ruthlessness in his eyes.

She knew he wanted her to go first in case he needed to protect her, and she considered fighting it, but like going first in the stairwell earlier, she didn't think they had the time. And one of them had to go first.

She straightened her maintenance uniform, hunched her shoulders as if she was weighed down by her cares and a long night of hard work, and pushed through the door.

The two black-clad guards turned as she stepped out into the dawn light. The sun had just risen, and she shielded her gaze as the angle of the rays hit her directly in the eyes.

It put her at a disadvantage, as the guards were backlit by the sunlight, and she dipped her head, and stepped between them.

"Hey. You're Rina Fattal."

She shook her head and kept going, but she had a sinking feeling she knew who the guard was who called out to her.

He was one of the two who'd tracked her and Sebastian down in Dar Raca and then eaten with them at the restaurant. The one who'd shot Sebastian with his laz.

Bauer.

"You are." Bauer's hand came down hard on her shoulder, and he jerked her around.

"Don't touch me." Her voice was icy.

"Looks like you're sneaking out again, all dressed up like a cleaner and all, and your daddy will be very pleased to have you delivered back."

"Bauer ..." The other guard looked uncertain.

"Me, Travi and Haber had to go out and get her just a couple of nights ago."

"I'm a free person. I can leave if I want."

Bauer shook his head. "This place is owned by the Cores, and your father is the head Cores exec. You are not a free person. None of us are."

He was quite right, but what she found startling was the gleeful way he said it, without pausing to consider what that meant for him as well as her.

His grip slid to her arm and he hauled her back toward the door.

She relented, letting him pull her along as she put her hand into her pocket.

The other guard went through the door first, looking back over his shoulder as he stepped inside. "What are we going to do? We can't leave our post."

He went down almost immediately, but Bauer didn't notice the laz hit because he was shoving Dee in behind him.

She stepped to the side, pulling her hand from her pocket, fist closed around her laz, but the door was already swinging shut, and Sebastian was right there, pinning Bauer back against the door.

"We meet again." He smiled, holding Bauer's gaze, and then shot him in the torso.

From the stairs behind him, they both heard the sound of running footsteps.

"I think the other guards have finished checking on their friends." He used his boot to shove Bauer aside so they could get the door open and then they were running through the lush gardens that surrounded the Tree.

SEBASTIAN HEARD a shout go up behind them, and guessed the guards on the other entrances had been ordered to hunt them down.

Dee kept up with him, and when he looked back, her face was focused and calm.

She'd told him before she was used to playing against high stakes, and she hadn't lied.

Laz fire flickered to his right as someone took a shot, and without conferring they both started to zigzag as they headed for the first line of buildings that surrounded the gardens.

They had a head start, but Sebastian knew there would be guards up ahead of them, as well as behind. There were guard stations along the wall separating Dar Raca from the settlement, and at the gate, plus guard patrols in Dar Raca itself.

The guards at the Tree entrance were only a small part of the whole.

He took the first alley they reached, and Dee followed. They had to slow down, because the alleys were a maze of boxes, refuse bins, storage lockers.

He took them south east, toward the building with secret tunnel access, and because dawn had just broken, it was still quiet and the streets were empty.

It worried him that there were no guards to be seen patrolling, and when they were forced to cross the bigger streets, no one was to be seen in either direction.

"Too quiet?" Dee whispered when he hesitated before they crossed the final road to get to the building.

He nodded.

They were pressed up against a building one street over from their destination, and she pointed to the back door. It was open slightly, prevented from closing by a small block of wood wedged into the frame.

Someone had wanted to come and go without signing in, he guessed.

"Go up to the roof and look?" she whispered.

He nodded, and they slipped through the door.

He was planning to take the stairs, but Dee shook her head, and called the lift.

He finally noticed the dark rings under her eyes, and she leaned back against the lift wall and closed her eyes as it seemed to heave itself laboriously up to the roof.

"How about now?" he murmured.

"Now?" She didn't open her eyes.

"For those sweet hellos." He drew her into his arms, kissed her forehead, her closed eyelids, her cheek, the corner of her mouth, and finally her lips.

They curved into a smile under his.

She leaned into him, and he could feel the exhaustion weighing her down.

"We deserve a holiday." She snuggled closer. "I haven't had a holiday in nearly two years."

Sebastian had never had a holiday. The possibility of it was tantalizing.

"Where would we go?"

"Somewhere warm, with a clear pool to swim in, and no one else around."

He brushed his lips on the top of her head. "I can do that. I'll even throw in a comfortable bed."

She laughed, low and throaty. "It's a deal." She pulled back as the doors opened. He saw her laz was in her hand, but the lift opened into a tiny hallway space, and it was empty. A door was set opposite the lift, and he stepped out into the still, cool morning air.

At this height, he could see the golden sunlight play over the tree-tops and the stir of life beyond the wall in the settlement.

He walked to the edge of the building, Dee right behind him, and they looked over the wall.

The building with the secret tunnel was surrounded by guards.

Sebastian could see people in the windows of the building, looking down with confusion and horror. A woman with two small children opened the front door to leave, freezing as a few of the guards turned their weapons in her direction, then scrambled back inside.

"I think they know about the tunnel." Dee's voice was dry.

"Someone told them, between us leaving last night and now."

The mole was burning his or her bridges. Maybe they saw the end was coming, one way or the other.

There was a sudden ripple in the attention of the guards. Most of them turned, some lifting a hand to their ear, and one fired off a shot down the road.

"Darren." Dee pointed to the left, and Sebastian caught a glimpse of Darren returning fire, and then he disappeared.

"They're on the run."

Dee leaned out over the wall a little, trying to see where they were headed, but Sebastian pulled her back, fearful one of the guards would notice them.

More of the guards around the building started moving, running after Darren and the others.

"Let's go."

When they were back in the lift, dropping down, he pulled out the crystal he'd stored the video footage on. Held it out.

She tilted her head to the side, looking at him with deep suspicion.

"I need to go help Vahn. It's the absolute least I can do. But I don't want to risk the footage not getting through to Caro. You need to take it for me. The guards are leaving the building wide open. Go around the back, slip in through the hole in the wall you used last night, and use the tunnel. Don't trust anyone on the other side. I don't know who the mole is, so never let your guard down. Get this to Caro, and get her to put it up on the board."

She didn't take it.

"Please, Dee. We need to split our focus here. I can help Vahn if I come up behind the guards. Cause some confusion. I might be able to give them a chance to go to ground."

"And what about you?" Her voice wavered, just a bit.

"I'm up for a holiday. I'm not going to do anything stupid."

"And yet, that's exactly what you're proposing." She stared at him steadily, then with sigh, took the crystal. "I'd do it for my team, so I understand. But . . ." She lifted an arm, sliding it around him and pulling him close. "Be careful. Please."

He kissed her, then pulled back as the lift suddenly stopped, the door opened and a surprised resident stepped in. They stood close together in silence to the ground floor, then walked out the front entrance behind the man, who looked back at them twice in suspicion.

"I'll see you at Jamari's. Go there as soon as you've given Caro the crystal. Don't tell anyone where you're going."

She nodded, gave him one last quick kiss and jogged away.

Sebastian turned in the direction of the gate, which is where Darren had been headed, most likely with Ruanne and Vahn in tow, and blended in with the foot traffic that had started to emerge from the buildings as the sun rose higher in the sky.

THIRTY-THREE

DEE DIDN'T KNOW if any guards were left out front of the building, but there weren't any left at the back.

She wriggled through the gap--it was harder getting in than getting out--and quickly stood when she heard footsteps up ahead.

She paused at the foyer entrance, looking out, and caught sight of a woman standing at the foot of the stairs.

"What are you doing?" The woman turned to her, her voice strident.

"I was looking out to see if the guards were still there." Dee hunched her shoulders.

The woman seemed to deflate. "Me, too. They're gone, though." She turned away and walked out the front door, and Dee waited for it to swing closed before she moved across to the basement door and quietly stepped inside.

If they had left anyone, it would be down here, or somewhere along the tunnel.

She didn't turn on the lights, but slid down the stairs with her back against the wall, taking each step carefully.

She was halfway through the boxes and crates when she heard someone clear their throat.

She sank down and moved forward even more cautiously.

The person ahead scuffled their feet and she tried to make them out in the darkness.

She could just see a darker shape against the gloom, standing against the far wall, blocking her exit into the tunnel.

He moved again, restless, and most likely bored.

They didn't expect trouble. Which was their mistake.

She'd set her laz to incapacitate rather than just stun, and she took aim and fired.

The guard fell back, smacking his head on the wall behind him and then sliding down it in a heap.

The secret door was wrenched open as Dee straightened up, the guard who'd pulled it open outlined perfectly against the faint light coming from somewhere in the tunnel.

"I said not to make a sound--"

She shot him and he collapsed.

She winced as she heard his head crack hard on the tunnel floor.

She didn't bother to try and close the door, or move the guard she'd shot, but she did check on the one in the tunnel, to make sure his face wasn't in the water.

Then she ran, keeping to the edges so she splashed less water, not just to reduce the noise she was making, but also to make it easier to hear if someone else was up ahead.

Her mind jumped to Sebastian, up above in a city swarming with guards, and it helped her push through the exhaustion that seemed to have a hold on her limbs.

She hadn't slept in too long. Hadn't eaten very much either. But Sebastian was up there, most likely under fire. She would get through, get to his friend Caro, no matter what.

Things were coming to a head, here, just as they had done a week ago on Garmen. She could sense it.

And it felt good.

She'd worked her whole life toward the goal of ending the Cores.

If she couldn't be there at the end on Garmen, she'd accept having a meaningful role in the Lassa takedown.

And she would enjoy every moment of it.

———

THERE WAS no one waiting inside the tunnel exit point like there had been when she and Sebastian had come through with Karr, but the ladder was impossible to miss because the lid wasn't flush over the hole and light streamed down, dancing on the water.

Dee pulled herself up, and shoved at the lid, tilting her head up to come face to face with a laz-wielding resistance member.

He blinked when he took her in, with her maintenance uniform and empty hands, and stepped back so she could come up.

"The tunnel's compromised," she told him. "The building was being guarded, and there were two guards in the basement, waiting at the entrance."

"What happened to them?" he asked, and she tapped her pocket. "Laz."

He put out his hand, as if she should give it to him, and she laughed and shook her head.

"No." She looked out of the enclosure door, saw there were people already gathering in the square in front of the board, waiting for the jobs list. "Where do I find Caro?"

He was frowning at her. "I don't know you, so I can't let you come through with a weapon."

She sighed. Nodded. Took it out, lifted it up and pointed it at him. "Where. Is. Caro?"

His eyes widened, and she wondered if he had been put on duty by the mole, because he was clearly incompetent.

"Why do you want to know?"

"I have a message for her from Sebastian."

He blinked, and then pointed a finger. "You're Sebastian's . . ." He cleared his throat. "You're the woman from Garmen."

"That's right. Now, please tell me, where do I find Caro?"

He thought about it. Nodded. "She's at headquarters. Just ask someone in the front room, they'll tell you where she is."

"Thank you." She stepped out and ran across the open space toward the crumbling building with washing strung across the windows.

She glanced back, but the guard hadn't followed her out.

Because everything about the situation made her suspicious, she skirted the front entrance, made her way around the building and came in through a side door.

The place still appeared to be an apartment building, with flowers growing in a pot in front of an apartment door.

Because she liked the look of it, she knocked, and Laschka opened up.

Dee guessed her face looked as surprised as Lasckha's did.

"Who is it?" Koan stepped into view behind her, and his eyes widened, as well.

"I've got a message for Caro. Where is she?"

Laschka's head jerked back in surprise at the lack of preamble, but she stepped forward.

"Come with me."

Dee followed her up wide stairs, could hear Koan following behind.

"How did you get free?"

"Sebastian and Darren helped me."

Laschka seemed to sag with relief. "Where are they?"

"Helping Vahn and Ruanne get out of the city. We had to split up."

Laschka stopped, mouth open. "Vahn is alive?"

She nodded. "They were keeping him in the same place as Lucia."

"Lucia would have told us if Vahn had been there." Koan tried to grab Dee's arm and she slid out of his reach.

"Lucia was never conscious, from the time she was taken, to the time she was returned. She didn't know Vahn was there with her."

"How do we know that's true?" Koan's lips formed a thin line.

"Dee gave herself up to the Cores to save Lucia. I saw her do it myself. I believe her." Laschka turned and kept going, then knocked lightly on a door just off the top of the stairs.

She opened it without waiting for a response. "Someone with a message for you, Caro."

Dee stepped in behind her, found herself in a room that looked like an electronics workshop. Caro was sitting at a workstation in from of a comm unit, and she turned to greet them.

She was tiny, her dark hair shot through with silver, the color even more striking against her dark skin.

"What's the message?" Her voice was rough, like she'd been shouting for hours.

"Vahn and Ruanne were being held in the Tree, and there is footage of them being beaten up while being questioned. But the really interesting part is at the end when Hanran Fattal admits he's selling out everyone but the top Cores execs to the Caruso. And even the top execs are being manipulated by him."

Lascka blew out a long breath. "You have that on record?"

"Yes." Dee didn't reach into her pocket for it, though. "Sebastian wanted you to put it up on the screen. So everyone in the settlement can see it. So they can wake up and understand what's going on. Without their involvement, the whole planet is about to fall."

Caro looked at her, saying nothing, and then turned to the comm unit, began to fly her fingers over the board. Then she gave a decisive nod. "Give me the data." She held out her hand, and Dee took the crystal out, and placed it carefully in her palm.

"Hmm." Caro inserted it, and suddenly from the speakers on the screen across the square came the sound of someone being struck. "Draw them in with the senseless violence, and they'll stay for the political emergency." Caro's voice held a hint of humor, despite the situation.

Koan and Laschka had turned, and were both standing at the window, looking out at the board themselves.

Dee held her hand out, and eyebrows raised in surprise, Caro pressed the crystal to release it, and gave it back. Dee put it in a front pocket and then walked to the window herself.

"The tunnel's been compromised." She spoke to Laschka, not bothering to even look at Koan. "There were two guards waiting in the basement, and before that, the whole of the building was surrounded by guards."

"How did you get through?" Laschka asked, eyes riveted to the screen.

"The guards caught sight of Darren and the others, and went after them. That's when Sebastian and I split up. He went to help Darren and Vahn."

"What about the two in the basement?" Koan asked.

"I shot them."

Laschka looked at her sharply. "Dead?"

"No. I don't kill if I don't have to." And she'd had to far too many times.

She looked below, saw the crowds were growing around the screen. They were silent, which was more disturbing than if they'd been muttering to each other.

She'd thought the number of people she'd seen there yesterday was a lot, but the crowd had swollen to at least double that, and it was still growing.

"What are we going to do about this?" Laschka murmured, gaze fixed below. "We need to give them a useful outlet. We need to be on the front line."

A ripple went through the crowd, and Dee realized someone had started firing from the gate.

"Are they shooting into the crowd?" She craned her neck to see, but she was at the wrong angle.

"Laschka, you go down there, find out what's going on. I'll find everyone in the building, call them in to help." Koan turned to Caro. "Will you try reach everyone out in the field?"

Caro nodded as Laschka took a last look below and then ran out the room.

"Caro, is the unit here capable of interplanetary comms?" Dee guessed the answer was no, or she and Sebastian wouldn't have had to go to the lengths they had to contact Leo, so she wasn't surprised when Caro shook her head.

"I wish."

On the screen outside, the long clip of Vahn and Ruanne being beaten was coming to an end. The crowd was more restless now, and making some noise at last. Dee could hear more firing, but it didn't seem to be aimed at the crowds, which made her wonder, who was it being aimed at?

"Go forward to the last ten minutes," she said to Caro. "That's the important part."

Caro's fingers flew, and suddenly there was Dee on the screen, laz pointed at Hanran Fattal, and he was spilling his secrets.

Koan had paused at the doorway, still looking out the window at the screen. He'd been murmuring into his comm set, quiet enough she couldn't hear what he was saying, but he turned, and there seemed to be almost a look of panic on his face. "This is going to bring down the Cores."

"I think you're right." Caro leaned back in her chair with satisfaction.

"I'll go down and help Laschka." Dee had done everything she could here. "Maybe there's a way to help Sebastian from this side of the wall."

"I still have to find everyone in the building." Koan moved with her.

When she reached the stairs, he put a hand on her shoulder.

"There's an office along here with a better view of the gate, if you want to see what's going on before you go down there?"

She nodded. "I would. They're firing on someone. I'd like to know who." Although she had a horrible suspicion.

He led the way, opened the door, and stepped back, as if leaving her to it while he went on his own way. She saw he was right, the view was better from here.

She'd just reached the window when the door slammed behind her.

She turned as the lock engaged.

"Hey!" She ran to it, pounded on it, but Koan was gone.

She spun around, leaning back against the door, and banged her head. Guess she'd just found the mole.

THIRTY-FOUR

DEE FORCED herself to think past the fury at herself for being so careless.

She took stock of the room. It looked like an office, but the desk was bare.

She sat on the chair and began opening draws.

One was locked, and she stood and looked around for something to break it open with.

She found a metal doorstop on the floor near the door, and used it as a lever to snap the lock.

There was a comm set inside, and she pulled it out and clipped it into the power source, heart beating a little too fast.

She clicked on the holo screen, tapped in the code for Leo's firm, and then, too anxious to sit still and see if she got through, she moved back to the window.

Most of the guards at the gate were now watching the screen, she saw. Caro had it on a loop, and she'd edited a little, showing shorter clips of Ruanne and Vahn's beatings, and then going in to Hanran Fattal's devastating confessions.

There was also a group of guards on the Dar Raca side, standing on the street leading through the gate, and they looked confused.

Some were pointing their weapons down the street, others were trying to see the screen themselves.

A hover swept down the hover track--she could feel the hum from the window--and then stuttered to a stop close to the building, still on the settlement side.

Dee wondered whether someone onboard had decided to stop so they could watch the screen as well, or whether they were going to put it in reverse, after looking at the way things were going down in Dar Raca.

There was a faint sound from the desk, and she ran back to it.

"Leo." She collapsed into the chair at the sight of his face, and her hand shook as she pulled out the crystal, and clicked it into place on the side of the unit. "I don't have time. I'm sending you something, and you need to get it out, especially to the Bodivas, but to the VSC in general. Especially the last part of the recording."

"What is it?" Leo didn't waste time asking unimportant questions, something she'd always admired about him.

"It's a confession by the top Cores exec here about his deal with the Caruso. What they're planning, and that the plan includes a kind of neglectful genocide. There's some footage of him beating up Ruanne and the previous head of the Lassian resistance, as well."

Leo leaned back, eyes open wide. "It's coming through."

She put her hands on the desk, and had to fist them to stop them shaking. "I'm hoping it'll force Bodivas to act, and soon. The Caruso already have landing pads here, they're already stealing the resources."

"You get somewhere safe, Dee. I'm going to make such a stink, the Bodivas will be begging to pick you up. Where are you now?"

"I'm in a sort of informal settlement just outside Dar Raca--"

There was a sound at the door behind her, and Dee stood up and turned, her body blocking the comm unit, and she pulled her laz.

Koan flung the door open and she shot him, but he stepped in, unharmed, and shot straight back.

She fell, and she could hear Leo's shout from behind her, Koan's roar of anger as he lunged forward. She hit the ground, with Leo issuing threats to Koan, and Koan switching the comm unit off.

"I thought Caro still had the crystal." Koan threw it on the floor and crushed it beneath his boot.

She tried to smile, but she couldn't move the muscles of her face.

Too late, she wanted to say.

She only hoped she was right.

SEBASTIAN KNEW WHERE DARREN, Vahn and Ruanne were.

It was hard to miss when the guards were so focused on the low wall beside the gate out of Dar Raca.

He guessed they'd tried to blend with the workers moving to and from the settlement, and someone had noticed.

He wondered if it was just that they'd stood out--Vahn and Ruanne certainly looked like they'd been in a fist fight--or whether someone had recognized them.

Some of the guards at the gate could have been on guard rotation in the Tree, watching them at some point.

It didn't matter. They were hunkered down, taking fire, and so far, he looked like the only one on their side.

The screen above the gate flickered to life, and Sebastian shifted in the crowd that had gathered to gape at the exchange of laz fire happening right in front of them.

He was in a mix of gen-pop heading home after a night shift, the more well-off workers who lived in Dar Raca itself, and a few people who looked like genuine Cores execs. Most of them didn't react to the screen coming on.

They thought it was the usual job auction.

The sound of fists striking flesh took a while to penetrate, but slowly they lost interest in the firefight and turned to the screen.

Sebastian smiled. It meant Dee was safe. That she'd made it through.

Everyone shuffled forward, trying to get a better angle.

That suited Sebastian. It got him closer to the wall where his friends were taking cover.

The guards saw the crowd moving, but Sebastian could see them hesitate, unsure what to do, and at least half of them were watching the screen.

On the other side of the gate, more of the gen-pop from the settlement were gathering, watching from the square, and as the numbers began to swell, the guards became twitchier.

"I didn't realize how many people had been forced out into the forest," a man beside him murmured.

Sebastian could see he was in a suit similar to the one Sebastian was wearing himself.

"Where did you think they'd gone?" he couldn't help but ask.

The man shrugged. "I thought they'd moved out to the pipelines. I was told the closure of the independent firms would be made up for in extra mining jobs."

"You were lied to," Sebastian told him. "And even that doesn't excuse you, because where did you think extra jobs were going to come from, if there were no new mines, and why would you think a mining job out in the forests would make up for taking someone's company away from them?"

The man stared at him in shock, and then looked away, his attention back on the screen.

Sebastian had to rein himself in. The faces of people he knew, children he knew, thin to the point of painful, haunted him, and he needed to shake off the ghosts at this moment, and help Vahn.

He kept to the edge of the crowd, laz at hip level, close against his body, as he angled himself and lined up a shot at the guard closest to the wall.

He fired, and while he didn't hit the guard full on, he went down, clutching his shoulder.

The other guards reacted, looking around wildly, some caught off guard because the screen had been holding their attention.

Vahn stuck his head out from behind the wall, and got off a shot, hit another guard, and ducked down.

"Shit." One of the guards looked at the two downed men, looked at the screen, which had looped through Hanran Fattal throwing his own guards, along with everyone who lived on Lassa, to the mercy of the Caruso, and holstered his laz. "I am done."

Sebastian wanted to tell him he'd made his decision six months at least too late, but no sense ruining the moment. Especially as it was in his favor.

"Get back here."

The guard ignored the order as he walked away, back into town, and Sebastian used the moment of frustration and indecision to shoot another guard.

A hum filled the air as a hover flew in from the hover base along the elevated track, and then slowed to a stop close to the resistance headquarters building.

Sebastian wondered if they had stopped to watch the screen, which Caro had looped around again.

He was lining up yet another shot when he saw the headquarter's window nearest the hover open.

The hover rose up off the hover track and moved across, the hand of the driver a trifle unsteady as it moved sideways and bumped into the wall, then rose a little to align the hover door with the window.

The view into the main seating area of the hover was clear from where he stood, and Sebastian watched as Koan stepped out of the building and into the hover carrying someone in his arms.

Not someone, Sebastian realized in horror as he made out the gray of the uniform, the dark hair swinging from a limp head. It was Dee.

Koan was the mole. And he had Dee.

THIRTY-FIVE

"YOU OWE ME."

Dee realized she'd drifted off for a while, because she was in a hover now, not the floor of Koan's office.

"Here's your payment in the form of invaluable advice. Get off this planet."

There was a moment of silence. "Are you joking? You said you were looking for a hover out to the pipelines."

"That was when I thought the worst that had happened today was that the gen-pop, along with the Cores guards, were about to learn a few home truths and discover that Vahn was still alive. The Cores won't hold on to power much longer than this afternoon. It was before I discovered that thanks to this interfering idiot," he shoved at Dee's shoulder, "the Bodivas have all the information they need to take Lassa back before the Breakaway treaty expires at the end of the week."

Dee kept her face lax, but her glee was immense. The full recording must have gone through. And Leo would make sure it got where it needed to go.

The information might not reach Bodivas in time to save her-- although she didn't understand why Koan had taken her at all--but it would mean Lassa would have the full force of the VSC coming to save it.

"So you're not going to hide out for a few months and then find a way off planet on a trader? You're leaving now? How?"

Dee cracked open her eyes to see who was talking.

She was lying on the floor of the hover, and she could feel the tips of Koan's boots against her back, so he must be sitting behind her. To catch a glimpse of the speaker, she'd have to tilt her head, so she didn't try, but he was sitting up front, and she guessed he was the driver.

"I did a quick deal with the Caruso after I found out what our Garmen friend here had shared with Bodivas and the VSC. The Caruso will give me some credits and get me off the planet, in exchange for a valuable shield."

"What shield is that?"

Koan shoved at her shoulder again.

"Her? What's so important about her?"

"According to the threats from the VSC official she was speaking to when I caught her passing on Hanran Fattal's incomprehensible confession, the full might of the VSC will rain down on me if I so much as hurt a hair on her head. It makes me think they won't shoot down a Caruso ship if she's onboard. That turns out to be as valuable to the Caruso as it is to me."

"I won't leave with the Caruso. I don't trust them."

Koan laughed. "You're not invited to. I don't care how you get off-planet, I'm just telling you it's the only way you won't be caught up in the mess."

"No one knows I helped you. I kept it to myself." The driver seemed to be trying to convince himself.

"If you say so." Koan didn't bother to hide his skepticism.

The driver said nothing in response, but the atmosphere seemed to sour and Koan didn't speak again either.

"Are you back with us, sunshine?" Koan shook her when the hover stopped, and Dee pretended to stir.

She could move, but was unsure how limber she was after the laz hit. Which reminded her. She'd hit him directly in the chest and he hadn't flinched. "You ... wearing ... anti-laz ...?" She kept her words slurred.

"Of course I'm wearing an anti-laz layer. I knew you'd shoot me when I stepped into the office." He hauled her to her feet, his big hand clamped hard on her shoulder, and she winced and stooped a little to ease the pain.

Koan pushed her out the door of the hover, and she stumbled out into a loading bay, into the growing heat of the day and the stink of hover afterburn. She flicked a wistful look at the hoverport building, remembering the serenity and cool of it from before.

"Walk." He put his hand in the center of her back and his laz to her neck, and herded her ahead of him, but she didn't have to fake the way her legs kept trying to crumple beneath her and the loss of balance as she walked.

The whole world seemed to be swaying around her.

She hunched over, crossing her arms over her chest and used the motion to surreptitiously pat at her pockets, to find out what Koan had or hadn't taken from her.

She almost sank to the hard surface of the launch pad in relief when she felt the shape of what she was looking for.

With a curse, Koan stepped to her side, hooked a hand under her armpit and dragged her the rest of the way to the dark Caruso warship that had towed her and Sebastian here to begin with.

It looked even bigger up close.

As they approached, a ramp extended and a door opened up.

A Caruson soldier stood in the doorway, massive laz cradled in his arms, the ridges of his thick skin clear in the bright morning sun. He stepped back to let them in.

"Where to?" Koan asked, and the soldier pointed to a room just off the entrance.

"Just her. You come with me." He spoke in a halting voice, unsure of the language, and Koan gave a nod, shoved Dee into the room.

She didn't bother turning, or protesting. She heard the door close behind her.

As soon as it shut completely, she looked around, trying to see if she was being watched remotely.

In the end she couldn't be sure if there were cameras on her or not, so she pretended to feel faint, putting a hand to her head, and staggering to a corner of the room.

It was really a cell, or possibly where soldiers about to deploy gathered to receive their final orders and wait to disembark. Benches had been clamped to the walls, and she sat down and then swung her legs up to face the far back corner, bending over her knees, curled up tight, so all anyone would see was the curve of her back and the top of her head.

She had to take a breath to steady herself as she fiddled in her pocket, trying to look like she was rocking from side to side in fear rather than up to no good.

The door opened, and she turned to look over her shoulder.

There was shouting out by the ship's ramp, orders being given.

"What is your name?" The Caruson who stood in the doorway looked more senior than the one who'd let them in--there was some insignia on his uniform. She guessed he was the ship's captain.

"Rina Fattal," she said.

The captain looked at Koan.

"She's lying. Her name is Dee and she's from Garmen. I know for a fact that she's important to the VSC."

"We'll see if that's true. Come with me." He gestured to Dee and she stood up, but too quickly, and she tipped over a little to the side.

"What's wrong with her?"

"I shot her with a laz."

The Caruson looked at her with professional interest. "What setting?"

"Lightest one."

"She's small and thin." The Caruson shrugged. "Can't take it, probably." He made the gesture again. "Come quickly."

Dee complied, following behind him, aware Koan was coming along behind her.

The captain stepped into what looked like a comms center, and pointed to the first Caruson woman Dee had seen, sitting next to a huge screen. "Hail the main Bodivas battleship."

"I can't be seen," Koan said, nervous.

"Then stand out of the way." The captain pointed, and Koan moved deeper into the room and stood behind the screen.

The tech bent over the panel in front of her, and Dee took stock.

The door to the comms unit was open, and just down the passage she could see the main entrance to the small warship was still open from when she and Koan had been let in. Soldiers were running in and out, and she guessed Koan had told them a Bodivas attack was likely and they were packing up to leave.

She didn't think she was going to get a better chance to execute her plan. The moment the ramp was lifted, her options were nonexistent.

Even if she had no idea, no idea at all, what would happen.

She tipped again, as if the floor was moving beneath her feet, fetching up against the captain.

"Sorry." Her voice came out a croak, her throat tight with fear and anticipation.

He put massive hands on her and set her away from him. "Sit." He pointed to a chair, and then staggered back himself.

Everyone--Koan, the tech, a soldier passing the doorway--stared at him as he ran into equipment behind him, sending some of it crashing to the floor.

"Are you all right--?"

He started screaming, the sound making Dee cover her ears, and he pulled the laz he'd shoved into a leg holster out. He aimed it at the soldier at the door and shot him.

"Admiral Yoto responding to your hail." The woman who suddenly blinked to life on the screen's eyes widened as the captain screamed again, swinging around to smash one of the panels behind him.

Dee caught her eye for one single heartbeat, then ducked under a desk as the captain stepped deeper into the room and, using his laz like a club, swung it at Koan.

She didn't know if he hit him or not, she was too busy drawing a second shot of venom into the syringe she'd taken off Hanran Fattal, but she saw the comms expert fall, lifeless, from her chair, and then the captain ran out the room. He turned deeper into the warship, and Dee scrambled out from under the desk.

She heard the Bodivas admiral call out to her, but she ignored the hail, flying out the room and running for the ramp.

The soldier who'd let them in was blocking the entrance, and he aimed his laz at her, but his attention kept flicking to the carnage that was clearly audible from the bowels of the ship.

"I'm just getting to safety," she said, lifting her hands in surrender. She turned back as the laz fire and screaming got louder, walking backward. "We need to get out of here."

"No. Get in the room." The soldier looked down the passage, then to her, and pointed to the cell he'd put her in earlier. "You can wait there."

"I'm sorry. No." She flinched back against him as laz fire scored the ceiling halfway down the passage, and depressed the syringe. Like the captain, he didn't seem to feel it.

He took a step forward, almost as if he'd forgotten she was there, and she darted around him and down the ramp, running in a zigzag as fast as she could go toward the hover track.

Behind her, she heard him scream, the sound over-scored by the sound of laz fire, and she felt the nausea build in her throat as she pushed herself far harder than her body wanted her to.

A sound swelled up behind her when she was halfway across the launch pad, and she stumbled to a stop and turned to look, saw a ship around the same size as the Caruson warship dropping from the sky like a raptor.

A light flicked over her, she caught sight of it on her arms and torso, and then the ship began flying in an upward curve and the Caruson warship she'd just left went up in a conflagration.

She was blown backward, twisting in midair to land with hands out, although she bashed her knee. She stayed still, head hanging down, on all fours, heaving in sour, burnt air, feeling the wash of heat, and then gingerly twisted to look behind her.

Her arms gave out and she flopped down.

She'd expected debris with the blast wave, but whatever was in the weapon used to blow the Caruso ship up, it had contained the blast. There was almost no debris at all.

To her right, the Bodivas warship, she assumed it was Bodivas, and if it wasn't, she didn't have any fight left in her, landed back down.

Troops ran out and she watched them with detachment as a few headed for the Caruson warship, and the rest headed for the hoverport building.

She leaned forward, head resting on her forearms, and felt the burn of the late-morning sun on her neck.

"Dee Vanuka?"

She twisted around, had to shield her eyes to look up at the woman who approached her.

"Who's asking?"

"Commander Delkin." Delkin put out her hand, and Dee grasped it, allowed herself to be hauled to her feet.

She tried not to cry out at the pain in her scraped hand, and Delkin looked at her sharply as she swallowed back the pain.

"Thanks for checking to make sure I wasn't in the warship before you blew it up."

"You saw the light scan?" Delkin sounded interested.

Dee nodded.

"You're a long way from home, I hear," Delkin said after the silence stretched out.

"Well, technically, yes."

"Technically?" Delkin raised her eyebrows in surprise.

"I've come to like it here."

They stood, side by side, looking at the Caruso ship, which was still red hot in places.

"Care to tell me how you engineered the freak-out on that thing?" Delkin nodded to it.

Dee lifted her shoulders in a shrug. "I have no idea what happened. They just went crazy."

Delkin snorted. "Not buying it. Admiral Yoto saw you."

Dee closed her eyes and rubbed the back of her hand over her forehead. "I'm not really in a state to be debriefed. No matter what happened, it's not going to help you one bit with the mess down here."

High above she saw a flicker of light, and she lifted her head. "Or up there."

"Seems Hanran Fattal was right about there being three Caruson warships hiding on the moons." Delkin lifted her own head, eyes narrowed.

"You don't seem too concerned."

Delkin turned back to her. "We have seven, so no."

Dee grinned. "And there Leo was, telling me you had one warship on the way."

Delkin didn't smile, but her eyes softened. "Never know who might be listening, so we might have underreported a little."

"Dee!"

Dee turned, saw Sebastian running toward her, saw Bodivas soldiers divert to intercept him.

She tapped Delkin's shoulder. "Hurt him, and you'll never know what I did to those Caruso." Dee started running herself, in a limping sort of fashion.

Delkin must have issued an order, because the soldiers pulled back, and Dee was able to slow to a walk.

Sebastian slowed, too, his gaze going over her, then over her shoulder to look at the Caruso ship. He was scowling as he got even closer.

"Uh uh." She waggled her finger.

"Uh uh, what?" He reached her, gently ran fingers down the side of her face.

"No frowns. We're both alive, and I have to say, I had serious doubts about that outcome a number of times."

"When I saw that fucker, Koan--"

She didn't have it in her to go up on tiptoe, so she hooked an arm around his neck and pulled him down, shut him up with a kiss.

"He's dead." She waved her hand behind her at the ship. "If the Caruson captain didn't kill him, the Bodivas did."

"*I* wanted to kill him."

She grinned. "There, there. It can't be helped."

He kissed her back, just a soft touch of his lips, and then pulled away, and she could see from his face, from the hardness in his eyes, Commander Delkin must be behind her.

She fitted herself under Sebastian's arm and turned to face her.

"Commander Delkin, this is Sebastian Xian. Leader of the Lassian Resistance."

Delkin couldn't hide her surprise, and Sebastian gave a curt nod. "Commander."

She gave the Bodivas greeting of clenched fist covered with the other hand, and Sebastian did the same.

"You're Bodivas born?" Delkin asked.

Sebastian nodded. "Was brought here when I was fourteen."

"You think the people of Lassa will listen to you?"

Sebastian pondered that. "Me, Vahn, and Ruanne Lex."

"Ruanne Lex being alive was a pleasant surprise," Delkin said.

"Dee and I rescued her earlier this morning."

Delkin tilted her head, her eyes on Dee. "We saw that on the video feed you sent through. You're a busy woman."

"Right now, she's a wounded woman. I need you to get her a medic and then we're going home to rest. Neither of us have slept in nearly two days."

Delkin looked her over again, and gave a nod. "Done." She spoke quietly into her comm unit and then stepped back. "I'll see you later."

Sebastian pulled her a little closer as the commander strode away, and a two-person team of medics raced toward them.

"Should I have asked her to take you to the ship? Treat you there before flying you out?" He looked down at her, eyes unreadable.

"Without taking me on the holiday you promised me first?" She kept her tone neutral.

He stared at her as if she'd lost her mind. "Are you being serious?"

She shot him a dirty look and elbowed him in the ribs. "No, I don't want to jump straight onboard a Bodivas warship. I'm invested here."

"Sorry." He rubbed his side. Turned to take in all the activity around them. "I don't know how to feel, now they're here."

"My guess is, a little put out, because they're going to try to take charge." She could see the tension in his face. "But what you have to remember is that between the VSC and the Cores, the VSC wins, every time."

He relaxed against her. "You're right. They're not the enemy."

She grinned up at him, then put her hand on her hip as she surveyed the burnt out Caruso warship. "And it'll be unlucky for them if they are."

THIRTY-SIX

"THIS ISN'T THE HOLIDAY." It was the second time Sebastian had said it. "It's a prelude to the holiday."

"All right. So noted." Dee was still limping a little, but otherwise felt almost herself again, enough that the walk Sebastian was leading her on through the forest was pleasant, rather than an ordeal.

Fluffy chirped from her shoulder, then jumped to the forest floor. When she landed and turned back to Dee, there was something in her mouth.

"You are quite the little hunter," Dee told her.

"Did you eventually tell Commander Delkin what you did to the Caruso?" Sebastian had stopped on the path, and Dee could just make out a track snaking off from where he stood.

She nodded. "It wouldn't have taken them long to figure it out for themselves." She scooped Fluffy up. "And I suppose Fluffy's venom might as well go somewhere useful. I think they're going to stockpile it in case it comes in handy in the future. They've asked us not to talk about it."

He nodded, held back a branch for her, and she stepped past him, feeling a sudden shiver of desire as she brushed against him.

There was no doubt this was an outing to get some alone time.

Since the Cores collapsed and the Bodivas took over, there had barely been a moment when they'd had any time to themselves.

The task ahead was massive, but there was a sense of relief, of optimism, that helped, even when disagreements arose and tempers frayed.

She heard the sound of water a few moments before she stepped between two massive trees and came upon a stream and a rock pool in the tiny clearing.

The sun shone through the branches, and thick rays of light lit the water with a golden glow.

"A prelude, huh?"

He came up behind her, pulled her back against him and nuzzled her neck. "Just for an hour or so. I did bring a comfortable bed, though."

"You did?" She twisted her head to look back at him in surprise.

"An inflatable. One of the Bodivas store masters gave it to me."

She curled her arm around his neck, and tipped her head back to kiss him. "How organized of you."

He turned her around, but there was none of the humor in his face she'd heard in his voice a moment before.

"Caro said you spoke to Leo earlier."

She nodded. "Just to touch base. Let him know what was going on."

"And what is going on?"

She looked into eyes filled with unspoken declarations.

"You mean, what do I plan to do?"

"Yes." He splayed a hand on her lower back, pulled her a little closer.

"What would you like me to do?" She thought she knew the answer. She needed to hear it.

"I want you to stay, Dee. I will literally do anything to convince you."

She smiled, feeling weightless as she stepped in even closer. "As it happens, you already have."

She looped her arms around his neck. "Meet the new head of Gaudier Transport on Lassa."

He gave a shout of happiness, swung her around, and then slowly lifted her top over her head. "When do you start?"

She lifted her face up to his and smiled. "After my holiday."

EXCERPT: SKY RAIDERS

BOOK ONE IN THE SKY RAIDERS SERIES

ONE

HE'D ASKED her to wait for him, and then he'd disappeared for two years.

As he reached the top of the pass and started down the steep path to the valley below, Garek wondered just how angry Taya would be.

That she would be angry enough to have taken someone else sat like week-old loaf in his stomach, heavy and sickening.

He'd had no choice, had come as soon as he could . . . he tried to shake off the chill that touched him, despite the bright day. He'd take her anger, her fury--he'd take it all if it meant he didn't find her with someone else.

He forced himself to pay attention as the path became steeper still, and frowned at how badly maintained the way had become, as if no one had repaired the damage a winter in the mountains could do to a narrow track. The spring thaw had come and gone, replaced by a golden summer, and the snow had retreated to the tops of the mountains.

Kas should have done something about the erosion by now, even though this path was a shortcut few besides the villagers knew of, cutting across the Crag and shaving hours off the journey through the foothills.

The familiar landscape tugged at something inside him. He hadn't thought himself sentimental, and though he'd missed Taya with an ache that hurt worse than a knife to flesh, he hadn't thought the sight of the rolling hills and high peaks would affect him. The crowds and enclosing stone walls of Garamundo had been something to bear stoically, but he was surprised how easy it was to breathe here, and it wasn't just because the air was sweet with the scent of summer grass.

When he'd left two years ago, the only thing he'd regretted was leaving Taya behind him, and he'd come back only to fetch her.

Fetch her and run, as fast as possible.

As far away from West Lathor as they could get.

The shadow cast by Garamundo had a long reach, certainly long enough to reach out and try to grab him again if he stayed here, and he'd sworn when they'd finally released him that he would never go back.

He wouldn't give them a chance to conscript him again.

He was halfway down the mountain when he noticed there were no leviks on the slopes.

He stopped a moment, shading his eyes against the bright midday light of the Star to search for any sign of their golden, curly coats.

He could find none.

A breeze rose up, swirling about him, and he was struck by the silence.

His hearing was exceptional, and there was no sound of life. No ring of a hammer on anvil, no murmur of voices from the street.

Impossible.

His home town was small, but not that small. Pan Nuk had at least a hundred inhabitants when he'd left. And it was directly below him. Hidden by the thick line of trees it would take him only ten minutes to reach, but there nonetheless.

He started to run.

At first he ran under his own steam, and then, as the silence seemed to deepen, become more sinister, he opened himself up to the Change and felt the curious, slow, honey-thick flow of the air around him, the inbetween, and he was suddenly at the village gates.

He drew back to himself, stumbled a little at the feeling of disorientation such a quick Change generated.

He stood still, looking around him carefully. Took it all in.

The ripped doors. The shutters hanging by a single hinge. The smashed pots and baskets lying in the street.

The emptiness.

While the city of Garamundo had held him, forced him to help them protect themselves from the sky raiders, the sky raiders had been helping themselves elsewhere.

Helping themselves to Taya.

TWO

THERE WOULD BE BLOOD.

Taya moved her gaze from Jerilia, weeping in soft, keening sobs, to the big Kardanx who gripped her arm, to the way Kas and the other men and women of the Illy began to gather to one side of the open area in front of the mine where they waited to be collected for the camp.

The Kardanx shifted his grip and Taya could see there were already dark smudges ringing Jerilia's upper arm where he held her.

The spike of anger that ripped through her made her gasp, made her force in a breath of dusty, cold air.

If she couldn't keep a cool head, she couldn't expect Kas and the others to do the same.

Behind the Kardanx, some of his fellow countrymen began to gather as well, their expressions more muted, more severe.

They didn't want trouble with the Illy. It seemed the big man who had grabbed Jerilia wasn't so worried.

Kas had already told him to let Jerilia go. Jerilia herself had demanded it. Taya looked into his eyes and knew he would not do it.

Perhaps if Jerilia hadn't screamed so loudly, made such a fuss. Perhaps if Kas's bellow of outrage hadn't made every head turn.

Or perhaps not.

Whatever the reason, to let her go now would be a loss of face the Kardanx would not be prepared to accept.

Taya could see it in the way his eyes narrowed, the way his mouth tightened. She had always had the gift of reading people's intentions from the way they moved their bodies, and the Kardanx was screaming pent up rage and defiance with every pore.

A small movement caught her eye. Kas, drawing something from the back of his pants, gripping it tightly in his fisted hand.

Was that a *knife*?

No.

She wouldn't let another she loved be hurt. Not because of the lust of a stupid Kardanx. The Kardanx were supposed to worship the Mother, but either this one wasn't an adherent to the belief, or he was simply one of the majority who twisted the meanings of their oaths so they could treat women with less respect. She saw the evidence before her now, in the way the Kardanx thought he could have Jerilia, even against her will.

Taya had heard another, even uglier whisper. That the reason there were only six women amongst all the Kardanx the sky raiders had taken was because the men had killed them, rather than have them taken by the enemy.

Taya had heard Kardanx men swore an oath to protect the Mother, and her avatars, all women, with their lives. But if they had killed their women to protect them, they were not honoring the Mother as an equal. They had killed them like they would kill their livestock so the invading army cannot use it. As they would burn their house, to give the enemy nothing to shield himself from the weather.

As one treats a possession, not a person, with their own will and choices.

The Kardanx took a step toward his own group, dragging Jerilia with him, and Kas and three others took a step forward.

The other Kardanx shouted something to their countryman, and he turned to look at them over his shoulder. He shouted back, and though Kardanx was close enough to Illian, it was said so fast Taya couldn't understand it. But the meaning was clear enough.

The Kardanx would not back down.

She wished, not for the first time, for Garek. Felt a need for him as strong as for her next breath. Then she shrugged off the paralysis of wanting something she could not have, and her gaze came to rest on their guard. When they'd first been brought here the metal skin of the two-legged, squat vehicle that enclosed him had been gleaming and new. Now she could see flakes of it falling off, and it was dull, corroded.

He was the only one on watch and his guns hung at his sides, mounted sleek and black on the stiff arms of his protective cover, above the pincers he could use as hands.

Kas took the first step out from the shouting group of the Illy, and without another moment's hesitation, Taya ran toward the sky raider.

He noticed her before she got to him, the head of the machine tipping down to look at her.

"Stop them." She looked straight up into the glass, and the dark tint faded to clear. For the first time, she found herself face to face with one of her captors.

Pale yellow eyes watched her with an interest that made her want to stumble back a step or two, turn tail and run.

She forced some saliva down her throat, worked her tongue off the roof of her mouth. "You need to stop it."

The robotic suit stayed still, but inside it, the sky raider tipped his head. "Why?"

The sibilant tones which made everything they said more frightening hissed over her. But now she'd been given a window into the helmet, she saw there was a disconnect between when the sky raider had spoken and when she'd heard the question.

It came to her in a flash that that wasn't how they sounded. They were using some device, some method of translating their language into Illian. It made her less afraid to know she wasn't dealing with something that sounded like she would expect a slither to sound like, if slithers could speak instead of hiss.

"We are different groups, we come from different parts of Barit. We are the Illy, they are the Kardanx. The Kardanx have different beliefs, different ways to us."

"We do not care." Again, his mouth moved and only after a beat did the hiss of his answer wash over her.

She shivered.

"Then you are stupid." She banged his leg with her fist in frustration, felt the gritty crunch of rusting metal. "If you want less work done in the mines, then you'll let that Kardanx take Jerilia. Because we're all mixed up in there. Kardanx and Illy together. And if he takes her, it will be against her will, and that will make us all feel like we have even less control than we already do. The Illy will fight the Kardanx. Fight them down in the shafts. Where you do not go."

She saw the pale yellow eyes blink in their narrow, sharp face that was otherwise not that different from her own, if you discounted the long, sharp incisors she caught the briefest glimpse of and the pale yellow fur that covered his face. He spoke again, although this time there was no hiss of reply to her.

She had the feeling he was talking to someone else. Getting advice. How he could do that, she didn't know. But then, most of what the sky raiders could do was new and magical to her.

He gave a sharp nod within his metallic cocoon, as if receiving an order, and then lifted both arms.

She heard something in the metallic suit whine. And the sky raider shifted, lifting up his arms. The barrel of one of his guns came level with her face.

But before she could think anything, feel any terror, the guard swung away from her and in two long steps was beside the Kardanx, gun leveled at his head.

"Let the woman go back to her kind." The hiss of the order fell into the silence that had descended, licking the air like a hungry tongue.

Without a word, the Kardanx released Jerilia, and she ran toward Kas and the others, stumbling in her haste.

They opened ranks for her, and then stepped back in to fill the gap, closing the line again.

"All who are the Illy, go this side. All who are Kardanx, go this side." He pointed with the guns, and Taya moved over to her group.

Some had been standing a little way away, watching without getting involved, and they began to move, pushing and weaving through each other to reach their people.

In the confusion, Taya saw one of the few Kardanx women in the camp slip amongst the Illy. The woman caught her eye and stumbled, and Taya realized her horror, and her anger, must have shown on her face.

If they sheltered one of the only Kardanx women left, if they took her to their side, that would be reason enough for another scene like the one today.

But hadn't she just seen how some of the Kardanx treated women? And hadn't she in these last few minutes come to the realization that the ugly whispers about men killing wives, sisters, mothers, and daughters was true?

Could she send a woman back to that against her will?

"Please." The woman was at her side faster than it seemed possible. Her hands came out to touch Taya's arm, and then drew back, fists clenched. "They don't want me anyway. They think me a witch. It's why I'm one of the few women in the group. I was living outside the village, and there was no man to kill me when the sky raiders came.

There was truth and desperation in her words. Her accent was thick, the vowels round and plump as a ripe plum, but she spoke Illian fluently.

Taya studied her, looking for some trick, some hidden motive. She was a few years older than Taya and her eyes were a pale, almost glacial green. Her skin was honey-gold, close to Taya's own skin tone. Her dark hair hung down her back with a glint of auburn in it.

With a grimace, knowing only trouble could come of it, Taya gave a quick nod and pushed the woman deeper into the crowd. She felt a brief, light touch of thanks on her shoulder, and the woman was gone, burrowing deep into the mass.

Silence fell as the last of the prisoners sorted themselves into Illy and Kardanx.

The Illy, with their equal mix of men and women, were the bigger group, because most of the Kardanx volunteered for night shift.

If it were true that for nearly every man standing here, at least one woman had died, the sky raiders must have had to attack many towns and villages in Kardai to get this many of them. And the blood must stain the ground in Kardai dark red.

Looking at the Kardanx, thinking of that many bodies, Taya felt the burn of nausea in her throat.

She should be thankful to Garamundo. Thankful for the protection they offered. Keeping the sky raiders away so that only a few places in West Lathor were hit.

But giving even a drop of thanks to Garamundo was beyond her because of Garek.

She felt something on her cheek, and lifted a hand to brush it away. Her finger came away with a single tear, and she rubbed it into the filthy tunic she wore.

The guard swiveled the head of his suit to her, one gun held steady on each group, then walked slowly back, so that he could see them all without having to turn. The glass of the dome that covered his head was opaque again. "We understand now. Your ways are different. It is decided. You do not mix. You do not fight. You work together peacefully. There must be no break in production." The sinister voice that came from the sky raider's suit drifted on the fading light of the evening as the Star sank down in the west. The threat in the words, the very sound of them, made her shiver.

In the distance, the transporter skimmed over the open ground toward them, bringing the night shift.

There must be no break in production.

She shivered again.

There had been a few demonstrations of what would happen if production should slow or even stop, right at the start.

She watched the Star as it lit the sky a deep violet, low on the horizon. She liked to think of it slipping away from them here on Shadow to rise in the east on Barit. Taking a part of her with it.

Kas came up next to her and put a hand on her arm, and when she looked across at him, she couldn't tell what he was thinking. He looked tired. Tired and worn.

She'd run to the enemy. Made a decision without consulting him first.

"I don't regret it."

Kas gave a slow nod. "This was the culmination of two weeks of antagonism." He blew out a breath, looked across at the Kardanx. "It was only a matter of time."

"Tell me." Taya's voice came out on a croak. "Are the rumors true? What they did to their women, that there are so few here?"

Kas looked away. "So I hear."

"Then I'm doubly glad I did it. That some man who has no woman in his bed because he slit her throat like a goat tried to take a woman from the Illy, rape her . . ." She couldn't finish the sentence, her throat too tight. She took a breath. "I'll deal with the sky raiders before I deal with them."

Her gaze was drawn to the big Kardanx, to his hands. She imagined him holding a woman against his chest, running a knife across her throat.

She could hear a singing in her ears, like the sound the massive sky raider ship had made when it hovered over Pan Nuk, and taken them all. A singing, soaring sound of rage.

"Taya."

She turned to Kas, and he took a half-step back.

"What?" The word came out slowly, and she frowned at him. "*What?*"

"You were . . ." Kas wet his lips, set his feet apart. "Taya, you were starting to call the Change."

270

ALSO BY MICHELLE DIENER

Science Fiction Novels

Sky Raiders series:

Sky Raiders

Calling the Change

Shadow Warrior

Class 5 series:

Dark Horse

Dark Deeds

Dark Minds

Verdant String series:

Interference & Insurgency Box Set

Breakaway

Breakeven

Historical Fiction Novels

Susanna Horenbout and John Parker series:

In a Treacherous Court

Keeper of the King's Secrets

In Defense of the Queen

To receive notification when Michelle Diener's next book is released, you can sign up to her new release notification list at michellediener.com.

ABOUT THE AUTHOR

Michelle Diener is an award winning author of historical fiction, science fiction and fantasy.

Michelle was born in London, grew up in South Africa and currently lives in Australia with her husband and children.

You can contact Michelle through her website or sign up to receive notification when she has a new book out on her New Release Notification page.

Connect with Michelle
www.michellediener.com

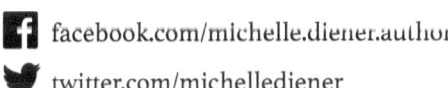 facebook.com/michelle.diener.author
twitter.com/michellediener

ACKNOWLEDGMENTS

Thank you so much to Edie, Diane, Justin and Jo for your eagle eyes and great suggestions as always, as well as to my awesome reader team! Thanks as always to EJR Digital Art for the truly beautiful cover!

www.ingramcontent.com/pod-product-compliance
Lightning Source LLC
Chambersburg PA
CBHW030634110726
47901CB00002B/442